A Place for Annika

Rebecca Velez

Sue,

Jesus has a place
for us!

Becky

Published in the U.S. by Rebecca Velez Books
Manchester, NH

Cover by Temitope fiverr.com/pro_design190

Scripture portions are taken from a combination of versions:
The New Revised Standard Version Bible, copyright © 1989 National Council of the Churches
of Christ in the United States of America. Used by permission. All rights reserved worldwide.
The New Century Version®. Copyright © 2005 by Thomas Nelson. Used by permission. All
rights reserved.

ISBN: 978-1-7322921-7-8 (print)
ISBN: 978-1-7322921-8-5 (digital)

Library of Congress Control Number: 2023921983

For Mom

We miss you.

"Lord, you have been our home since the beginning."
PSALM 90:1 (NCV)

Contents

Glossary

Adelsverein—society of nobles dedicated to the emigration of Germans to Texas

Äpfel—apple

Bürgermeister—chief magistrate

Danke—thank you

Dom—church

Dummkopf—dummy

Ell—length of fabric which varied by region, 22-25 ½ inches in various German cities, 45 inches in England

Frau—Mrs.

Fraülein—Miss

Gasthaus—restaurant

Gute Nacht—good night

Guten Abend—good evening

Guten Morgen—good morning

Guten Tag—good afternoon

Hallo—hello

Herr—Mr.

Ja—yes

Kaffee—coffee

Kinder—children

Kirche—church

Kleid—dress

Kuchen—cake

Liebling—darling

Mutter—mother

Nein—no

Onkel—uncle

Oma—grandmother

Opa—grandfather

Pfeffernüsse—spice cookies

Pfennige—pennies

Sehr—very

Schloss—castle

Stollen—a sweet bread with nuts and candied fruits, often served for Christmas

Tante—aunt

Thaler—a silver coin

Vater—father

Verrückt—crazy, insane

Wunderbar—wonderful

Weihnachten—Christmas

Wilkommen—welcome

Characters

Beckers (Herr, Frau, Paul, Lucie)—bakers in Braunfels

Engels (Frau, Greta)—seamstress proprietors of Engel's Kleider Shop

Hoffmanns (Herr, Frau, Dorothea, Ulrich)—family renting Annika an attic apartment in Wetzlar

Huber (Fritz)—farmer in Braunfels

Kellers (Herr, Frau, Rosa)—banking family renting Annika a room in Wetzlar

Langes (Vater, Annika, Matt, Dora, Charlotte, Helmuth)—farmers in Braunfels

Roths (Gerry, Hans, Frieda, Max)—furniture makers neighboring the Langes

Schäfers (Margarete, Ida)—daughters of a shepherd

Schumachers (Herr, Olga)—cobbler and seamstress in Wetzlar

Seidels (Herr, Frau)—haberdashery owners in Limburg

Steins (Frau, Herr, Frank, Ehrich, Lina, Elsa)—apple orchard owners neighboring the Langes

Webers (Oskar, Alma, Gustav, Erwin)—weavers in Wetzlar

Webers (Onkel, Hertha, Paula, Klara, Conrad, Ella)—weavers in Wetzlar

Winters (Liza, Josef, Kate)—family in Braunfels

Zeiglers (Otto, Adele)—brewery owners

Chapter 1

Floating in step with her partner on the packed-dirt floor, Annika scanned the young men and women in the half-timbered barn, her crimson dress whirling to the steps of a lively polka. She stiffened as Ehrich and Margarete appeared through the barn door.

Werner glanced in their direction. "Keep smiling, *Liebling*." He appraised Margarete's dress. "She's worn that blue thing too often. You look marvelous in your new creation. And I... I am the most dashing figure of the evening in my military uniform."

Annika couldn't help but smile at her cousin's audacity. They bowed to each other as the dance ended before Werner passed Annika to her next partner, a gangly farm boy.

Annika tried to pay attention to his talk of fields and rainfall as she tracked Ehrich from the corner of her eye. After the farmer stomped on her toes for a second time, she pleaded for a rest. The boy immediately led her to a barrel of beer in a corner of the barn. Several couples were sitting on benches while a group of men discussed the best crops for their region.

Lucie scooted over on a bench so Annika could sit and massage her foot while her partner filled a mug with beer. "I wish these boys would manage the steps better," Annika complained.

"More like Ehrich?" her friend teased.

"Or Werner," Annika replied loftily.

"Don't worry. He'll ask you to dance, probably a waltz so he can hold you close."

"Werner's already fulfilled his obligation to me."

"You know I'm not talking about Werner." Lucie gestured to tall, flaxen-haired Ehrich dancing with a petite blond. She peered into Annika's face. "You're not worried? Seriously! He invited you to walk just last week."

"I brought his *Oma* some bone broth because she'd been under the weather. He simply walked me home." Annika tucked her foot beneath her petticoat and smoothed her woolen skirt. "Of course, I did time my delivery to coincide with the afternoon chores on his grandparents' farm."

Lucie gave her a playful nudge. "Of course you did. I wouldn't expect anything less from you. But you're still a little young for him, no?"

Lucie had touched on a sore spot. Annika was only seventeen. Margarete was already eighteen, marriageable age for women in Braunfels, and her family was well connected to the council and *Bürgermeister*, who would need to grant permission. Ehrich was twenty-three, already eligible for marriage for a year. Annika had hoped he was waiting for her. She longed to establish a home of her own.

The clumsy farmer thrust a foaming mug into Annika's hand, sloshing beer onto her treasured dress. "Be careful," she reprimanded. After a few minutes of stilted conversation, he took the hint that he wasn't wanted and went to find another partner. Annika shared the stein of beer with Lucie while they decided which men they wanted to dance with.

Soon, a country dance was called, and all the men and women formed lines that weaved in and out. Several handsome men asked Annika for subsequent dances, and the night was half over before she found herself cooling off in the crisp autumn air at the barn's entrance while her latest partner secured refreshments.

Ehrich materialized beside her.

"It's a beautiful night." Annika pointed to the moonlit pasture.

"I'd rather admire the beauty here."

Annika's heart did a little flip.

"Is that a new dress? It's very becoming." Ehrich eyed her appreciatively.

Annika's cheeks heated. "Yes, I made it myself."

"You're a very clever seamstress."

Annika wanted to hear more, but her partner had returned with a luscious-looking piece of *Streuselkuchen* to share with her.

"Save me the next waltz, Anna," Ehrich said as he sauntered back to the dance floor.

Annika tried to concentrate on her partner's description of his thriving cobbler's shop. Eventually she gave up and simply nodded as she satisfied her hunger with the apricot jam-covered cake, dreaming of the next waltz.

She didn't have long to wait. The fiddlers began a Mozart waltz, and Ehrich took her in his arms and guided her smoothly around the dance floor. He pulled her a little closer, and Annika longed to lay her head on his shoulder. He was the perfect height for her tall frame. She felt safe in his embrace and never wanted the waltz to end.

But as she already knew, perfection couldn't last. It always popped like the soap bubbles on washing day.

With a sense of loss, she parted from Ehrich and joined a country jig. Since it was one of her favorites, and Werner kept making outrageous faces at her as everyone switched partners, she was soon laughing with the other couples. But her delight burst when the dance ended and she spied Ehrich glowering near the beer keg.

Lucie latched onto her arm and guided her in the opposite direction. "Werner's doing you a huge favor."

"What do you mean?" Annika tucked stray hairs back into her looped braids.

"He's showing Ehrich how desirable you are. You outshone every other girl in that jig."

Annika's brow wrinkled. "But that makes no sense. Werner's my cousin. There's nothing between us."

Lucie smirked. "Ehrich doesn't know that. And he's a *distant* cousin."

Understanding dawning, Annika squeezed Lucie's arm. "Are you having fun?"

Lucie nodded. "Of course. Fritz has asked me to dance twice, and he said to save him the last waltz." Her cheeks colored.

"You look so pretty tonight."

"Thanks to the way you styled my hair."

Annika studied her friend's blue eyes and rosy cheeks. "No, it's something shining from inside you, Lucie. You're sparkling tonight."

"I think I've found the man I want to marry," Lucie whispered.

"It's about time," Annika teased. "You're nineteen and can have your pick. The town council will let you marry anyone you want. I'm just the daughter of a poor farmer who used to be a soldier."

"Maybe, but I'm not nearly as beautiful as you. You already have beaux falling at your feet. Plus, you can sew like no other girl our age."

"And you and your mom are the best bakers in the village. What man can resist a *Hausfrau* who can fill him up with

Kuchen? That reminds me—when are you going to share your recipe for Pfeffernüsse? I think I can handle baking some of those."

Lucie pretended to pout. "I've got to keep a few secrets to give me an edge. I already gave you advice about your *Stollen*, didn't I?"

"Yes, and I appreciate it, but it still doesn't taste as good as yours, so I think I need something simpler." Annika dropped her voice. "Here comes Fritz."

The wiry farmer joined them at the barn's entrance. "*Guten Abend*, Annika. Hello again, Lucie. I'd like to accompany you home at the end of the night, if you don't already have an escort."

Lucie nodded with a radiant smile. "I'd like that."

A muscular blond entered the barn. He offered Annika his arm. "May I have this dance, Beautiful?"

Although they hadn't been properly introduced, she accepted in order to stoke Ehrich's jealousy. "I'm Annika Lange. You're not from Braunfels, are you?"

"My name is Gustav Weber. My aunt purchased some furniture from the Roths. I helped Gerry carry it into her home, and we got to talking. He invited me to tonight's festivities."

"The Roths make the best Biedermeier furniture in Braunfels."

Gustav led Annika to the dance floor. "I was impressed by their workmanship."

"Your family are weavers?"

"*Ja.* Of fine linen."

"There's nothing like linen on a hot day."

Gustav threw back his head and laughed. "My family

couldn't agree more, and my cousin likes how well linen holds color. She's experimenting with new dyes. Some of the results are stunning."

Gustav bowed to her as their dance ended. "It's been a pleasure, *Fraülein* Lange. I hope to see you again soon."

Lucie grabbed her hand and pulled her into the next folk dance. "He was very handsome."

Annika smiled enigmatically.

As she exchanged partners with the dance's movements, she came face-to-face with Ehrich. "Would you like to walk home with a group of us headed in your farm's direction?"

Annika nodded regally. "That would be a lovely end to the evening. Thank you for thinking of me." She had no doubt Margarete would be part of the group, but at least Ehrich had included her too.

Ehrich claimed Margarete for the last waltz while Annika found herself in the cobbler's arms.

The young men and women drank their final mugs of beer and finished the last crumbs of cookies and cakes. After the ladies gathered their platters, the crowd dispersed.

Annika found herself headed down the road with about a dozen other partygoers.

"Did you have a good time?" Margarete asked Annika as they picked their way along the rutted road by the light of Ehrich's lantern.

"Ja. And you?"

"Ja, *sehr*. I'm looking forward to the dance at the school. We'll have a piano there. The waltzes sound better with the piano."

Ehrich steered Annika around a large pothole. She kept hold of his arm. "The moon will be nearly full that weekend. If the weather's good, we'll be able to open the doors and dance outside in the schoolyard, too."

"Here we are, Annika. See you at church tomorrow," Margarete said as they reached the lane to Annika's family's farm.

"*Gute Nacht,*" everyone called into the crisp fall air.

As their old farm dog Bruno came to greet her, Annika's feet crunched through the beech leaves, easily picking their way up the familiar wagon track. The dog lay down in front of the door while Annika slipped inside. She crept up to the attic as her father snored in the downstairs bedroom.

In a matter of minutes, she snuggled into the down mattress she and her mother had stuffed with goose feathers and fingered the worn quilt her Oma had stitched. It had covered Annika's bed for the dozen years since her grandparents passed. It was worn through in places, but she shouldn't need it much longer since she and her mother had started a quilt to crown her marriage bed. She had stuffed the incomplete blue and tan coverlet into a cherry-wood chest and shoved it under the eaves the day of her mother's funeral.

I wish you were here now, Mutter. I miss you. Home doesn't feel the same at all. We didn't finish my wedding quilt. And I need your advice about how to catch a husband...

Chapter 2

Hurry, Annika. There's a storm coming. We're all going to the Steins to pick their *Äpfel*."

Annika stopped mulching her garden and jumped into the back of her neighbors' wagon.

"*Opa's* bones are telling him this is going to be a bad one," fourteen-year-old Max announced from the front bench seat as his older brother Hans clucked to the horse.

"We left in such a hurry, my hair's a mess," sixteen-year-old Frieda lamented.

"Sit here in front of me, and I'll braid it." As Frieda shifted position, Annika looked back at her unfinished task. Their remaining crops would survive a bad rainstorm, but if there were high winds, the Kleins' *Äpfel* could end up on the ground. They wouldn't be good for eating although they could still be used for baking or cider.

When they arrived, Annika spied Ehrich bringing two ladders from the direction of the barn. Margarete was also watching him as she emptied an apronful of apples into the Steins' wagon, which sat between two rows of trees. Her younger sister Ida and the two Stein girls were working nearby.

Ehrich set a ladder against a tree whose lower branches had been picked clean. The top boughs groaned with the rosy fruit. "Max, this ladder's not strong enough to hold a grown man. Do you want to give it a try? Be careful, and mind that fourth rung."

Max scampered up the ladder. "It's fine for me. I don't think

I can balance a basket up here though. Who wants to catch my Äpfel?"

"I will," Annika offered, thankful her older brothers had played catch with her. She positioned herself to Max's right and caught the first apple he tossed. She set it on the ground to catch the next one.

"Here's a crate," Ehrich said, setting a wooden crate near her feet. "Good catch," he added, as Annika pulled a wild throw out of the air.

"Sorry," Max called.

The crate was full before Max climbed down, so Annika piled the overflow on the ground. When Ehrich took the box to the wagon, she stuffed the extras into her apron and scampered after him. "It's a good harvest."

"And thanks to all of you, we might actually get to enjoy it. With *Vater* being laid up and Frank away building railroads, all the work's behind." Ehrich handed her an empty basket. "I'm going to take this load to the cellar, pack it in barrels, and free up some crates."

Margarete appeared on the other side of the wagon. "I'll give you a hand. The girls can finish the last of what's down low."

Ehrich looked up the row. Hans was standing on a sturdy ladder tossing fruit to his sister, who was missing a fair number. "Too bad more of you can't catch like Annika."

Annika pinkened with pleasure. Margarete shrugged.

"Elsa," Ehrich called to his youngest sister, "Come help me and Margarete unload Äpfel."

Elsa carried their basket of apples over to the wagon. "They're too high for me to reach."

Ehrich took the basket and tipped the apples into the bed. "That's okay. I need your help, and after we're done unloading, you can fetch drinks, and we'll bring them back for everyone.

You'll be the most popular girl here."

The ten-year-old beamed. "And maybe some of Mutter's *Apfëlkuchen*, too."

Ehrich boosted her into the wagon.

Annika watched with dismay as Margarete claimed a place on the front bench seat. Ehrich vaulted up next to her and grabbed the reins.

"Hey, Annika. I need you over here." Max had moved the ladder and scurried up the next tree.

Annika positioned herself so Max could toss the fruit without twisting. They fell into a smooth rhythm and stripped the upper branches.

When Max descended, Hans called, "The sky looks angry, and the wind's increasing. Won't be long before it'll be too wet and windy to finish up." He motioned for the two girls who'd finished picking the lower branches. "Can either of you catch?"

"Of course we can," Lina Stein said.

"Just not as well as Annika," Ida added.

"Max and I will pick faster. Just don't fall, Max. Mother will have a fit if you break something while I'm looking after you."

"If we had another ladder, I could pick," Annika offered. "We'd have three teams instead of two. I'm not much heavier than Max, so I could use a ladder like his." Although tall, Annika had a willowy build like the other women in her family.

Hans eyed her skeptically. He pointed to a tree with spreading branches. "Max, if I give you a boost, can you climb high enough to grab most of those Äpfel? Safely?"

"Sure," Max answered. Max stepped into Hans' interlaced fingers and scrambled up to a sturdy branch.

Hans turned his attention back to Annika. "Are you sure

you want to do this?"

Throat dry, Annika nodded. Hans moved the rickety ladder to a smaller tree and secured it against a strong branch. He held it steady while Annika slowly ascended. Reaching the top, she grasped the branch and tugged on an apple. Trying to assure her audience, as well as herself, she tried to breathe confidence into her voice. "Whoever's catching for me should stand over there." She waved toward a grassy spot directly in her line of sight.

Lina moved into position.

"Ready?" Annika asked.

When Lina nodded, Annika gently tossed her the apple. Lina looked surprised when she caught it. Ida clapped.

"Impressive," Hans praised. "Don't even try to reach all the fruit from there, Annika. I'll move the ladder after you finish this side. The goal right now is to pick as much of the harvest as quickly as possible...without anyone getting hurt," he added sternly. "Hear that, Max?"

When Ehrich, Margarete, and Elsa returned with the empty wagon and a jug of water and slices of Apfëlkuchen, the harvesters had completed their three trees, and Max had moved onto a fourth. They weren't picked clean, but most of the Äpfel were in baskets or piles on the ground waiting for the crates Ehrich's crew had emptied.

"You got a lot done," Ehrich said in surprise.

"Turns out this girl is just as good at climbing as she is at catching." Hans offered Annika the metal cup.

Ehrich's eyebrows raised. "Truly? Is the ladder holding up?"

Annika laughed. "Are you saying I'm fat?"

Ehrich stammered. "No such thing...I..."

Annika swallowed another bite of Kuchen. "If I eat any more of your Mutter's delicious treats..."

Hans glanced at the lowering clouds. "No more treats for now. I'd be surprised if we get to more than three trees, although we can pick faster now since we'll have two people to throw to."

"All right." Ehrich took a last swig of water. "I'll gather everything you and Elsa already picked, and then I'll catch for Annika. Margarete, you help Max."

Annika couldn't suppress her smile at Margarete's pout. Ehrich carefully positioned the ladder for Annika and stood behind her as she climbed. Satisfied with its stability, he quickly loaded the produce and distributed the empty boxes. Then he stepped up next to Lina and managed to catch every red orb lobbed to him. When Lina bobbled a catch, he reached out and plucked it out of the air. Annika had to grasp two thick branches while she and Lina laughed at his antics.

When Annika descended and Ehrich took the crate to the wagon, she measured the progress of the other groups. Hans, his sister Frieda, and Elsa had nearly finished another tree. Since Hans was tall, he could reach almost every piece of fruit from the ladder. Although Elsa dropped many of hers, Hans and his sister worked efficiently.

"Can't you girls catch anything?" an exasperated Max asked his team.

Ida's perturbed voice came from the other side of the tree. "We're doing our best. It would help if your aim were better."

"Standing on two branches doesn't allow for the best aim, unless you want me tumbling down, Ida Schäfer."

Annika moved over for a closer look. Ida was standing too far to the side. Poor Max had to twist to see her.

"Why don't you try standing underneath him, so he can just drop the Äpfel?" Ana suggested. She stood slightly to Max's right and spread open her brown work apron. "Drop it right here."

"Finally, a girl with a brain," Max muttered.

"What did you say, Max Roth?" Ida demanded, hands on her hips.

Annika bit back a smile at the sparks flaring between the two.

"If you stand over here, it will be easier." Max shifted so he was standing more comfortably, plucked an apple, and dropped it into Annika's apron.

Ida grimaced but moved next to Annika.

"I'd best get back to my tree, so you don't outpace me too much." Annika returned to where the ladder had been. "Hey, where's the ladder?"

A voice answered from the next row of trees. "We moved it over here."

When Annika went around Max's tree, she saw Lina standing off to the side as Margarete tottered on the fourth rung. "That's the wobbly rung, Margarete. Come down one."

"Nonsense." Margarete reached toward a cluster of apples. "I won't be able to reach much down there—"

The rung collapsed, and Margarete slid downward. "Eee—" Teetering backward, she fell.

Hans scurried down his ladder, Max vaulted out of his tree, and everyone ran toward the ruckus.

Ida tried to pull the ladder off Margarete, but Margarete moaned.

"Her legs are tangled in the ladder. Just hold it off her face while I check for broken bones." Annika probed Margarete's exposed legs. "Does this hurt?"

"Pull my skirt down," Margarete hissed, eyes tightly shut.

Annika complied but kept probing underneath. "I don't feel any breaks, but something might be sprained."

Hans extricated her from the ladder.

"Can you sit up?" Ehrich asked, concern in his light blue eyes.

Margarete took a deep breath. "I think so, if you'll help me."

Ehrich slid his strong hands behind her back and slowly pushed her upright.

"Can you wiggle your toes?" Annika asked.

Margarete wiggled the toes of both feet. "Nothing more to see here," she said, struggling to stand. Annika supported her on one side and Ehrich on the other, but Margarete gasped in pain and clutched Ehrich's arm, favoring her left leg.

"Let's take her up to Mutter and get her a cold compress," Lina said.

"I'll bring the wagon over." Ehrich grabbed a crate and disappeared into the next row of trees.

After Annika took Hans' place on the ladder, Hans and Max gathered the remaining crates and baskets of Äpfel. As soon as the wagon pulled away with Ehrich and his sisters in the front and Margarete and Ida in the back, fat raindrops began to fall.

"I think we'll have a few more minutes." Hans hoisted Max into a tree and exchanged places with Annika. He threw apples as fast as Annika could catch them while Max dropped several apronfuls into Frieda's lap.

Annika was beginning to feel damp when Ehrich returned in the wagon. They scooped up the remaining harvest and ran for the wagon. The girls scrambled into the back with Max, and Ehrich draped a thick blanket over their heads.

"Hold on!" Ehrich urged the horse to a trot and drove into the barn as the storm unleashed its fury. The men jumped down, shook the water off like dogs, and assisted the girls. Ehrich rubbed down the plow horse, soothing him as thunder roared and rain rattled the roof. The group settled on benches and hay to wait out the worst of the storm.

Hans kept pacing to the door to check the storm clouds. "We've got to get home for the evening milking, Max. Dad and Gerry left to deliver furniture in Wetzlar. If they didn't make it back before this, they may bed down somewhere for the night."

"How many milk cows do you have now?" Annika hugged herself against the colder air blowing through the open barn door.

"Just the two."

"Your ma can handle two milk cows, especially after seven of you Roths," Annika teased.

"Ja, but she's home alone, and she was feeling poorly. Vater said to take good care of her, and here I am half an hour away."

"We Steins appreciate the help. The rain'll let up, and we'll lend you some cloaks and send you on your way." Ehrich chewed a stalk of hay as he sized up the harvest. "I'm going to give you a basket of Äpfel for your trouble. You too, Annika."

"Just a small one. I didn't do as much as Hans, Frieda, and Max, and it's just me and Vater anyway."

Ehrich dropped his voice for Annika's ears alone. "You saved as many Äpfel as me or Hans. You're amazing."

Warmth spread through Annika. No one had complimented her like that since her Mutter had passed. Vater was a man of few words, and he saved them for the weather and livestock. She stood and brushed hay from her skirt.

"It's slowing down. Let's make a run for it to the house." Hans beckoned to Frieda.

"Watch out for the branches down in the yard." Ehrich set his cap back on his head. He outran them through the puddles and flung the kitchen door wide so they could dash inside.

Margarete was sitting in front of the kitchen hearth, foot propped on a stool with a cloth wrapped around it. Elsa was stirring a pot over the fire while Ida, Lina, and *Frau* Stein worked at the kitchen table.

"Can you stay for dinner?" Frau Stein deftly chopped apples and threw them into a pan with some sliced pork.

Annika's mouth watered at the sight of pork. They hadn't eaten pork all summer, and their hogs still needed butchering this fall.

"I'm sorry, ma'am, but we have to get home." Hans took a mug of beer from Elsa.

"How are we going to get home?" Ida asked Margarete. "You can't walk, and Vater will be gathering up the sheep."

"Ehrich will take you home later," Frau Stein said. "Once I'm sure your foot's all right. I can't believe you were up on a ladder. Annika, if you hadn't started this whole thing..."

Annika froze as she accepted a stein from Elsa, all her previous warm feelings draining from her body into the cold, oaken floor, leaving her chilled.

Noticing her shiver, Ehrich pulled another chair in front of the fire. "Come, sit, Annika, and you too, Frieda. Mutter, Annika did the work of a man today. We should be grateful." He looked out the tiny window at the renewed downpour. "We're not going to get many more good Äpfel after tonight's storm."

His mother pursed her lips. "We're thankful, of course, to all of you." She continued to fuss as she added onions and herbs. "But better to be ladies and keep your feet on the ground."

Lina patted her mother's arm. "Of course, Mutter. Annika and Margarete never would have climbed the ladder if it weren't necessary."

Annika slid her bare feet to the warmth of the hearth.

Chapter 3

You have to sit still if you want your hair to look right."
Annika struggled to capture wisps of Lucie's fly-away
hair.

Lucie crossed her arms and pressed herself into the chair. "I
feel like I may float away."

"Or jump up and dance a jig." Annika sighed and attempted
to re-loop Lucie's braid.

"I can't believe Fritz already spoke with Vater. This is my
first social as a betrothed woman. I can dance with Fritz or
sit and eat with him, and no one will be urging me to partner
with boys who step on my toes while they stare at my bust. I
don't have to wonder who will bring me home or wait for my
brothers and cousins to take pity on me when no one asks me
to dance."

Annika paused with pins in her mouth and hands in mid-
air. She never lacked for partners so had no idea the torments
Lucie experienced.

"I'm sure Paul's happy, too. It was his turn to escort me,
but he almost never dances since Gretchen died." Lucie's older
brother stood morosely in the corner at every event, quaffing
beer and talking with the men. Brothers abounded in Lucie's
family, just like Annika's. Paul never attended if another of
Lucie's brothers could chaperone her, but they were married
with families of their own. "Ehrich should have more dances
for you, with Margarete staying off her ankle. Do you think
she'll even bother to come?"

Annika fastened the last braid in place. "I'm sure she'll try—

if she gets a ride. She can still gossip and eat, maybe even dance a couple times since it's only a sprain. Now, take a look in the mirror and tell me what you think."

Lucie hopped up and peered into the mirror on her mother's bedroom wall. "It looks amazing, like it always does when you style it. You'll help me get ready on my wedding day, won't you?"

"I wouldn't miss it. And I'm going to sew you a dress that will be the envy of every bride in Braunfels!"

"Mutter said we can go to Wetzlar next month to look for fabric when Paul lays in supplies for the bakery. You'll come too, won't you?"

"I haven't been to Wetzlar in ages. What fun!" Annika took her turn in front of the mirror and patted a few golden strands into place. "I wonder if I should have worn my new red dress, but I hated to wear the same thing to two frolics in a row."

"You look great in this blue one. It brings out your eyes."

"Because my eyes aren't truly blue like yours."

"Yours are more interesting. It's like they reflect the sky, Annika. Blue some days and gray on others."

Annika laughed. "You're much better at compliments than the boys in this town. You need to give lessons on wooing a girl. One farmer told me my hair was as fine as his best horse's."

Lucie and Annika fell on the bed in a fit of giggles.

Lucie's mother knocked on the door. "Fritz is here. Are you girls ready yet?"

Lucie jumped up. "Yes, Mutter."

The young women descended the stairs and donned their shawls in the front room where Fritz waited.

"I'm the luckiest man at the dance to be escorting the two prettiest girls," he said.

"Get on with you." Lucie smiled and blushed.

Lucie's mother handed her a cake. "You two have a good night and make sure you come in quietly. Your Vater and Paul have to be up early tomorrow to start the ovens. As long as you're at the counter by half past eight, you can sleep in a bit."

Lucie kissed her mother's cheek. "Thank you, Mutter. We won't disturb you."

Annika grabbed a basket of cookies she had baked at home, and the three young people stepped out into the blustery dusk.

Annika pulled her wool shawl tighter and wished she'd brought her cloak. A killing frost would hit her garden any night now. To distract herself from Fritz and Lucie's affectionate cuddling, she fell behind a few steps and examined the goods offered in the Vogels' store windows. A machine-loomed gingham caught her eye. It would make a pretty tablecloth for the newlyweds, if she had enough money saved up from her sewing. She'd have to ask the price next time she purchased salt or sugar.

The main thoroughfare of Braunfels was quiet, although she could hear music from the *Gasthaus* several streets away. As they turned onto the next street, activity increased with walkers and wagons converging on the school.

"Guten Abend!" floated on the wind along with the yellow beech leaves.

A blond young man fell into step by Annika. "Hello, Fraülein Lange."

Annika's pulse quickened. "Guten Abend, *Herr* Weber."

"So you remember me?" Gustav's mouth quirked into a smile.

"Of course. How could I forget the weaver from..." Annika switched the basket of cookies to her other arm. "I don't believe you mentioned where you were from, just that Gerry invited you to our last social."

"You have a good memory. I met him in Wetzlar, which is home."

"Do you work with other weavers?"

"My Vater and *Onkel* are master weavers and have passed on the trade to three of us boys. The women of our family spin the thread."

"Annika's the best seamstress in Braunfels." Lucie chimed in, having paused in the schoolyard to let Annika catch up.

Fritz shook Gustav's hand. "Herr Weber, allow me to present my betrothed, Lucie Becker."

Gustav bowed. "Felicitations on your engagement. I met Herrn Huber last month but didn't have the pleasure of an introduction to you, Fraülein Becker. I can see that Fritz has beaten me to one of the fair flowers of Braunfels." He gestured to the open door with a flourish. "But let's not stand out in the cold."

Annika and Lucie preceded the men into the schoolroom. Benches lined the walls, and fiddlers and accordion players shared a corner with an upright piano. A basket sat on its shiny top to collect donations for the musicians, who were warming up their instruments.

Treats loaded the instructor's desk in the far corner. Lucie set the *Bienenstich* dripping with honey and almonds in the center. Annika placed her homemade cinnamon cookies next to the cake while the men helped themselves to ale from the beer barrel.

As the instruments segued into a lively polka, couples began twirling around the dance floor. After the women laid their shawls on a bench, Lucie and Fritz joined the throng.

"Shall we?" Gustav offered Annika his hand.

"Certainly."

Gustav was a good dancer for a large man, and his hands were gentle on Annika. "You look as beautiful as I remember."

"I wore a new dress last month. This one doesn't compare."

"I respectfully disagree. Did you design this one yourself?"

"Ja."

"It's very becoming, and it brings out your lovely eyes, which seem to change constantly, like the water in the North Sea."

Annika blushed. "I've never seen the North Sea."

"It's mesmerizing. I hope you'll see it someday." He thought for a moment. "They also remind me of the winter sky."

Annika laughed. "I've heard that before."

"Another admirer?"

"Something like that."

The dance ended, and a folk dance began with women lined up on one side and men on the other. Annika was still beaming when she came face-to-face with a frowning Ehrich. "Who was that?" he whispered when the lines intertwined.

"Gustav Weber, a weaver from Wetzlar."

"What's his business in Braunfels?"

"Hans Roth invited him."

"Humph." The couples separated back into their lines and moved two steps to the right.

Annika didn't see Ehrich again until he found her resting with a mug of cider and chatting with Lucie and Fritz. "May I have the first waltz?"

Margarete interrupted from nearby. "I thought you promised that to me?"

Ehrich looked startled. "I asked if you'd like to try one dance..."

"I can hardly dance a jig or a polka. I'll have to start with a slow, smooth dance to see how my ankle holds up, so that means a waltz." Margarete fluffed her skirts.

"So it does. Forgive me, ladies. Could I have the pleasure of the second waltz, Annika?" he said.

"Ja." Annika glared at her rival.

Fritz cleared his throat, and Annika gulped the rest of her cider and fiddled with the empty cup in her hands. "I can tell this didn't come from the Stein orchard," she finally said.

"Yes," Margarete agreed. "It's a little too sweet. Your family makes the best cider in Hessen, Ehrich."

Ehrich bowed. "If the weather's fine, we plan to press cider on Thursday. We'd be pleased to have all of you come out to the orchard and turn the work into a celebration."

"That sounds lovely." Margarete beamed.

"I'd like to spend time outside before it gets too cold. Would you have time to pick me up and press cider for a few hours, Fritz?" Lucie asked.

"I'll make time." Fritz and Lucie's eyes locked.

"The two of you are so sweet," Margarete said.

Werner latched onto Annika's arm as he passed. "Are you ready to polka, Anna?" Werner guided her to the dance floor where they became the center of attention with their intricate steps and turns.

Annika almost forgot about Ehrich until she glanced back at the bench she'd just vacated. Her eyes met Ehrich's.

Margarete was passing him a stein of cider. Lina was whispering in his ear.

The next time Annika caught a glimpse of the bench, Margarete was surrounded by young men, but Ehrich wasn't among them.

"He's a few couples behind us with his sister," Werner informed her.

Annika turned her head and smiled at Lina. "How do you always know what I'm thinking?"

"Because I've been doing it for years, *Cousine*."

Annika tried to swat him, but he nimbly backed away. "Don't be tangling our feet. You'd ruin my reputation as a dancer."

Annika laughed. "No one could do that. We all know you're the best partner here. Thanks for rescuing me back there."

"My pleasure. You make me look good." Werner winked and handed her off to the cobbler as a folk dance began.

Annika tried to converse pleasantly, but she was worried about the first waltz, which would come up any time. Although she was curious about how Margarete would fare with her ankle, she didn't want to have to sit out and watch. Hopefully, someone would claim her as it started.

As she'd suspected, the instruments transitioned from the folk dance into a Strauss waltz. She moved to the side as everyone else found her prearranged partner. Margarete was moving gracefully without any hint of a limp.

"Darn!"

"Pardon me?" a familiar deep voice asked from her side.

Annika startled. "Nothing. Just talking to myself."

Gustav chuckled. "If you also find yourself without a partner, Fraülein, shall we?" He gestured toward the other couples.

Annika nodded.

Gustav positioned them on the dance floor. He placed a hand on her waist and she on his upper arm. His muscles belied his occupation as a weaver. Looking straight ahead, her eyes fell on his dimples. She adjusted her gaze up just a fraction.

"You're refreshingly tall, Fraülein. I don't have to stoop to dance with you."

"I'm glad I can give you a break from all our petite Braunfels beauties, Herr Weber."

"It's good to stand tall and proud on an evening like this one."

Realizing he must have overheard Margarete's remarks after Ehrich's offer to waltz, Annika flushed. "I agree, of course."

"Your nemesis seems to be moving a bit slowly."

"Does she?"

"I don't think she'll be dancing much after this one."

Annika feigned a sorry look.

Gustav's mouth quirked up in one corner. "You don't have to pretend with me."

"I'm not sure I could fool you if I wanted to."

The waltz ended, and the musicians took a break for refreshments. Gustav walked her back to Lucie's side. "You look like a girl who would like some Kuchen. Would you care for some too, Fraülein Becker?"

"My betrothed has gone to get us some, but *danke*, Herr Weber."

When Gustav left, Lucie smiled dreamily. "I love being able to say that...my betrothed."

Annika sat and rubbed her feet. "I wish my future was settled."

Lucie dropped her voice. "I did a lot of praying about a spouse. I've watched my parents be partners in running the bakery and raising us." She gestured with her hands. "I wanted a good man who's not just going to order me around. I want someone who will listen to what I think about our children and livelihood."

Annika slipped her shoe back on. "How do you know Fritz will do that?"

"I told him I wanted to continue working at my family's bakery. He's going to make sure I can come into town two days a week, at least until the babies come. I'll bring home bread from the bakery, so I won't have as much to do at home."

"I'm really glad for you, Lucie. I just want to find someone who can support a family and doesn't drink much." Annika's eyes sparkled. "Handsome and charming go without saying."

"Of course." Lucie's smile sobered. "You should try praying. I'll add my prayers to yours."

"I pray every Sunday at church. And before meals, of course. I can't really ask Vater to add a spouse to those prayers."

"I pray before I fall asleep."

"I used to...when Mutter was alive. Now I talk to her sometimes."

"Praying to God can be just like talking to your Mutter. Tell him what's on your mind."

"I never thought of it like that."

Gustav and Fritz returned with Kuchen. The night flew by until the second and last waltz.

Annika and Ehrich took their place among the other couples. *God, please make Ehrich want to marry me.* Annika's face hurt from smiling by the time the waltz and last folk dance ended. Ehrich had lined up across from her for that dance too.

"I brought the wagon," Ehrich said. "Do you need a lift home?"

"Danke, but I'm staying with Lucie tonight."

Lina bounced over to them. "Margarete's asking when we can leave. She's tired and her ankle hurts." She rolled her eyes. "I don't see why Mutter said we had to bring her."

"Why don't you see if the Roths are ready? Gerry, Hans, and Frieda are hitching a ride with us, too."

Lucie darted through the crowd, and Ehrich turned back to Annika. "Mother said Margarete shouldn't miss all the fun tonight even if she couldn't dance much. She thinks we owe her since she fell in our orchard."

"Sounds like she overdid it." Annika turned away.

"Annika, you'll come on Thursday, won't you?"

"If Vater can spare me."

"Tell him you'll bring home some cider." Ehrich winked. "I'll see you Thursday if the weather's good. If not, I'll let you know the day."

Chapter 4

Thursday dawned overcast but dry, so after Annika prepared breakfast and tidied the kitchen, she took the shortcut through fields and a patch of woods to the Steins' orchard.

Elsa ran to greet her, apron full of apples. "Didn't you wear an old apron, Annika? Mutter gave me one of hers. It holds so many Äpfel, and it doesn't matter how dirty it gets."

Annika glanced down at her own painstakingly embroidered apron. Bright red and orange flowers decorated the scalloped hem. "Aren't you smart? I didn't even think to grab an old one. I'll have to put the apples into the wagon or a basket."

"Maybe Ehrich will let you crank the press. He said I could have a turn when his arm gets tired."

"I might let the men show off their muscles with that job. Who else is here?"

"Lucie and Fritz." Elsa made a face. "Margarete and Ida. Margarete's sitting in the kitchen with Mutter because of her ankle. Mutter said she'd send her out later to supervise. Like we need to be told what to do. Even I know what to do, and I'm the youngest. I've been doin' it every autumn since I can remember."

"You're the expert then. Tell me where to start."

"We'll fill up the wagon with the fruit on the ground. The storm knocked everything out of the trees, so you don't need to climb any ladders today. Ehrich's setting up the press with

Fritz."

Annika followed Elsa to the wagon. Lucie, Ida, and Lina were gathering fruit on the other side.

"*Morgen!*" they greeted each other.

Lucie waved Annika over to her side. "Frau Stein also wants to make applesauce, so any fruit that's barely bruised can go in these baskets." She dropped her voice. "Mutter told me never mind bringing home cider but try to wrangle some Äpfel for strudel."

Annika's mouth watered at the thought of the flaky cinnamon treat from Becker's bakery.

"Anything for the hogs goes in that trough." Lina pointed to an old feed trough.

"That's all there is to it." Elsa skipped to a tree. "We don't need *supervised.*"

"Mutter's just trying to include Margarete." Lina soothed her little sister.

Fritz emerged through the trees. "Press is all set up next row over. Ehrich figures by the time we pick up the drops in this row, we can get the press started. He went back to the house for a few minutes."

The group bent to their task—the only sounds the buzz of bees and the thump of apples against the wood of the wagon or feed trough.

Laughing and a deep bass voice announced the arrival of Margarete, Ehrich, and Frau Stein to the nearby press. The sound of knives being sharpened drowned out Ehrich's approach. He had hefted a full basket into each arm before Annika realized he was there.

"Hallo, Annika. Could you bring this third basket?"

Annika followed Ehrich to a large apple press where his mother and Margarete waited. "Guten Morgen, Frau Stein,

Margarete."

Frau Stein studied her, unsmiling. "Would you like to borrow an apron, Annika?"

Annika set her basket beside Ehrich's and ran her fingers over her apron's fine orange and red threads. "*Nein*, danke. I'll be careful. Would you like more help here or should I go back to picking up Äpfel?"

"We're all set. Margarete's quick with a knife."

Dismissed, she turned to go, Ehrich falling into step beside her. He cleared his throat. "I appreciate your coming."

"Thank you for inviting me. It's a beautiful morning."

"Ja, on days like these I'm glad to be a farmer. Crisp air, not too hot or cold." He breathed deeply. "Smells like Äpfel and grass. It's the freezing cold days I wish I were baking bread or working in a machine shop."

"Wouldn't be pleasant in the heat of summer."

"True, true." Having reached the group, Ehrich bent to start picking up drops. Annika joined him.

After clearing all the apples under the first row of trees, Ehrich jumped into the wagon, pulled Elsa up beside him and started driving down the row and around to the press in the middle of the next row. Everyone else cut across and took a water break.

"Can't wait to taste the cider." Fritz smacked his lips.

"Neither can I." Ehrich opened the tailgate and started rolling a few Äpfel into a wooden tub half-filled with water. "Especially once it's hard."

Frau Stein swatted at her son.

"Scold all you want, Mutter, but you look forward to it, too. Last year's is gone."

"Your Vater finished it just last week. It was a good harvest last year. Looks about the same this year, praise God." She and Lina swished the apples around in the water, removing the dirt. Then they rolled them onto a scarred, wooden table.

After a pile accumulated, Frau Stein began cutting the bad spots out, dropping the rotten pieces into the hogs' trough. Lina continued washing. Margarete swiftly quartered the fruit and threw it into the hopper on top of the press.

Everyone else continued picking up apples. The sun had peeked out and was warming up the day. Even after laying aside their coats and shawls, the pickers were starting to feel heated.

"I should put my foot up." Margarete climbed into the front of the wagon. "Why don't you take my place, Annika?"

"I'd be happy to." Annika took the remaining knife from the table and began slicing. She tried to adjust to the feel of the iron, wishing for the familiar knife in her kitchen, but this one seemed clumsy. Possibly not sharp enough? But she'd heard the knives being sharpened. She redoubled her efforts but lagged far behind Frau Stein.

"Tsk, tsk." Frau Stein dumped more leavings into the trough. "Can't you keep up, child?"

Annika blushed. To her relief, Ehrich and most of the others had moved down the row and were involved in conversation.

But Margarete was still nearby. "Ehrich, can you get me down? Annika needs help."

The sun's warmth seemed to double in strength. Annika could feel sweat between her shoulder blades. She wiped her slick hands on her apron as Ehrich lifted Margarete from the wagon.

Margarete bustled over with her knife. "We'll catch up in no time." True to her word, the pile of apples vanished within minutes. "No problem at all!" She sent Annika a pointed look.

Ehrich paused after pouring another basket of drops into the wagon bed. "I'm going to send Elsa to stand in the front of the wagon and roll the fruit toward you." He checked the hopper full of apples. "Almost ready to press. Fill it to here." He indicated a line near the top. "Then you can pile more Äpfel in this basket." He set his empty basket next to Margarete. "I'll be right back."

When he returned with Elsa and another basket of apples, he opened the press and pushed the fruit onto it. Satisfied with the number of apples, he snapped it shut and began cranking. A dribble of liquid became a steady flow. When it slowed, he reversed the cranking until he could remove the pulp and fill the press with more fruit. He began the process again.

Annika's fascination with his rippling muscles was broken when Frau Stein said, "We're all caught up here, Annika. Help Elsa push the Äpfel toward us."

Blushing again, Annika climbed into the front of the wagon and knelt on the seat. When Elsa leaned so far forward that she nearly tumbled into the apples, Annika caught her dress and hauled her back onto the seat. "Careful. Let's clear a place to stand in the wagon bed, so we don't have to reach so far."

"Ehrich said we were getting the dangerous job."

"Maybe we could use a rake to push the Äpfel?"

Frau Stein frowned. "It will take longer to fetch it than just sticking to your task."

"I thought there might be one down here in the orchard."

"There's not."

Elsa watched as Annika pushed the apples forward. "Watch out for the wasps, Anna. I don't want to get stung like I did last year. My hand swelled up like a pig's bladder balloon."

"I think you'll fit in this little space I cleared. You can use it to move some more Äpfel so I can stand with you."

Elsa started to scramble over the wagon seat, but a huge wasp flew in front of her face. Panicked, she flailed her arms. Annika swatted the threat away, but the wasp landed on the rump of the farm horse. The poor beast jerked, swishing her tail. The wagon shifted, and Elsa plunged to the ground with a sickening snap.

Frau Stein rushed to her side. "My baby! My baby's dead!"

Annika leaned over the wagon's side. Taking in Elsa's white face, she feared the woman was right.

Ehrich rushed over to his little sister. "She's breathing, Mutter. Calm down. It looks like she injured her arm." Elsa's right arm was bent at an impossible angle. "Fritz, go get the doctor. Elsa's hurt," he yelled.

Lucie and Ida joined the small group as Fritz dashed toward the barn and thundered out minutes later, saddleless, on his buggy horse.

"Elsa, Elsa, can you talk to Mutter?" Frau Stein cried. Looking up, she spied Annika. "Get off our property! You're nothing but trouble."

Elsa moaned.

"Mutter, this wasn't Annika's fault. Leave her be and lower your voice for Elsa's sake." Ehrich laid his hand on Elsa's back. "It's all right, Liebling. You took a fall."

Elsa mumbled. "Hurts. Am I stung?"

"No, you didn't get stung. What hurts? Do you think you can sit up?"

Annika crept down the other side of the wagon. Should she leave?

Lucie rounded the wagon. "Just ignore her. People say things they don't mean when they're upset."

Lina joined them. "Elsa's sitting up. Ida went to fetch a bucket of cold water. Let's keep pressing the Äpfel while Mutter tends to her."

Lucie and Annika took over for Frau Stein while Lina and Margarete resumed their tasks. Ehrich soon joined them at the press. Annika's hands shook so much she feared she'd cut herself and prove Frau Stein correct.

"Maybe you should wash for a while, Anna." Lina switched jobs with her. "Ehrich, this knife didn't get sharpened," she said, running the blade over her thumb.

Ehrich examined it. "You're right. No wonder you were having trouble, Annika." He ran it over the whetstone and offered it back to Annika.

She shook her head. "I'll stick to washing for now."

Fritz returned with the doctor who splinted Elsa's arm and prescribed rest. Ehrich gently carried her up to the house.

He returned with cold water, bread, and cheese. "Doc thinks she hit her head but should be fine. Mutter's keeping a watch on her. Sorry about Mutter. She's extra protective of Elsa."

The group worked hard the rest of the afternoon and finished in time for the afternoon milking. Fritz swiftly packed Lucie, Margarete, and Ida along with jugs of cider and a basket of Äpfel for strudel into his buggy so he could drop off the women before hurrying to his chores.

Ehrich, Lina, and Annika stored barrels of cider in the cellar. "I wish I could give you a ride home, Annika, but Lina and I have to milk, feed the chickens, and slop the hogs while Elsa rests. Leave your jugs here, and I'll run them over sometime in the next few days."

Cheered at the thought of seeing him again soon, Annika set off at a brisk pace to return home and prepare supper.

Her father was still working in the barn, so she stoked embers on the hearth and added twigs to heat leftover turnip soup. She floured the table and retrieved a clump of yeast starter to make rolls before setting the table.

When her Vater got to the table, he grabbed his stein. "Where's the cider, girl? I don't want water. I've had a hankering all day for fresh cider."

"The Steins filled those big jugs for us. Ehrich didn't want me to carry them home, but he didn't have time to drive me." Annika ladled up a bowl of soup, trying to gauge if her father was going to lash out and cuff her. "Elsa had a mishap and broke her arm, but he'll bring them by real soon." Undecided about her father's frame of mind, she set the bowl to cool on the hearth and dished up another.

Her father grumbled but sat in his chair. She put the perfectly browned rolls on a square cloth on the table.

"Smells good."

She released a pent-up breath and retrieved the bowls. They bowed their heads and prayed aloud in unison. "Come, Lord Jesus, be our guest, and let these Thy gifts to us be blessed."

Annika tacked on a silent plea. *Please, God, let Ehrich choose me for his wife and make his Mutter like me.*

Chapter 5

Annika inhaled the aroma of chocolate at one of Wetzlar's chocolatiers as Frau Becker dickered over supplies for the bakery. She looked longingly at the chocolate bars in the display but knew she couldn't spend any of her coins if she were to afford the cloth for Lucie and Fritz's wedding present.

Lucie bustled up to her friend. "Mutter says we can visit the haberdashery while she finishes up here. I'd like to get Fritz a gift."

The women combed over the men's ties, cravats, and handkerchiefs. Lucie finally selected a red and blue silk tie. "I know it's dear, but Fritz can wear it for our wedding and to church afterwards." Lucie handed the clerk a princely sum. "One little extravagance for my groom. Now let's go to Engel's *Kleider* Shop."

Paul and Frau Becker met them outside the haberdashery. After he accompanied them to the dressmaker's, he departed for a nearby Gasthaus to enjoy a beer.

Annika ran her hands over the woolens and linens and eyed the silks in the glass case. She had never sewn silk. If the Beckers splurged for Lucie's wedding, the slippery material could be difficult. To her relief, Lucie and her mother focused on the linen. Pale green, blue, or pink were the final choices. Linen would need ironed constantly as she sewed, but at least she was familiar with it.

Frau Becker draped the different colors over Lucie's shoulder and around her narrow waist. "Which color suits her best, Annika?"

"Either the blue or the pink is equally becoming. Which do you prefer, Lucie?"

"Blue would be more practical." Lucie sighed.

"Remember we're going to purchase wool for an everyday dress. Let's see if it comes in either of these colors before you make a final decision." Frau Becker moved down the counter to examine the woolens.

The bell on the shop door announced another patron.

"Herr Weber, it's good to see you. So, your Vater finally sent you over with the cloth he promised me." The plump dressmaker beamed. "Ladies, you'll want to look at this fine linen too. It's in such demand I have trouble keeping it in stock." She removed the red from the pile of fabrics. "This is already spoken for."

After accepting payment from the shopkeeper, Gustav lingered. "Fraülein Lange, Fraülein Becker, it's always a pleasure to see you. Do you come to Wetzlar often?"

"Nein, not often at all. It's such a surprise to see the one person I'm acquainted with in this city." Annika sensed Lucie's mother behind her, so she stepped aside. "Frau Becker, may I present Gustav Weber? Lucie, Fritz, and I met him this fall at the socials in Braunfels."

"I'm delighted to meet you." Gustav bowed over her hand.

Frau Becker inclined her head regally.

"Are you making purchases for the upcoming wedding?"

Lucie fingered the Webers' cloth. "Ja. Fritz and I have set the date for November 30. Annika has a lot of sewing to do."

"Perhaps I can be of some service in my profession as a weaver." Gustav examined the cloth on the counter. "All these? Or are you trying to make your final selections?"

"We've decided on a blue woolen, so it will be the pink linen for Lucie's big day." Frau Becker turned to Annika. "Do you think you can finish two dresses by the end of November?"

"If Lucie does the plain sewing and doesn't choose styles that are too difficult. Did you see a style you like?" Annika gestured toward the dress forms.

Lucie and her mother flitted to the opposite side of the shop.

Before Annika could follow them, Gustav cleared his throat and whispered, "Do you trust me?"

Annika looked into his cornflower blue eyes.

Gustav persisted. "Could I show you something before you finalize your purchases?"

"Certainly."

"Can you convince Lucie to buy only the wool and then meet me at the Gasthaus on the corner?"

"I think so. Lucie's older brother Paul is already there, waiting to drive us home."

"Good. I'll find him, and when you're done here, he and I will escort you to my family's business. It's not far." Gustav tipped his hat and left the shop.

"Annika, I found the perfect style!" Lucie pulled her friend toward a display at the window. "Come see."

Annika glanced at the shopkeeper who was deep in conversation with another customer. "Coming, dear, but listen, Gustav said to buy just the blue material. He wants to show us something. He's gone to find Paul now, so we can all go to his family's shop."

"What do you think it is?"

"If I had to guess, I'd say linen he thinks would suit you better."

Lucie's eyes sparkled. "A prettier shade?"

"Maybe. We'll have to go see."

Annika examined the pointed waistline and full skirt of the dress Lucie liked. While the Beckers purchased the wool, she inspected the cape-like pelerine that covered the bodice of the dress. It would be a little tricky, but she should be able to do it.

The ladies examined the goods in the storefront windows as they ambled down the street to find Paul and Gustav. After a stein of beer, they departed on foot for the Weber shop.

Humming emanated from the brick building. Gustav flung open the door and ushered them inside. A distinguished, middle-aged man set down his shuttle and left his loom. Three other looms kept up their clackety-clack accompanied by six spinning wheels on the other side of the room.

Gustav made the introductions to his father Oskar Weber. "Vater, could they see the fine pink linen you crafted last week? Fraülein Becker marries at the end of the month and is looking for material for a special dress to be sewn by Fraülein Lange."

"I'm so pleased you're choosing linen, Fraülein. Let me fetch it from upstairs." The man strode up the narrow staircase.

"We have a storage closet near our living quarters for our best pieces. Vater's very proud of this particular cloth. It's a color we've never achieved before. My sister's been experimenting with dyes."

Herr Weber returned, handling the champagne pink linen like his firstborn.

Lucie's intake of breath revealed her opinion.

"You like it?" Herr Weber smiled. "I'd be honored to have it grace a bride."

"Let's talk about the details." Frau Becker gestured him toward a private nook in the open room.

Noting Lucie's tension, Gustav said, "Vater will give you a

good price. Without a merchant as middleman, we can sell it for not much more than the cloth you were considering at Engel's."

Annika patted Lucie's hand. "This pink cloth is much better workmanship."

Lucie continued to watch her mother anxiously until Herr Weber wrapped the cloth in brown paper. Frau Becker handed him some coins and took the package.

"Danke." Lucie smiled at Gustav.

"Our family's contribution to the wedding."

"You'll have to join us and see the lovely dress Annika creates. November thirtieth at two in the afternoon."

"I wouldn't miss it." Gustav bowed over Lucie's hand but directed his gaze at Annika.

Paul cleared his throat. "Mutter, we should get going. Our supplies will be loaded, and we want to reach home before too late."

"It's taken a little longer than I planned, but I'm so pleased with the results of our shopping trip. We've gotten everything we needed, and thanks to you, young man," Frau Becker nodded at Gustav, "a bargain. We'll see you on Lucie's big day."

Chapter 6

A week after their trip to Wetzlar, Lucie pulled up to Annika's farmhouse in her family's buggy. Annika had spent hours bent over the dress, perfecting every detail. Her back and shoulders ached, but the look on her friend's face made the effort worthwhile.

"Annika, I can't believe this is my dress!"

Annika pulled it over Lucie's head and inserted a few pins. "I haven't started the pelerine."

"I like it without." Lucie twisted this way and that, trying to see the back in the mirror.

"The pelerine will keep you warm on your wedding day. I'm not letting you cover up this dress with a shawl."

"Never!" Lucie hugged her. "How many petticoats should I wear with this skirt? Come into town with me to pick them out. I need a few other things as well."

"Let's see how it looks with two." Annika sighed. "I don't think I can go. Papa's been complaining about his meals. I have to put more time into dinner today."

Noting her friend's red-rimmed eyes, Lucie said, "You need a break. These tiny stitches are going to make you cross-eyed. We'll stop by the bakery. Mutter will give us some bread and goodies, and I put a stew on this morning. You can bring some of that home."

Annika kneaded her back as she surveyed the kitchen and sitting room which were strewn with bits of material and thread.

"Please, Anna. I'll help you tidy up before we go, and I'll bring you home, too."

Annika carefully slid the dress up over Lucie's head and stored it in the loft. Lucie redressed, and the girls flew around the room, throwing the sewing supplies into a basket. They grabbed their cloaks and scrambled into the buggy.

As Lucie guided the gray carriage horse, Annika took a deep breath of the crisp autumn air. She hadn't spent much time outside in the past week other than caring for her chickens. She missed her walks through the crunchy red and gold leaves. She closed her eyes to reduce the sun's glare but tilted her face to soak up the sunshine.

She was almost asleep when Lucie drew Tilli to a halt and hopped down from the buggy. "We're here." She tied the reins to the post in front of the Vogel's general store. "Mutter and I saw some ready-made petticoats here. I bought one with a pretty edging at the beginning of the summer, so I can wear it on top. A stiff, plain one for underneath shouldn't be hard to find."

Annika folded up the lap robe and laid it on the seat before climbing down. If she could get the gingham for Lucie's gift today, she could save a trip into town and have more time to work on hemming the tablecloth. She'd have to buy it while Lucie was occupied.

Lucie led the way to the dry goods and started examining petticoats. Annika helped her select a stiff wool one for fullness and warmth. When Lucie moved away from the cloth to the display of shoes, Annika whispered instructions to Frau Vogel. Then she positioned herself between Lucy and the shopkeeper so Lucie wouldn't catch a glimpse of the gingham.

Oblivious, Lucie dithered between white and pale pink shoes.

"Do you have anything else to wear pink shoes with?"

41

Annika asked.

"Good point. White it is." After putting the petticoat on her family's store account, Lucie used coins to pay for the shoes. "Anna, remind me to put a coin in my new shoe on my wedding day."

"We won't forget." Annika smiled over the custom which was supposed to ensure wealth for the new couple.

While Lucie untied Tilli from the hitching rail, Annika paid for her purchase. Lucie drove them up the street to the bakery and, after a few words with her mother, disappeared into their living quarters to dish up some stew. Annika lingered over the glass counter displaying bread and pastry.

"We have plenty of wheat or rye bread, Annika. Which does your Vater prefer?" Frau Becker asked.

"Rye bread will be a nice change. Danke."

"No thanks necessary. We can give you baked goods each week until the wedding. I know you don't have long to do all we're asking."

Beyond grateful, Annika also accepted some small cakes. Lucie reappeared with a crock just as bells jingled to announce the next customer.

"Guten Abend," Ehrich greeted them.

"Ehrich, I'm glad to see you." Lucie handed the crock of stew to Annika. "I was going to take Annika home, but I realized I have more dinner preparations."

"I'm going home from here, so she can ride with me. Are you finished in town, Annika?"

"Ja, danke, Ehrich." She made a face at Lucie when Ehrich turned to the display case. Her friend beamed and mouthed, "You're welcome."

Frau Becker struggled to keep a straight face. She cleared her throat. "What would you like today, Ehrich?"

42

"Elsa asked for macaroons."

"How is she?" Frau Becker slid out a tray of cookies.

"She's able to bend her arm. Doc said to keep it in the sling a few more days and then let her use it a bit, see how things go."

"Bless her. We've been praying for her every night, haven't we, Lucie?"

"Ja, we have." Lucie tied on an apron.

Frau Becker picked up one cookie. "How many macaroons would you like, Ehrich?"

"Six, danke."

Lucie carefully wrapped the cookies in paper while Annika retrieved her package from Lucie's buggy. When Ehrich emerged from Becker's, he helped her into the wagon and draped a lap robe over both of them. "It's getting nippy. We'll have snow before we know it."

"I love the first snow of the season."

Ehrich chuckled. "Is there anything you don't love?"

"Dirty dishes, foxes in my chicken house, grumps..." Annika ticked off her response on her fingers. "Why do you ask?"

"You're so enthusiastic about everything—dancing, apple picking, Lucie's wedding. Don't worry. It's a good trait." Ehrich captured her restless fingers in his hand.

"I wish Vater thought so."

"Your mother had the same joy. You must remind him of his loss." Ehrich gave her hand a brief squeeze.

"I never thought of it that way. I seem to annoy him."

"I could see that happening when you were a schoolgirl chattering like a magpie," he teased. "You used to drive us all a little *verrückt*, but you've curbed that tendency. Unless you still jabber away at home?"

Annika elbowed him in the gut. "I most certainly do not."

"Hey! I forgot you always were one to defend yourself."

"I got into my share of scrapes at school. Comes with having older brothers." Annika sobered. "Honestly, it's awful at home, like all the joy got sucked out when the fever took Mutter."

"At least your Mutter was full of life when she was alive."

Annika pictured Frau Stein's sour expression. "Ja. I just wish…"

When she left her thought unfinished, Ehrich said, "We'll both be able to marry soon and establish new families, happy ones, I hope."

Annika went very still, except for the butterflies in her stomach, and tried to catch a glimpse of his expression from the corner of her eye. Neither spoke until he pulled into her lane.

"Thank you for the ride, Ehrich."

"You're welcome, Anna."

Annika's hand burned at his touch when he helped her descend from the wagon. He carried the warm crock she'd kept at her feet while she brought the bag from the bakery and her package. Thankful the house was tidy, she waved him inside. "Just set it on the table, please."

After following her instructions, he stood with hat in hand. "I've got to get back for chores, but I'm glad we bumped into each other. Save me a waltz at the wedding."

As she watched his departure from her small window, Annika's heart was already dancing.

Chapter 7

Basking in the success of Lucie's wedding dress, Annika watched the short service binding her friend to Fritz for the rest of their lives. Emerging into the bright afternoon light from the candlelit stone chapel, Annika followed the bride and groom's procession to the nearby Gasthaus.

Her Vater trailed behind with several cronies, boasting of the ale he'd consume. Annika hoped he wouldn't create a disturbance. She shuddered at the thought of returning home with him. She usually spent the night with Lucie in the apartment over the bakery after an occasion like this, but tonight her friend would sleep beside her husband in her new home. Annika shivered again.

"Do you need a coat?" A friendly voice interrupted her thoughts.

"Nein, danke, Herr Weber. Lucie will be so pleased you came."

Gustav fell into step beside her. "I wouldn't have missed this for all the silkworms in France."

"It was only a village wedding. I'm sure your family's been involved in finer weddings in Wetzlar."

"We have, and I must say, you've made a huge misstep today, Fraülein."

Annika's heart plummeted. "What mistake did I make?"

Gustav bent closer. "You've upstaged the bride."

"Ach. Lucie's dress is the best I've made!"

"That's not what I meant. You, in your simpler red dress, are outshining the bride." Gustav shot her a cocky look. "It's not your fault. God gifted you with beauty. Lucie was pretty today but still couldn't compare."

Feeling off balance, Annika wrapped her arms around her middle. "Have you already been into the ale?"

"I'm stone-cold sober, Fraülein, and, as you've said, I've been to many fine weddings, so you need to take my word on this." He glanced behind them. "And my arm, or you'll be trampled by the revelers behind us."

Annika reluctantly took his arm, and they moved forward. Gustav patted her arm. "Your creation is exquisite, Annika. Well done!"

Annika released her breath and smiled. "Danke."

"Daughter!" her father's voice roared behind them.

Annika pulled away from Gustav and hurried to her father. "What can I do for you, Vater?"

"Who's that?" Her father pointed at Gustav, who'd moved to the side of the street.

As they came abreast of Gustav, Annika said, "Vater, may I present Gustav Weber?"

Her father snorted.

"Gustav, this is my Vater, Wolff Lange. Gerry invited Gustav to one of our dances this fall. Gustav's family sold Lucie the linen for her wedding gown."

"Pleased to meet you, sir."

"Didn't Lucie go into Wetzlar to shop for this wedding?"

"Ja, I happened to see her at Engel's Kleider Shop. She was buying cloth when I was delivering linen. My family owns a weaving establishment in Wetzlar."

Wolff's eyes lighted. "Do they now? Tell me a bit about your family, son."

"My Vater and Onkel run the business together. The women spin the thread. We men weave and sell the linen."

"Brothers?"

"One younger brother."

Wolff clapped Gustav on the back. "We're glad you've joined the festivities today. Sorry about earlier. I thought I knew all the young men interested in my Annika."

Annika dropped her eyes to the ground, trying to hide her flaming cheeks.

"I understand, Herr Lange. One of my cousins is about Annika's age. We all keep an eye out for her."

Gustav and her father ducked to enter the Gasthaus. The scent of venison and pork greeted them. Rolls and pastries towered on trays accompanied by bowls of steaming vegetables. "Enjoy the feast, son. The Beckers are important tradespeople, and they're putting on an enormous send-off for their only daughter." He headed toward the men surrounding the barrel of ale.

Gustav turned back to Annika, but Frau Becker intervened. "Lucie's looking for you, Annika. She's in the back room."

"Save me a dance, Annika," Gustav said.

Annika nodded as she made her way through the crowd to a tiny room where Lucie was gulping down water.

"Are you okay?"

"Feeling a little faint, and Fritz caught the hem of my dress with his boot. Can you fix it?"

Annika examined the dirtied hem. "It didn't rip." She drew a needle and thread from her reticule. "Good thing your Mutter told me to bring these, just in case." She quickly stitched the hem. "Are you ready to join the celebration?"

"Ja. I caught my breath. I'm just hungry. We didn't take time to eat much this morning. Come on. You must be hungry, too."

Annika's stomach gurgled in agreement. "It all smells delicious."

Lucie linked an arm through Annika's and led her to the buffet. She and Annika piled tin plates with goodies and sat at the table with the groom and his family. The Beckers were darting around seeing to their guests. Paul stood at the ale barrel, filling steins.

A few instruments played while everyone ate. Then a fiddler joined them. "Gentlemen, find a partner for the polka," he bellowed.

Annika found herself dancing with one of Fritz's brothers. After a few folk dances, a Mozart waltz began. Ehrich materialized at her side. "May I claim this waltz?"

Annika took his arm. "I'm glad to see Elsa running around with her friends."

"You'd never know she'd been hurt." Ehrich held her closer than he ever had. "You did a good job with Lucie's gown."

"Danke."

"Have you begun one for yourself yet?"

"Nein. The dress fabric often depends on the season." Feeling encouraged by his interest, Annika plunged ahead. "I won't be eighteen until the end of April. I'm hoping for a spring or early summer wedding when the church can be filled with flowers, instead of just candles and greenery."

"That's a busy time of year on a farm."

"A wedding only takes one day, and I'd be able to work on my husband's farm all summer."

"If your Vater will let you go at that time of year."

Annika finished the last steps of the dance woodenly.

Werner swooped into her line of vision. "You look overheated, Annika. Let me take you outside."

Tears clouded Annika's eyes as she clung to her cousin's arm. He guided her through the throng and sat her on a bench.

"Do you mind if I have a smoke?"

Gazing at the night sky, Annika drew in a deep breath. "Nein, go ahead."

Werner removed tobacco from the pouch of his dress uniform and deftly rolled it in thin, brown paper. He cupped a match at its end and managed to light it despite the breeze. "Do you want to talk about it?" He ground out the match with the heel of his boot.

Annika remained mute.

"No, well then, you listen. I can see you've set your cap for that farmer. Are you sure that's what you want, Anna?"

She found her tongue. "Ehrich's a good man."

"I know he is, and handsome as well, though his Mutter doesn't seem to like us Langes. But you're a beautiful girl. You have other options."

"All our family knows is farming, Werner."

"You'd do any farmer proud, Liebling, but you also have a gift with needle and thread. You could do other things with your life."

"I want Ehrich," Annika whispered.

"Sometimes life doesn't work out the way we want. And sometimes that's for the best."

"You don't think he's going to marry me, do you, Werner? What have you heard?"

"Nothing! I don't know one way or the other. I just want you to know you have other choices." Werner stomped on his cigarette stump. "Me, I belong to the Prussian army right now, and they're calling me away to Berlin. This is our last chat for a while."

"I'm going to miss you so much. I'll write to you."

"You'd better! And I don't want a string of heartsick letters. I want happy letters full of amusing stories."

Annika enfolded him in a hug. "I'll try."

"I know you will. Now let's go back inside and take a look at your options. Are you sure you don't fancy city living? That Weber fellow keeps looking your way."

Chapter 8

When Annika woke to a chill December morning, she decided to take her quilt downstairs and put it on the quilting frame after her morning tasks were completed.

She could hear her mother's voice as she began her task. *Morgenstund hat Gold im Mund.* "Morning hours are worth gold" was what her mother used to say when Annika tried to snuggle back into her warm bed on cold winter mornings.

Today she had leapt out of bed with excitement. Ehrich had taken her for a sleigh ride in the first snow a few days ago. They had cuddled together and laughed to the accompaniment of the bells he'd attached to the horse's harness. Surely, she would be a bride by June.

Later that morning, she struggled to position the three layers of quilt smoothly. This step was always easier to do with someone else. *Oh, Mutter, I wish you were here.*

She could ask friends to quilt with her. Whom could she invite? Lucie was a busy newlywed.

A knock at the door interrupted her thoughts.

"Lina!" Annika swung the door wide. "I'm so glad to see you. Come in and I'll get you some Kaffee. Brrr. It's cold out there."

"Danke, Annika. I'd welcome a cup of Kaffee." Lina unwound her scarf. "Are you trying to frame your quilt by yourself? I can stay a bit to help."

"You're a godsend." Annika handed Lina a full mug. She

tugged one corner of the quilt. "Every time I get one part straight, another gets bunched up."

Lina wrapped her cold fingers around the mug and took a couple of swallows before approaching the frame. "Where do you want me to hold it?"

"Hold the short side in place while I attach the opposite side." Annika pulled until she was satisfied the stars lined up. She clamped the quilt to the frame. "I was just thinking about inviting a few girls over to quilt. Could you help me get started today? Vater won't want this to be out for long."

"I have about an hour." Lina fingered the yellow and blue stars. "This is gorgeous. So much prettier than Margarete's bridal quilt."

Annika froze.

"She showed it to me on Tuesday. She's going to have trouble finishing it by..." Lina grabbed Annika's hands. "I'm so sorry, Anna. I didn't want you to find out in church on Sunday, so I told Mutter I needed a long walk. I'd much rather have you for a sister."

Tears pooled in Annika's eyes. "Ehrich's marrying Margarete?"

"Ja," Lina whispered.

The joy of the morning slipped away, leaving Annika with a lump in her stomach. She turned her eyes from Lina's pitying gaze to the quilt.

"As soon as you turn eighteen, you'll be a bride, too. All the fellows are sweet on you."

"We just went for a sleigh ride. I thought he was having a good time." Annika bit her lip.

"He did. He was in high spirits until Mutter got to him. She said he'd do better to marry Margarete and have a warm bed this winter and a bun in the oven by summer."

Annika's anger began to simmer. "But he's a grown man. He doesn't have to do what she suggests."

"No, but Mutter makes us miserable if we don't do things her way. You know whoever marries Ehrich will have to live in our house. It's plenty big enough, but..."

"Your mother would rather work with Margarete."

"You know Margarete. She flatters Mutter, even though she's mean behind her back. Elsa's devastated. I would have sent her if Mutter didn't let me leave this morning. We both wanted *you* for our sister, but we're stuck with Margarete."

After sitting quietly for several minutes and sipping her coffee, Lina stood and washed her cup at the sink. "I know this is hard. Unless you want company, I'll leave now. I'm going to invite a couple of our friends and we'll come back Monday or Tuesday to quilt, whichever day suits you. It will let everyone know that you *will* be getting married soon."

Receiving no reply, Lina bent to kiss Annika's cheek. "I can't believe my brother is such a *dummkopf*."

"When is their big day?"

"December 29th." Lina brushed back Annika's hair. "You'll be much happier somewhere other than my Mutter's kitchen. She's my Mutter, and I love her, but I'm looking forward to getting out of there when I marry."

Lina let herself out. Annika buried her face in her hands and wept.

On Sunday, Annika set out for a long walk. She and Vater had eaten lunch in silence, and he was napping. If he knew something was wrong, he didn't say anything. Annika hadn't heard much of the sermon. Her thoughts were still swirling with the news of Ehrich and Margarete.

It was cold but bright. Annika took a basket and went

down to the stream to gather holly for the coming *Weihnachten* season. She usually waited a few more weeks, but this would make the cottage festive for the quilting on Tuesday afternoon. Lina and Lucie had gathered a few friends. They should be able to finish the quilt so Annika could tuck it back in its chest in the attic. If only she could box up her hurt along with it.

After cutting holly and evergreen boughs, Annika decided to go home by the longer route on the road instead of fighting through any more thickets.

She was halfway home when she heard a wagon behind her. She ignored it until it drew up beside her.

"Whoa!" Ehrich's bass voice rumbled.

Annika closed her eyes.

"Hi, Anna. Would you like a lift?"

"Nein, danke."

"I'd really like to talk to you."

Annika faced him and glared. "Well then, talk."

Ehrich climbed down from the seat and ran his hand through his blond hair. Annika backed away from him. "I wanted you to know it was a hard decision. Mutter had very definite ideas about...things."

"So Lina told me."

"I'm sorry, Anna."

"You should be," Annika whispered under her breath as she stepped off the dirt road to pass him.

"What did you say?" Ehrich reached toward her.

Annika side-stepped. "Goodbye, Ehrich."

On Thursday, Vater hitched Blackie to the wagon so Annika could buy supplies at Vogel's. After making her purchases, including thread to replace the spool used on her completed quilt, Annika stopped by the bakery. Lucie usually worked at Becker's on Thursdays. Since there were no other customers, Lucie brought out mugs of coffee, and the two friends chatted. Lucie was wrapping up a couple slices of Äpfel strudel for Annika and her father when Margarete swept into the shop.

"*Guten Tag*," she greeted the twosome. "I've come to pick out a few things for my wedding feast. Ehrich and I are marrying late morning, so something appropriate for luncheon." She turned to Annika. "Of course, we're only inviting a small selection of guests, relatives mostly. You do understand."

Annika's hands fisted but she smiled back. "Of course I do, Margarete. A sheepherder's family can't afford to feed the whole town. I wouldn't want to impose." She turned to her friend. "Blackie's been standing in the cold long enough. I'll see you soon."

"Have a good day, Margarete," she added as she passed the red-faced girl. "I would recommend a color other than crimson for your gown. It simply doesn't become you."

"Ehrich likes how I look in any old thing," Margarete called after her. "But for your information, I'm going to have a beautiful, new, blue dress to complement my eyes."

Annika's hands were shaking as she loosed Blackie's reins from the hitching post. She shouldn't have provoked Margarete, but really, the girl had asked for it. Not that Annika would have gone to the wedding. If invited, she would have made up an excuse not to attend.

Annika backed the rig up too quickly.

"Watch where you're going!"

Mortified, Annika halted Blackie.

"It's a good thing I remembered what a verrückt driver you are." A tall, emaciated man vaulted into the seat beside her.

"You're not going to run over your own brother, are you?"

"Matt!" Annika dropped the reins and threw her arms around her older brother. "What are you doing here? We weren't expecting you. Where are Dora and the *Kinder*?"

"Still a magpie." Matt picked up the reins in one mammoth hand and clamped the other around his sister. "But all grown up as lovely as Mutter. Dora's at her Mutter's with the children. I sent Vater word that the farmland I was working changed owners and the new one turned us out."

"Right before winter? What about the harvest?"

"Wasn't good in Prussia this year. Especially for those of us growing potatoes. The tubers have blight. Vater said the harvest here was decent, he's getting on in years and could use me, so to come on home."

Annika squealed. "I'm so glad you're here, but Vater didn't tell me. I don't have anything prepared."

"We'll stay with Dora's family a couple nights. I can't see her Mutter lettin' us go right away. She latched onto the baby, and she's not giving up little Helmuth anytime soon. I'll bring Dora out to the farm tomorrow so you ladies can make some plans."

"We'll need to stuff some fresh mattresses and figure out where to put everyone."

Matt handed her the reins. "Can you be depended on to drive home without running anyone else down?" He winked.

"I didn't run you over!"

"It was a close call." Matt jumped down. "See you tomorrow, little sister."

Annika thrust the package of strudel at her brother. "A little treat for your homecoming."

His eyes lit up. "It's been a long time since I've had anything sweet."

"Make sure you share." She pulled Blackie away to the infectious sound of her favorite brother's laugh.

Chapter 9

Annika flitted around the farmhouse, trying to clean to Dora's fastidious standards. With the quilting on Tuesday, she'd skipped cleaning the floor. She wrestled the rag rug out the back door and took out her angst over Ehrich, beating the dirt out of it. Leaving it to air, she raced back inside and scrubbed the windows and the floor.

Exhausted, she plopped down at the wooden table with a mug of Kaffee. The bedrooms would have to wait. She didn't have time since she needed to start dinner. She ran out in the cold and lugged in the rug, laying it between the horsehair sofa and the fireplace. Then she started to chop vegetables for a soup. Too busy to eat, she sampled a bite here and there.

It was mid-afternoon by the time she put the dough that had been rising all day into the Dutch oven so she'd have something to offer her brother's family. She was starting to heat water to wash a few dishes when Dora knocked at the door. Annika ushered her tiny sister-in-law to a seat in front of the fire. It looked like a stiff winter wind would blow Dora away.

"I'm so glad you're here. Would you like a cup of warm milk?" When Dora hesitated, Annika swung a small pot over embers on the side of the hearth. "I was just about to have some myself to use up the morning milk. Have a cup with me."

Dora nodded and leaned back in the rocker, closing her eyes. "Your Vater and Matt will be along eventually. He's showing Matt some things that need done."

When the milk was hot, Annika knelt at Dora's side. "Are

you all right?"

"Ma says I'm exhausted and undernourished. I can't remember feeling any other way." She gave Annika a thin smile and wrapped her fingers around the mug. "It's a hard thing when the crops fail. I'm glad the new owner turned us out so we could come home. I'm not sure Helmuth would have survived the winter. My milk's not steady, and the goat died."

Appalled, Annika took Dora's free hand. "Everything will be all right now. I baked some rolls. Would you like one? Let me go out to the cellar and find jam to go with it."

In the root cellar, Annika counted the crocks of preserves and jams. She'd been proud of the abundance when there were only two mouths to feed. The bounty could stretch to three, but four adults and a growing child? One a nursing mother and the other a man in his prime. *God, help us.*

A ray of hope lightened her heart as she remembered the coins the Beckers had paid for Lucie's dress. She could use them for food. Surely, the Beckers would also give her day-old baked goods. Vater wouldn't like it, so she'd have to get them without his knowledge, but she would make sure they all had enough. The cow was still giving milk. By the time she ran dry, the goats would be birthing.

She grabbed a crock of strawberry jam and returned to the house just as the men were coming from the barn. Bruno was prancing around Matt's feet like he was a puppy again.

Chapter 10

"Helmuth's crying," Charlotte complained as she burrowed into Annika's side.

"He's probably teething." Annika repositioned herself on the narrow bed. She needed to get Matt and Vater to build a bigger bedframe. She enjoyed three-year-old Charlotte's warmth, but the old bed was too small. Since she didn't have sisters, she'd never needed to share it.

She put an arm around her niece and hummed a lullaby until Charlotte fell back to sleep. Tired as she was, Annika couldn't seem to join her. It was only three days until Weihnachten, and she had so much to do.

Dora was getting stronger, but the brunt of the work fell on Annika. Not that she minded. The joy in their home eclipsed any sacrifices she had to make. Charlotte chattered and giggled, and Helmuth gave drooly baby smiles to anyone who held him. The baby delighted his grandmother, who visited regularly, bringing food to stretch their supplies. Matt's face looked less pinched. He worked long hours, but his relaxed, easy manner brought out the best in Vater, who was drinking less and smiling more, especially at his grandchildren. It would be the best Christmas since Mutter died.

When Annika pushed away the sadness and reached for happy memories of her mother at the holidays, she had to stop herself from bolting upright before she disturbed Charlotte. She had forgotten the Stollen Mutter made every Weihnachten. She would have to go into town tomorrow to get a few ingredients.

At least the trip would give her a chance to pick up a stick of candy for Charlotte. Other than that, Annika was scrambling for gifts. It was a good thing she'd already knitted Vater warm mittens and a hat. With the leftover yarn, she was halfway through a tiny cap for Helmuth. Since the wool was from Margarete's sheep, Annika felt like a bone was stuck in her throat every time she knitted with it, but it couldn't be wasted. Thankfully, it was almost gone.

It was only a week until the wedding. Margarete would make a beautiful bride. Annika wished for an ice storm even though it was too early in the season. She shifted to her back and finally fell asleep to dream of Ehrich.

By Christmas Eve, Annika had baked the Stollen, finished Helmuth's cap, started a blue scarf for Matt, and fashioned a rag doll for Charlotte. She would knit Dora a matching scarf later. It was the best she could do. Matt and Vater had shot a buck, so there was plenty for their Weihnachten feast. Sprigs of holly decorated their cottage, and all was ready when the entire family piled into the wagon for the short drive to church.

The chapel was bathed in candlelight and smelled of evergreens. The songs cheered Annika. Every parishioner listened in hushed anticipation as Pastor Brandt read the nativity story in his mellifluous voice and explained prophecies fulfilled in the Christ child. He kept the sermon short for the children's sake. As soon as they were released, they burst out the back door, eager for the treats awaiting them at home. The adults lingered to wish each other *Frohe Weihnachten*.

Annika found Lucie and wrapped her in a hug. "Frohe Weihnachten, Frau Huber."

Lucie dimpled. "How are things going with your family?"

"Good. Dora looks better, don't you think?"

Lucie studied Dora as she chatted with her Mutter. "Ja. More color in her cheeks, but she still needs to put on weight. If you come to the bakery this Thursday, Mutter said you can have all the Weihnachten goods that don't sell. If you heat them, they shouldn't seem stale."

"Danke. Dora needs to be able to feed Helmuth. That little one sure is fussy. We think he's teething."

"Mutter will know something for him to suck on that will quiet him down. She's not here tonight, but I'll find out for Thursday."

"What would I do without you?"

Lucie looked guilty. She hesitated before blurting, "You wouldn't have an escort to the dinner dance tomorrow."

"What?" Annika spun around to face her friend. "You know I don't want to go to any socials now."

"I know. I know, but I overheard Margarete saying she's too busy to go, so you won't have to deal with her and Ehrich. You don't want people to think you're mooning over him. You need to get out there. Find someone even better."

"Lucie!" Annika moaned. "What poor sop did you get to take me?"

"Paul. He won't want to dance much, but he'll take good care of you. He'll come pick you up at dusk."

Annika could concede Lucie's points. She shouldn't cower at home, and Paul would be an excellent chaperone. He was like an older brother. She'd be completely comfortable with him.

"Say you'll go."

"Okay."

Lucie started to put on her gloves. "And wear your red dress. It's perfect for Christmas."

Annika made a small curtsey. "Yes, ma'am. Is there

anything else you'd like to arrange about my night?"

"I almost forgot. You don't need to bring any food. Mutter will send a cake with Paul."

Chapter 11

Annika was ready at the appointed time in spite of "assistance" from Charlotte. Dora had finally rescued Annika from Charlotte's attempts to brush her waist-length hair.

"Come help me in the kitchen, Liebling. Since *Tante's* going out, I need you to scrub this pot and set the table." Dora winked at Annika as she herded Charlotte to the sink. "You look beautiful, Annika." She fingered her braid. "My hair's gotten so thin."

The transformation of Dora's once-shining golden locks to lackluster strands was another result of her hunger. Dora had confided that it fell out in chunks on their trip home to Braunfels.

"You're looking better every day. Before you know it, your hair will be full and glossy. You were the prettiest girl in the village when Matt married you."

"I just want to have enough milk for Helmuth and strength to pull my weight around here."

"You're doing plenty. I'm glad you're all here."

Dora stirred venison stew. "You've been so kind, Anna. I'm sorry you're having to share everything, even your bed."

Annika finished her preparations and grasped her sister-in-law's hands. "Your being here is the best thing that's happened all year." When Dora hugged her, Annika realized Lucie was right about Dora's slight weight. "And now that we have the bigger wood frame Matt gave me for Weihnachten and the bigger ticking you and your mom stuffed, we'll be very comfortable, won't we, Charlotte?"

"I like sleeping with Tante Anna." Charlotte played in the water.

Noise outside the door signaled Paul's arrival. Annika bundled up in her cloak. "I'll run out so he doesn't have to leave the warm buggy. Bye."

"Have fun!"

As soon as they entered the school, Annika spied Lucie in her wedding dress. "So, you insist I come tonight just to outshine me in the very dress I sewed for you!" she teased.

"Nobody's going to outshine you, tonight, Anna. You're the princess of this dance." Lucie pulled her toward tables set up for the feast, with a roasted boar provided by the town's butcher.

"There's almost as much food as there was at your wedding," Annika whispered as they seated themselves on the bench next to Fritz. "I feel bad I didn't bring anything."

"Nonsense. Here's Paul with the cake." Lucie waved to her brother and pointed to a table laden with desserts. "Set it down on that table for later, Paul."

The foursome filled their plates with the delectable fare. Annika was glad Paul wouldn't notice how much she ate as she devoured her mound of food. She'd gotten by with a piece of thick bread and jam for lunch so there would be more for Matt and Dora. She might need to sit out the first dance or two to avoid a stomachache.

As Annika satisfied her hunger, Lucie chattered about her Christmas morning. "Vater promised us Tilli's next foal!"

"That will be such a blessing on the farm," Fritz said. "Our family's horses are getting older. There's one we're trying to breed. If she foals, we could have a new pair for plowing."

"Tilli's last foal Jaeger was a good one. Vater gave him to me. He pulled the carriage tonight." Paul attacked the pork on his plate with gusto.

"Jaeger's a handsome fellow," Annika said.

Paul nodded. "And he was easy to train. Tilli tends to pass down her tractable disposition."

The musicians began tuning their instruments. Paul finished his meal, went to drop a coin in their basket, and procured a stein of beer.

"May I have your first free dance?"

The hairs on Annika's neck prickled. She glanced over her shoulder. "Hallo, Herr Weber. I'm sitting this one out, but you may have the next."

Gustav looked over to the beer barrel where Paul was engrossed in conversation with the other men. "Looks like your escort may be tied up for a while; though with the prettiest girl here, I'd have thought he'd pay more attention to you."

"Paul is Lucie's brother. He brought me as a favor to her."

Gustav quirked his blond eyebrows.

"Long story, and he's not much of a dancer, but I'm determined to relax for this first dance any way."

"Busy day?"

"Ja." Annika told him all about her brother's return.

Gustav listened intently. "Does your house have enough room for all of you?"

"We have plenty of space. Seven of us used to live there. Vater moved up to my brothers' bedroom, so Matt, Dora and the baby can have his downstairs' sleeping space. Charlotte sleeps with me."

"Lucky girl!"

Annika blushed.

Lucie leaned over Annika. "Keep it proper, Herr Weber, or I won't let you know when our next social is."

Gustav tried to look contrite. "Yes, Frau Huber. I apologize." But his eyes conveyed mirth.

"Can I trust you to behave while I dance with my husband?"

"I promise to be a better escort than your brother."

Lucie glanced at the men laughing raucously around the keg. "That shouldn't be hard."

Gustav became serious. "You know I'll treat Fraülein Lange well. Otherwise, you wouldn't have invited me."

"They'll be fine, dear. Come dance with your husband." Fritz took her hand and led her away.

Discomfited that Lucie had planned this meeting, Annika blurted out, "You're far from your family on Weihnachten."

"We celebrated together last night. I entertained my cousins' children a bit this morning. Then I hired a horse and rode over here."

"Sounds cold."

"It was worth it."

Scrambling for a safe topic, she said, "Have you seen one of the new steam engines everyone is talking about?"

"Ja. In Frankfurt. I'm going to ride a train one of these days."

"Our doctor says it's not healthy to travel at such a fast rate."

Gustav threw his head back and laughed. Annika had to join in.

"How old is the good doctor?"

Annika pictured the stooped, white-haired man. "I don't

know, but he may have been present at my Opa's birth."

"Railroads are the wave of the future. The older generation and nobles just don't realize it. Most wanted to dig more canals."

"I like traveling by water, not that I've done it very often, but I like watching the shore."

"Trains will be timesavers, and more goods will be transported than could go by canal. That will free up the canals for leisure."

Persuaded by his enthusiasm, Annika found herself agreeing. "Vater thought the doctor was talking nonsense."

"So, when's your next trip into Wetzlar?"

"We don't have any planned." Annika nibbled on a roll.

"Why not? Isn't it the slow season on a farm?"

"Ja, but Vater and Matt are doing a lot of repair work." Annika hesitated.

"I feel like there something you aren't telling me."

"With Matt's family coming, it's just… There's no money for anything that's not absolutely necessary."

Gustav pursed his lips and fell into thought. "I might have some good news for you on that front. Remember the dressmaker you visited with Lucie?"

"Ja."

"She lost one of her seamstresses. With the recommendation of our family, I think she might hire you, if you were able to start soon."

Annika's eyes widened. "I've never even considered such a thing."

"Will you think about it?"

"Definitely. I'll think on it, mention it to Vater." Annika

finished her bread and pushed her plate away. "But where would I live?"

"I know a family who owns a big house near the dressmaker's. Their children have grown and moved out. Their youngest daughter married my cousin Conrad. Would you like me to make inquiries?"

"I guess it couldn't hurt."

Gustav beamed at her and offered his arm. "Are you ready to dance?"

Chapter 12

I 'm glad you convinced me to attend the Weihnachten dance." Annika sipped tea in Lucie's kitchen. The newlyweds had moved into the cozy, wood-beamed house behind the main farmhouse. The cottage had been empty since Fritz's grandparents passed away. "I received an interesting proposal."

Lucie's eyebrows shot up.

"Not a marriage proposal. A potential job."

"Really?" Lucie offered Annika a plate of gingerbread cookies.

Annika bit into the Pfeffernüsse and groaned. "Will I ever be able to bake anything half this good?"

"Maybe not, but I'll never be able to sew like you. Now tell me about this possible job."

"Gustav told me the dressmaker in Wetzlar needs another seamstress. He thinks I could get the position, if I act fast."

"What are you going to do?"

"I mentioned it to Vater yesterday. He thought it was a good idea. He must realize how short on food we'll be by spring if we all stay at the farm." Annika savored the gingerbread. "Dora can keep house for him. If she wasn't there, he'd never even consider it."

Lucie threw her arms around Annika. "I'll miss you so much."

"And I you, but you have Fritz now. Maybe you could come

into Wetzlar with Paul when he buys supplies. And I don't have the job yet. It might already be filled." She wiped crumbs from the front of her dress. "But I hope not." She stood. "I need to get home and help Dora with dinner."

"It's going to be a cold walk home."

"It was worth it." Tears formed in Annika's eyes. "Your Pfeffernüsse has to be the best in all of Hessen Baden."

Lucie laugh-sobbed and dabbed both their faces with the corner of her apron. "No crying. Your tears will freeze out there." She wound a scarf around Annika's neck. "Go with God," she whispered.

Annika nodded mutely and stumbled out the door toward home.

After the initial shock of the crystal cold, Annika tried to keep warm by walking briskly. She was glad to hear the jingle of harness bells behind her until she realized it was Ehrich stopping beside her.

"Hallo, Annika."

"Guten Tag." Annika kept walking.

"I have some warm bricks and an extra blanket. Could I give you a ride home?"

In spite of her woolen socks and boots, Annika's feet ached with the cold. "I don't think your betrothed would like that."

"You're my neighbor, Annika. Neighbors help each other. We can't avoid each other."

"Actually, we can. I'm planning to take a job in Wetzlar as a seamstress."

"Then you can't let your fingers freeze. Get in the wagon."

Acknowledging his wisdom, Annika reluctantly climbed into the wagon. Ehrich scooted a hot brick to her side of the footboard. "Why are you out walking in this cold?"

"I needed to see Lucie."

"A visit's worth frostbite?"

"I might not see her again for months." Annika propped her feet on the brick and hunched beneath the horse blanket to protect herself from the wind.

"I never pictured you as leaving here."

Annika hadn't either, but she'd pictured herself as his wife plenty of times, and that wasn't going to happen. "Things change." She began to pray the job was still available but stopped mid-thought. God hadn't answered her prayers to become Ehrich's wife. She was on her own.

"So you're leaving soon?"

"I hope to. It depends on Vater."

"He seems…lighter since Matt came home."

"Ja. The children even make him laugh."

"That's good. A man needs laughter in his house." Ehrich cleared his throat. "How'd you find out about this job?"

"It's a shop I visited with Lucie. Since the Webers supply them with cloth, Gustav let me know about the position at the Weihnachten dance."

"He's still traveling to Braunfels' dances?"

"He's come to the last few."

"Long way, and there must be bigger events in Wetzlar."

"I don't know what happens in the city, but I may find out soon."

"Just be careful, Annika. The Roths don't know Herr Weber personally. They crossed paths while doing business."

"It's no concern of yours," Annika said icily.

Ehrich clenched his jaw.

They rode silently until they reached the turn-off to

Annika's house. "Let me out here. I'll be fine going up the lane."

"Okay. I'd like to chat with Matt about his farming experiences out east, but that will have to wait. There's so much to do..."

"Of course there is. You're getting married." Annika threw off the blanket. "My fingers and toes thank you." She hopped down and darted up the lane.

Chapter 13

Annika fidgeted as Frau Engel inspected her work through spectacles perched on the end of her nose.

"This is very fine." The dressmaker turned her attention to Annika. "Have you sewn any dresses in the new styles?" She gestured to the dress forms scattered around the shop.

Annika pointed to the gown with the pelerine. "I sewed one of those last month." She removed a sheet of paper from her reticule. "My client sent a glowing report."

Frau Engel scanned the letter. "A bridal gown! We create a couple wedding dresses every month."

She stared down her long nose at Annika. "The position pays one and a half *thalers* a week. If business is slow, we won't have work for you since you're the newest girl. Of course, if your sewing is superior..."

The middle-aged widow returned Lucie's letter. "We don't provide lodging. You said you're from Braunfels?"

"I have a place to stay."

"It must be a respectable home. It goes without saying we expect the highest decorum from our seamstresses. If there's a hint of loose morals, you'll be terminated without references. Are these terms acceptable?"

"Ja, Frau Engel."

"We'll do a two-week trial period. If things are satisfactory for both of us, I'll hire you on a long-term basis. Go settle into your lodging, and we'll see you on Saturday at eight."

"Danke." Relief flooding her, Annika left to rejoin Paul, who was waiting outside the shop in the cold. "I'm hired for the next two weeks. If I like it and they like me, I'll have the job."

"I'm sure it will work out. I've been watching the patrons and spoke with one of the husbands. His wife has only high praise for this establishment." His mouth quirked up on one side. "Let's go by the Webers and get the address of the place you'll be staying before we get your bag." He offered her his arm.

The first fortnight flew by as Annika settled into her new routine. Every day she rose and cooked breakfast with Frau Keller. Then she walked five minutes to Engel's, which was sandwiched between a cobbler and a printer.

The seamstresses arrived at eight and worked until six. They were allowed a short break for lunch.

Two of the seamstresses, Olga and Johanna, were married. Annika and the exceedingly plain Greta Engel were not. Greta was fifteen and had been working since she was ten. Her father had died two years ago, leaving her mother Engel's Kleider Shop.

Greta chattered incessantly, which was useful at first, but soon began to grate on Annika's nerves. The older seamstresses ignored her as they cut and stitched. Occasionally, her mother would hush her, which relieved Annika, whose head ached every afternoon the first week.

Olga noticed Annika's discomfort and suggested she take a break from sewing in the afternoons by saving some cutting work. "In time, you'll be able to sew for longer periods, but it's still good to give your eyes a break."

Frau Engel took care of most of the customer fittings with Olga's help. For their best clients, the dressmakers would even make house calls.

Annika enjoyed handling the fabrics and looked forward to learning the new styles. The shop kept paper patterns, so she had less guesswork than with Lucie's gown. The seamstresses changed positions often, and the workroom's light from windows paned with glass was better than at the Lange farm. They were also allowed two lanterns on cloudy days, which were frequent this time of year.

On the day before Annika's trial period ended, Frau Engel asked her to stay for a few minutes after the others left. Before the two married women departed together, Olga gave Annika a surreptitious nod of approval. Annika relaxed and kneaded her back as she waited for Frau Engel to finish with the last customer of the day.

Frau Engel bustled into the workroom. "I'm sorry to keep you waiting. I thought Frau Zeigler would never decide, but at least she chose an expensive linen.

"We're very pleased with your sewing. Would you like to stay on? We have plenty of dresses ordered for the next few months."

"Ja. I enjoy working here very much. Thank you for the opportunity."

"I'll see you tomorrow. I'll pay your wages twice a month beginning tomorrow."

Annika floated out of the workroom but stopped short in the showroom when she saw how dark it was. The shop clock showed half past six. She swallowed hard. As an extra precaution, she grabbed an umbrella from beside the door and peered into the street. Numerous townspeople were hurrying around on errands or toward home. Annika stepped into the street, clutching the umbrella. When someone spoke her name, she whirled around, umbrella pointed at the intruder.

"I come in peace." Gustav held his hands up in surrender. "Everything all right?"

Annika lowered the umbrella and waited until the pounding of her heart lessened. "Everything is better than all right. You just startled me."

"I thought you always returned to the Kellers before now, so I was waiting to speak with you. When Frau Keller realized how dark it had gotten, she sent me to escort you."

"This is the latest I've ever been. Frau Engel wanted to talk to me, but there was a late client." Annika started walking. "I got the job! Thank you for telling me about it. It's a good place to work."

Gustav fell into step with her. "Do you miss the farm?"

"I miss my family. I can do without getting up early to do farm chores. I like not having to cook. I know I'll need to again someday, but for now I'll enjoy the break. Frau Keller is an excellent cook, and I'm learning some new recipes from her. The Kellers are great people. They treat me like family."

Gustav gave her a sideways glance. "I knew they would. I wouldn't have recommended them otherwise."

"I didn't mean..."

"I'm teasing you. Relax."

"It's just that they could provide a decent place to stay without being so welcoming. After we attended Sunday services at Wetzlar Cathedral, they included me at their family lunch."

"Frau Keller misses her daughters."

"Ja, but how did you know?"

"I talked to her at my cousin's wedding. She seemed a little sad. When I struck up a conversation, she admitted she was dreading having an empty house. That was over the summer, so I hadn't even met you yet, but I remembered her comment when the position at Engel's opened up and I thought of you to fill it."

"It all worked out very neatly."

"Wouldn't your friend Lucie say providentially?"

"Probably, but I think you're largely to thank, so danke." Annika noticed there were fewer pedestrians as they moved into the residential area. "How do you know Lucie would say that?"

"She's said it a few times in my presence." Gustav shrugged. "Would you like to know why I was at the Kellers' waiting for you?"

Annika laughed. "I'd forgotten about that! Yes, please."

"There's a skating party on the Dill River tomorrow. My family is going. Would you like to come?"

"I don't get off work until six."

"Most of us also plan to work all afternoon. I can come by the Kellers for you."

Annika took a deep breath of the crisp air. "I'd like that. I miss the outdoors. It's strange being cooped up inside all the time."

"Do you know how to skate, or should I bring the skating chair?"

Annika rolled her eyes. "What do you take me for? I'm a country girl. Of course I can skate, although I've never skated on a river before."

"It's been unusually cold, so it's quite safe."

"In Braunfels, we skate on ponds. The Roths used to host skating parties all the time."

"I remember seeing the pond on their property. Did you bring your skates?"

"Nein. I wasn't sure I'd get the job, so I brought the bare minimum. Maybe the Kellers have a pair lying around."

"My Tante isn't going, so I'll bring you hers."

The couple stopped in front of the Kellers' half-timbered, three-story home. "Thank you for the invitation and for walking me home. I was a bit nervous." Annika brandished the umbrella.

"The days are already lengthening, so you should be all right from now on."

Annika opened the door. "Gute Nacht. I'll see you tomorrow."

Chapter 14

The next evening was clear and cold, perfect for skating. After donning every piece of wool clothing she owned, down to two petticoats and warm stockings, Annika set off with Gustav. They strolled through a business section of Wetzlar Annika had never seen. The skaters were using the pier of a shipping company to descend to the frozen water.

"There are several of these piers." Gustav helped Annika maneuver down a ladder to the ice. He handed her a pair of the skates that had been slung over his shoulder. "You can lean on a piling to strap these on." He set the lantern he'd been carrying on the ice, and Annika quickly buckled the blades to her boots with the leather straps. Frau Weber's skates were well made, better than Annika's pair at home.

Gustav picked up the lantern. "Let's see if we can find my family. They usually stay between this pier and the bridge."

Annika had no difficulty keeping pace with him. A steady flow of skaters moved up and down the Dill, always staying to the right. A few were stopped along the sides with crying children. Some of the men were pushing ladies or children in skating chairs. As they passed a third chair, the occupant cried, "Gustav! Hallo."

Annika and Gustav slowed. The lantern in the rider's lap illuminated an attractive face framed by an ornate fur hat and brown curls.

"Hi, Adele. Have you seen my family?"

"Nein. Who's your friend?" Adele emphasized the last word of her query.

"Annika Lange, this is Adele Zeigler and her brother Otto."

"Is this the new seamstress I've heard about?"

"Ja. She works at Engel's." Gustav studied the skaters traveling in the opposite direction. "There's my cousin's family now. See you later." He executed a sweeping turn, and Annika followed effortlessly. The couple then sped to catch up with the family group of eight.

In the ensuing introductions to three of Gustav's cousins and their children, Annika didn't get the chance to ask about Adele. She and Gustav ended up flanking his five-year-old nephew, hands linked.

"He's been out here for hours. I think he's getting tired," his mother confided. "I know I'm ready to go back. Harbin, when we reach the pier, it's time to go home for some soup and bread."

"Okay," the little boy replied. "Oma said she was bakin' something special. I want to see what it is. Are you coming too, Gustav?"

"We just got here. We haven't even made one loop yet. How many have you made?"

"Twelve!"

"No wonder you're ready for dinner."

"I could eat a whole...a whole goat!"

Annika laughed with the other adults.

"Save some for the rest of us."

"Don't worry. A goat would fit in the huge pot Oma's making soup in. Do you think she'll let me have a piece of whatever she baked before everyone else gets back?" Harbin tripped, but Annika and Gustav kept him from falling.

"I think you'll be able to persuade her. You can tell her I'll be a while, though I don't think we'll skate as much as you did."

Gustav's cousin Klara, her husband, and their two children peeled away from the group at the next pier.

"It's cold out here. I've had enough for today, too." Gustav's fifteen-year-old cousin Ella joined her older sister's family. "Mutter said to bring Annika by for some soup, so we'll see you both later."

"Did Harbin's little sister skate as much as he did?" Annika asked when only Gustav's oldest cousin Paula, her husband, and their seven-year-old were left.

"No!" Paula laughed. "Her dad brought her for a little while after he finished working. She spent most of the day getting under our feet while we spun thread. In spite of that, the new thread is turning out well. I can't wait to dye it the new pink."

"My friend bought pink linen for the dress she wore on her wedding day. I've never worked with such fine fabric."

Paula beamed. "We were very pleased with that fabric. I'll have to show you the plum-colored linen we created last month."

"I think I've seen it. Did you sell some of it to Engel's Kleider Shop?"

"Ja." Gustav began skating backwards in front of them. "I brought it in last week."

"Show off!" Paula said.

Gustav laughed and took his place beside Annika.

"Will you show me how to do that?" his nephew Alfons pleaded.

"Sometime when the river's not so crowded."

"In the daylight," Paula added.

"We can come for a while tomorrow, if the weather holds," his dad promised.

"On the Lord's Day?" Paula glared at her husband.

"We won't go far. The fresh air will be good for him. If we can take walks on the Sabbath, we can skate."

Gustav took Annika's hand and sped up to leave the bickering behind them. "Sorry about that."

"It's not a problem. It's good to be in the middle of a family again. Leaving mine was the one thing I dreaded about taking this job."

"In that case, you should eat with us tonight."

"I wouldn't miss it."

Adele's skating chair drew up beside them. "Here you are again. I saw your family, Gustav. I suppose you found them?"

"Ja." Gustav sounded annoyed.

"I can't keep up this pace long, Adele. Want to get out and skate?" Otto was huffing and puffing.

"Perhaps Gustav would spell you." Adele sent Gustav a coquettish look.

"I'd be delighted to switch places with him." Otto steered the chair to the side of the river and turned to Annika.

Annika took the lantern from Gustav to avoid Otto's outstretched hand. "I'm fine on my own, danke. In Braunfels, we learn to skate young."

"Of course she'll do fine on her own," Adele said. "Country girls are much more…"

"Healthy," Gustav finished. "You really should learn to skate. It would keep you warmer too."

"You'll have to teach me sometime."

Even in the dark, Annika could sense Gustav's frustration as he reluctantly began pushing the chair.

"I already tried, Adele. You have to be willing to take some falls."

"I bruise far too easily."

Paula and her family caught up with them. "Gustav, I'm having trouble with one of my skates. Since they used to be yours, could you take a look?"

"Absolutely. Otto, sorry I can't be of more assistance. Better not block the flow." Gustav slid the chair toward him. "We'll see you folks later."

The Weber group retreated to the river's edge.

"Thanks, Paula." He examined her skate and tightened a buckle. "Better?"

Paula giggled. "You owe me."

"Don't I know it! Let's skate to the other side and reverse direction, so we don't run into them again."

When Alfons claimed Gustav's attention, Annika glided over beside Paula. "What was all that about?"

"Gustav took Adele on a few outings—a dance, a concert, and a skating night like this one. She became attached and continues to flirt with him, even though he hasn't asked for her company for months. Don't pay any attention to her. She's a pretty girl, but she's a pampered priss, not a good prospect for Gus."

Annika chewed on those words as they took a half dozen more laps, racing for short distances and reveling in the brisk air. All too soon, Paula said, "My toes are freezing. I need to head back."

"I'm hungry." Alfons grabbed Gustav's hand. "How about you?"

"What do you think, Annika? Are you ready to call it a night?"

"I am getting tired. It's been a long week."

After removing their skates at the pier and readjusting hats and scarves for maximum warmth, they set off for the Webers'.

"Come in by the fire," Frau Weber greeted them. Her husband and Harbin were bent over a backgammon board near the hearth but moved over to make room. Annika peeled off her outer clothes and stretched her hands to the flames.

"Can we have strudel now, Oma?" Harbin begged.

Frau Weber chuckled. "Let everyone have some soup first. Then we'll cut the strudel."

Gustav tousled his hair. "I guess she made you wait."

Harbin gave a huge sigh. "Ja, but she gave me a cookie to tide me over." He skipped over to the huge mahogany table and plopped down next to Alfons.

"That's good. We wouldn't want you to starve while you were waiting." Gustav took his place at the table next to Annika.

After everyone found a seat, Gustav's Onkel said, "Let's pray."

Everyone bowed his head. "Come, Lord Jesus, be our guest, and let these Thy gifts to us be blessed."

Chapter 15

Frau Engel stuck her head into the workroom a fortnight later. "Annika, you have a visitor."

Assuming it was Gustav, Annika stopped to smooth her hair in the small mirror in the hall.

To her surprise, it was Paul standing awkwardly in the showroom amidst the fabrics and lace.

"Paul, how lovely to see someone from home." Annika greeted him with a smile.

Paul kneaded his wool cap in his hands as if he were in the bakery working dough.

"Nothing's wrong, is it?" Annika asked.

"Nein, your Vater and family send their greetings. Dora sent you the box you asked me to fetch for you after you got the job here."

"I'd forgotten about that. It will be such a relief to have a few more of my things."

"How are you getting on?"

"I'm well." Annika glanced at Frau Engel, who was restocking fabric.

Frau Engel frowned as she folded a royal blue wool. "You may leave for lunch, Annika, if you'd like, to catch up with the news from home."

"Danke. I'll go and get my cloak, Paul."

When Annika emerged in her winter garb, the two headed for his wagon parked at the chocolatier.

"Is your employer always so pleasant?"

Annika's silvery laugh split the air. "You caught her on a good day. I suspect she let me leave because it's slow. I never dreamed you would show up today. You're back for supplies early."

"Ja. It wasn't so terrible cold, and we've all been wondering how you're getting on, so Mutter shooed me out of the house, scolding me to get your trunk out of her way."

"Did she pack me a bag of treats?"

A smile lurked at the corners of Paul's lips. "Of course. She considers you a daughter."

"I'm glad. It will be a taste of home. The bakeries here are good, but they can't touch Becker's."

Paul beamed. "Now that the formidable frau's not listening in, how is work?"

"It really is a pleasant place. The hours aren't too demanding. The other women aren't difficult to work with, and I started learning a new style of dress this week."

"It's always good to learn new things. And how about your lodging?"

"The Kellers have taken me in like I'm their own daughter. I attend church with them and eat a big meal with their entire family afterwards. The food is good, and my bedroom's comfortable. There's even a chair I can sew or read in. I couldn't have asked for a better situation."

"So the Weber fellow did right by you. Do you see much of him?"

"He delivers cloth to the shop sometimes. I went skating with his family once and ate with them afterwards. His nephews make me laugh." Annika sighed. "I do miss my family and friends in Braunfels. What news is there?"

"Let's see. Lina says she misses you. She spends some time

with Dora, especially since the Steins' house has had so many changes. Herr Stein died right after the wedding."

"Oh no!" Annika stopped short in the road. "He was always kind to me."

"Let's not get run over." Paul took her arm and propelled her forward. "I'm a dummkopf. I shouldn't have told you until you were sitting down."

Annika's mind raced with questions. "Let's get my chest and then have lunch at the Kellers. I'm sure there are some eggs I can scramble to go with your Mutter's treats."

When they reached the Kellers' home, Frau Keller welcomed them warmly. "There are plenty of eggs and a couple of slices of ham and bread for you to share for lunch."

"Won't you join us? Frau Becker sent strudel and other goodies from their bakery."

"Save me a piece for dinner, dear. I have a meeting at the church. The maid is cleaning, so it won't be improper for Herr Becker to stay."

Under Frau Keller's watchful eye, Paul set Annika's trunk in her bedroom. Frau Keller left for her meeting after the young people retired to the kitchen. Annika donned an apron and scrambled eggs and fried ham slices.

They sat across the long oak table from each other. "This is a solid, warm house." Paul studied the stone hearth and large room.

"Ja." Annika pushed her food around her porcelain plate. "So how is Frau Stein?"

"She took to her bed for a day or two after nursing her husband to his end, but she's up and about again, ornery as ever."

"How about...the rest of the family?" Annika couldn't believe he was going to make her ask about Ehrich.

"Elsa was quite sad at the funeral, poor mite. Lina's at her wit's end trying to keep the peace between her Mutter and Margarete. When I stopped by, Ehrich was in the barn mending harness. It was nippy, but I imagine he needed the peace and quiet."

Annika's mouth twitched upward. "Is that why men spend so much time outdoors?"

"Sometimes." There was a gleam in Paul's eye.

Annika sobered. "I didn't realize Herr Stein was so close to the end."

"Nobody did. He was at the wedding."

"Did you go?"

"We weren't invited. Frau Schäfer told Mutter it was going to be 'a small affair.'" Paul stuck his nose in the air and mimicked Margarete's mother's voice.

"Margarete informed me of the same."

"I heard. Lucie said she wasn't going even if she were invited. Since the Steins had just attended her wedding, she thought they might reciprocate."

"But they didn't?"

"Nein."

A strained silence fell. Annika took a bite of comforting strudel. "This is heavenly."

"It really is, isn't it? Even Lucie can't make strudel like Mutter." Paul wolfed his down while gazing out the window at the wall of the house next door. "I don't think I could ever live in a city like this. I need some elbow room. I like living outside of town in my cottage."

Annika studied his lanky frame and giggled. "You can swing your elbows quite a distance."

"Have you seen any of the advertisements or articles about

all the land available in the New World?"

"Ja. With all the Germans going hungry, some are emigrating. Why do you ask?"

"I'm thinking about going. A group of nobles called the *Adelsverein* are offering land to new settlers in a place called Texas. It costs a hundred twenty American dollars for a single man, and they set him up with supplies for the first year. Prince Solms has been commissioned to find the right place to establish a German colony."

"I don't think I want to live in Wetzlar forever, but I also don't want to cross an ocean to find a little breathing room." Annika picked up their plates and washed them as Paul finished his coffee. "The city does have its advantages. The Kellers took me to a concert at the cathedral last weekend. It's impressive, even though the bell tower hasn't been completed." She stacked the plates in a cupboard. "How would your parents run the bakery without you?"

"Luther's being discharged soon. He'll need a job. From his letters, it sounds like he's longing for peace and quiet after life in a garrison town. I imagine he'll find a wife and settle down. Me, I'm ready for an adventure."

"Will you farm?"

"Ja, in order to earn the land in Texas, it must be built on and cultivated. But I'm going to keep my eyes open for opportunities for a bakery, in case the rest of the family decides to come."

Annika felt like the wind had been knocked out of her. The cuckoo clock in the parlor struck one. "I've got to get back to work, Paul. Thank you for bringing my trunk and the news from home." They wrapped up in their winter wear and chatted about other neighbors on the way to Engel's.

"Lucie will come with me when it's not so cold," Paul promised when he left Annika at the door of Engel's.

"Tell her I look forward to it."

Chapter 16

What an amazing dress! You'll have so many partners," Greta said, her admiration tinged with envy over Annika's red frock with its intricate pleated skirt.

"You look nice, too." Annika fibbed, realizing she should have offered to style Greta's hair, which was pulled back tightly from her angular face. "Your dress is the perfect color for you." Greta wore a dark blue dress that brought out her eyes.

Greta smiled. "Mutter said she'll create a new spring dress for me when there's a lull between customers' dresses."

"Do you have a material in mind?"

"Maybe an ivory or pink linen."

"I think you'd look darling in a medium pink. Have you chosen a design?"

"Not yet. I'm waiting for the new magazines, so I can have the latest style. Mutter says I need to look my best to attract a husband."

"Don't the young ladies in Wetzlar wait until they're eighteen to marry?"

"Usually, but the matches happen when we're sixteen or seventeen."

"I see. And we're meeting some of your friends tonight?"

"Ja. They'll be at the Gasthaus. The fellows will escort us home, in a group, of course."

"Is there a young man you have your eye on?"

"Nein. I've known them since they wore short pants." Greta flashed a smile. "I'm hoping to meet someone new."

"Sounds like fun." The girls whooshed into the warm eatery from the dusky street. Smells of sausage and sauerkraut and beer greeted them.

"Are you hungry?" Greta headed to a group on the other side of the room.

"Starved," Annika admitted.

"The musicians won't be here yet, so there's time to order dinner." Greta slid to the middle of a bench next to a pretty brunette, leaving room for Annika on the end. "This is Minna." Greta introduced Annika to the other three girls and four boys. Several were related. They ranged in age from fifteen to twenty.

"The fellows ordered a platter of sausage for the table," Minna said. "We can all chip in."

Everyone talked about his week. The men worked in shops or trades. The girls helped at home or in family businesses. When the heaping platter of bratwurst arrived, conversation dwindled, except for Greta's lively chatter.

Sated after a sausage, Annika studied her surroundings. The Gasthaus was a cavernous room with dark timbers framing the ceiling. The floor was oak polished smooth over the years by many dancing feet. Half the area was cleared of the long oak tables that were now crammed in front of the bar. Kegs of beer lined the wall next to double doors that led to a kitchen.

When the fiddles and accordions had tuned up, Minna's older brother led Annika to the dance floor. He was an adept dancer, unlike her next partner, who already seemed tipsy from the beer.

Annika was almost glad to see Otto approaching. At least he was steady on his feet, but he held her too tightly. Annika longed for a partner like Werner or Ehrich. Thinking of Werner reminded her she needed to write and let him know how her job was going. She had dropped him a quick note when she first moved to Wetzlar. When Otto's hand roved too far, she pretended to stumble and broke free of his grip. "I need a rest."

"I'll get you a drink."

"No need. We have a pitcher at our table." Annika sped back to the safety of Greta and a few of the others. They chatted until a waltz began. To her consternation, Annika saw Otto headed her way. "Whatever you do, don't agree to a dance with him," she whispered to Greta, mind racing. She would have to plead a stomachache.

Tensed against Otto's approach, Annika relaxed when she heard a familiar voice. "Hallo, Otto. How are you?"

"Fine, Gustav. And you? I've come to ask Fraülein Lange for another dance."

"I believe Annika promised the first waltz of the evening to me." Gustav turned to Annika and raised his eyebrows. "If, of course, you're feeling up to it."

"Ja. This waltz is one of my favorites." She followed Gustav to the dance floor.

Taking one of her hands in his and resting the other on her waist, Gustav deftly guided them into the crush of couples. "It's my fault you met that scamp. He's annoyed every eligible woman in Wetzlar, so he's always looking for newcomers."

Annika giggled. "That bad? Or are you adding to the truth again?"

"Well, he focuses on the prettiest ones."

"And his sister?"

"Has set her cap for me, unfortunately." Gustav spun her gently.

Annika eyed Otto, who had chosen a buxom blonde for his partner. His suit was the latest cut and made of good cloth. A gold watch chain protruded from his pocket. "They seem well off."

"They are. The family owns a brewery, not far from the spot we met them."

"A brewery on the river. No wonder they're doing well."

"Ja. It's been in their family for several generations." Gustav grimaced. "And I apologize for stretching the truth back there. You seemed to need rescuing, and it's the best I could come up with on the spur of the moment."

"I'm very grateful. How did you know about my...er... distress?"

"I was dancing nearby when I saw you stumble. I've been to several dances with you and never witnessed a misstep on your part. Since your dashing cousin isn't here to rescue you, I thought I'd try." Gustav grinned at her. "It was fortuitous timing since I *was* planning to ask you to dance."

Pleased that he'd been watching her, Annika couldn't think of a response. She studied the nearby dancers. Some wore elaborate frocks and waistcoats. Others dressed in their threadbare best. "I hope he doesn't talk one of the younger girls into dancing with him."

"Don't worry. The Wetzlar women are wise to his ways."

Annika giggled. "Are you a poet, too?"

"Absolutely not. And if I were, I'd find better use of my talent, like flattering a beautiful woman." Gustav's warm appraisal made Annika blush. "And anyway, I need to keep away from his sister."

Annika joined him in laughter. "Now I believe *that's* the truth."

Chapter 17

While the women were eating their lunches on Tuesday, the bell in the shop signaled a customer.

Frau Engel looked at her half-eaten boiled egg and roll longingly. "Go see if you can wait on this customer, Olga. If she requires my expertise, tell her I'll be available in five minutes, loudly enough so I can hear."

Olga returned moments later. "It's Gustav with a delivery. He'd like a word with Greta and Annika. I'm sure he'll be happy to linger until you can pay him for the cloth, so go ahead and enjoy your last few bites."

Greta hurried to the storefront. Her mother shook her head in consternation but couldn't reprimand her with a mouth full of food. Annika wiped her face and fingers on a handkerchief and followed more sedately.

Gustav gave a little bow. "My family would like to invite you both to a dance and dinner next Saturday. It will start at five o'clock in our workshop. Don't be concerned about being late. I know you both work Saturdays."

"How kind of you to include us, Gustav," Annika said. "May I bring a dessert?"

"I'm sure Mutter would appreciate that. I'll let her know."

Greta's smile stretched from ear to ear. "I'll bake something too."

"Excellent."

Frau Engel bustled into the room with payment for the cloth.

"Mutter, Gustav's invited us to a dance next Saturday," Greta said breathlessly.

Turning her attention to Gustav, Frau Engel frowned. "Are you trying to steal from me?"

"No, ma'am."

"I'm going to have to let them leave a couple hours early. You have no idea how long it takes young ladies to prepare for a dance."

"Since it's just me and my brother, I'm sure I don't." Gustav's mouth quirked. "I have heard my female cousins complain about it a time or two."

Frau Engel harrumphed.

"I'm sure they'll work extra hard all morning." Gustav gave her his most charming smile. "But it can't take two such lovely ladies all that long."

Annika had to bite her lip to keep from laughing. Today Greta's hair was arranged in an unappealing way that emphasized her rather large ears. Breadcrumbs dotted her bodice.

Frau Engel handed Gustav his payment. "If it's just this once. You girls can't get into the habit of leaving early every Saturday."

Gustav accepted the coins. "I have more deliveries to make, so I must be going."

Greta started jumping up and down as soon as the door closed.

"Hush! You don't want to seem overeager," her mother hissed.

Annika turned away and straightened one of the mannequin's dresses to hide her smile.

"This is my first private dance in our larger circle," Greta explained.

Her mother pursed her lips. "I'm going to make you a new yellow bodice to go with your blue skirt. We have linen left over from the dress we just finished for Minna's aunt."

"That will look divine. Will you help me with my hair, Annika? Yours always looks amazing."

"Certainly. If you don't mind, Frau Engel, I could bring my party clothes here, and Greta and I could get ready and walk over together."

"Excellent. That will save time." Frau Engel fingered the new cloth. "Let's get back to work, ladies. Those dresses aren't going to sew themselves."

Greta was all thumbs the day of the party.

"Go keep an eye on the gingerbread so it doesn't burn." When her daughter bounced up the stairs, Frau Engel picked up the blue linen Greta had been working on. She tsked and scrubbed at the blood stain Greta had left after pricking her finger.

Annika bent over her task at the sunny window, fingers flying nimbly to placate her employer. Why had Gustav invited both her and Greta? If he wanted just Annika's company, he could have extended the invitation at the Kellers'. If Greta was the desired invitee as part of his family's business circle, he could have ignored Annika and extended the invitation to Greta. Was he interested in Annika? More importantly, was she interested in him? How did Greta figure into all this?

Annika's thoughts churned all morning. She only took a few bites of her lunch roll. She listed all his good qualities and compared him to the men in Braunfels. He came out favorably. She blocked Ehrich from her comparisons. He wasn't eligible.

"Mutter, can Annika style my hair now?" Greta called from upstairs.

Frau Engel inspected Annika's work. "You've gotten a lot done. Just finish the seam in the sleeve you're working on, and you may go." She lowered her voice. "No cut in pay."

"Danke."

Olga and Johanna paused.

"I let you go early to care for your children on Thursday, Johanna. And you may go as soon as Tuesday's fitting is done, Olga. You'll be close to home anyway. No sense in your walking all the way back here after that house call."

Annika clipped the thread, laid the bodice on a shelf, and climbed the steep stairway, enjoying the smell of gingerbread.

Greta was standing in the kitchen in her petticoats, brushing her walnut-colored hair.

Annika sat until Greta finished. "Would you like to try a loose chignon?"

"Whatever you think."

Annika parted Greta's hair in the middle and swept each side back loosely, covering half of Greta's ears. She gathered the hair in one hand and twisted it up and around, securing it with two pins.

"How's that?"

Greta studied her hair in a mirror. "Better than I'd hoped. It hides my ears. Mother says they're not my best feature."

"You just need to know how to accent your best features and downplay others." Annika added additional hair pins.

"You're so good at this."

"My best friend Lucie and I got ready for dances together all the time. I always did her hair. It's a lot like yours."

"I need to slice the gingerbread. Would you like a little piece?"

"Ja. My stomach's starting to rumble. I was too nervous to

eat lunch."

Greta cut the gingerbread and arranged it on a plate. "What do you think of Gustav?"

"He's charming and a good dancer. He was kind enough to help..." Annika broke off, realizing the shop had lost a fabric sale due to Gustav's goodheartedness. "...with his nephews when we went skating."

"He seems like a good prospect. His brother Erwin is just as handsome...and closer to my age." Greta's face took on a dreamy look.

Annika nibbled her gingerbread. "What do you know about the Weber family?"

"They're well respected, part of the weavers' guild. Erwin's grandparents started their business. Mutter likes the quality of their linen better than other suppliers, and they fill our orders just as quickly."

"Do you know what happened to Gustav and Erwin's mother?"

"She died of an illness about ten years ago. Mutter told me all about the family when we were discussing my marriage prospects."

Annika began plaiting her own hair. "So how does Erwin Weber measure up?"

"He's a good prospect. The problem is he's not the eldest, but Gustav's too old to be interested in me. I think he might be interested in you."

"From what you told me about how couples pair up here, Gustav seems a little old to be unattached."

"Some of the men aren't in a hurry. Gustav will take a pretty girl a few places and then switch to another. He just hasn't settled down. You're beautiful, and an excellent seamstress. You'd fit in well with the Webers."

Annika pinned her braids into loops. "Danke, but there are plenty of gorgeous girls from Wetzlar, like Adele."

Greta snorted. "Adele and Gustav are old news. She couldn't hold his attention."

Annika's stomach churned. If an attractive, wealthy city girl couldn't win Gustav, how could she? Though it would be satisfying to marry into a guild family in the city. Better than a Braunfels farmer. Could she live in a city for the rest of her life?

No reason to get her hopes up. Best see how tonight went first.

Annika put a mittened hand on Greta's sleeve to restrain her from charging through the Webers' front door.

"It's freezing, Annika."

"I know, but let them open the door for us…so we can make an entrance." Annika could hear footsteps approaching the door. "Ready?"

Harbin threw the door open. "Hallo, Annika. Hallo, Annika's friend. May I take your cloaks?"

Annika swept into the workroom regally with Greta clinging to her arm. Weaving equipment had been moved to the sides and hidden under lengths of cloth. Candelabra cast romantic shadows, and smells of ham and baked cinnamon apples greeted the women.

Alfons took the gingerbread and Annika's contribution of Streuselkuchen to the end of a long buffet table. Harbin bounded upstairs with their cloaks, pausing halfway to holler at Gustav. "They're here."

Gustav excused himself from his conversation with an older couple and approached the two. "We're delighted you're here. Thank you for coming."

A blond-haired man who resembled Gustav bounded over

to them. "Hallo, Greta. You look great tonight."

Greta pinkened.

"Erwin, this is Fraülein Annika Lange." Gustav said. "Annika, my brother Erwin. He was out with friends the night you met most of my family."

"I'm pleased to meet you, Erwin."

"The pleasure is all mine. Greta, there's a spot for you with the guests our age. Could I get you a drink?" The younger couple moved off, Greta exclaiming over the evergreens hung on the walls.

A silvery laugh escaped from Annika. "It's not often I feel old."

"Oof!" Gustav exhaled as Harbin ran full tilt into his legs. "There are a lot of people here. You should slow down." He turned the little fellow around and sent him in his mother's direction. "I thought you said you lived with your niece and nephew. My nephews' unbounded energy reminds me how old I am every day."

"Your nephews are quite different from my quiet little niece. My nephew is an infant, so perhaps when he's older."

"I imagine so. Just one of the many fascinating differences between boys and girls." Gustav gave her a grin that made her insides quiver. "I haven't fixed myself a plate yet, so let's go get some food and find a place to sit...with guests closer to our own age, of course."

Annika laughed again and followed him to the table. As he heaped his own plate with ham, apples, beans, and bread, Annika accepted smaller portions of everything. The night was off to a promising start.

When Gustav went to secure steins of beer, she studied the other guests. About half were her Vater's age. A few were from the generation before. The rest were young people, including a half dozen children. Harbin was trying to charm a blond-haired girl hiding behind her mother's emerald skirts.

As the evening wore on, she spotted Alfons leading the children to sample every dessert. Gustav's aunt shooed them away and signaled the musicians to strike up a lively jig that soon had all the children dancing.

"A folk song we can all join will be next." Gustav handed Annika a metal stein engraved with a buck.

The folk song was followed by a polka which Annika danced with Gustav's Vater. Gustav claimed her for the first waltz. Then there were more group dances. Alfons asked to polka with her.

Annika chatted with Rosa, whom she knew from Sunday lunches at the Kellers'. She had married Gustav's cousin Conrad over the summer. After being given six months to set up housekeeping in a snug apartment on a street between the Kellers and Webers, she was being taught to spin linen thread.

"I do whatever chores I have at home before I come here and spin. I like eating lunch with everyone, instead of home by myself. Sometimes I bring bread or soup. Other times they have a pot of something bubbling upstairs. After lunch, we women work a few more hours before going home to start dinner and finish up chores like taking down the day's laundry. Sometimes I visit Mutter before I come to work. I'm always busy, but it's not too much."

Annika thought about the constant grind of a farmer's wife.

"And at night, Conrad and I cuddle up in our feather bed." Rosa gave Annika a sideways glance. "I love married life."

"I'm glad it agrees with you so well." Annika's eyes followed Gustav as he danced with his cousins.

Conrad was headed their way with a besotted look on his handsome face. "Excuse me for stealing my wife away." He whisked Rosa away to dance.

Annika hoped someone would look at her that way someday. Ehrich never had.

As consolation, Annika took a bite of chocolate cake that melted in her mouth. Chocolate was a luxury she didn't often get in Braunfels, but in Wetzlar there were two chocolatiers. She should buy some to take to her family. When would she be able to visit? Maybe May Day. That would be the perfect time to be back in the country. Would she be able to endure an entire spring cooped up in the city?

"Aren't you having a good time, Annika?" Gustav plopped down beside her.

"Oh, yes!"

"So why the furrowed brow and sad eyes?"

"I was thinking of home and wondering how spring will be in the city. I'm sure I'll miss the fields and flowers."

"Wetzlar is at her best in the spring. There are plenty of charming places to walk." Gustav bent closer. "And boat rides on the Dill."

"That's one thing Braunfels doesn't have. But what about wildflowers?"

"Stunning. I will make sure you see the wildflowers every Sunday, and you can pick some to admire all week long. If you are agreeable..."

Was he suggesting courtship? If he wanted to see her every weekend...

"I'm traveling next week. With your permission, I'll stop and speak with your Vater on my way through Braunfels."

Annika gazed at him, thunderstruck. He had thought this out. He must be serious. "I would like that. Could I send letters with you to my family and Lucie?"

"I would be happy to deliver them." Another waltz began. "May I have this dance?"

"Certainly." *I might give you all of them.*

Chapter 18

I t snowed the next night. Annika was glad for her fur-lined boots as she walked to Engel's Monday morning. Although it was the end of February, spring seemed far away.

Greta gabbled on and on about the dance. "I had partners for every dance except two. They all danced *supremely*, better than the clods you get at the Gasthaus. Did you have good dance partners, Annika?"

Not waiting for a response, she gushed on. "I just wish Erwin had danced with me more. Don't you think he was the handsomest man of my age? I think Gustav, Erwin, and their cousin all tied for most handsome. Rosa Keller is a lucky woman."

When Frau Engel shushed her, Greta became sullen.

Annika spent the morning dropping pins and scissors and searching the floors with one of the oil lamps. Her need for the lamp hindered the other's progress since it was a gloomy day.

When Annika was on hands and knees for the third time, Frau Engel announced, "Let's break for lunch early. Greta, would you like to heat some hard cider for everyone? I think we need a pick-me-up."

Olga joined Annika in her hunt for the elusive pins while the others scattered. "What has you in such a tizzy?"

Annika leaned back on her knees. "Believe it or not, spring."

Olga gestured to the window where fat snowflakes drifted from leaden skies. "You have a month before the crocuses appear."

"I know."

"So, this is what we can expect for the next month?" Olga's chubby face registered concern.

"No, no. Of course not. I'll get myself together." Annika gave herself a shake. "At the dance, I was thinking about missing spring out on the farm. Gustav noticed and started talking about all the great spring activities in Wetzlar. The next thing I knew he'd offered to talk with my Vater so I could accompany him."

Olga's eyebrows shot up. "Are you worried about your Vater's response?"

"A little."

"What would you like it to be?"

"I would like to get better acquainted with Gustav."

"We'll pray your Vater says yes."

Annika grimaced and resumed looking for pins.

"What's wrong?"

"The last man I prayed about married someone else two months ago."

"Right around the time you started working here." Olga laid a motherly hand on Annika's shoulder. "I'm sorry. Sometimes God says 'no' for a reason we don't understand at the time."

"I'm not sure He cares."

"He always cares."

Greta popped through the door. "Mutter says to come upstairs to fill your mugs. She's afraid I'll drop the pot if I try to bring it down."

"We'll be right there," Olga said. When Greta headed back up the stairs, Olga turned her attention back to Annika. "I know God would like to hear your prayers, but until you're able, I'll pray for you."

Annika shrugged. "I think we've found all the pins. Let's go get some cider."

When Annika arrived at the shop Wednesday morning, there was a packet of letters for her. One from Dora, one from Lucie, and one in a man's unfamiliar handwriting. She snatched the one from Dora first, hoping it contained Vater's answer.

Dear Annika,

You can't imagine how much we miss you. The house isn't the same without your presence. Even Vater has commented on it. Speaking of Vater, he has given Gustav permission to court you. He says Gustav is a solid marriage prospect.

Annika was surprised her father had noticed her absence since Dora was there to do her work. Well, at least Wetzlar wasn't far. If Gustav could pop into Braunfels so often, she could go see her family occasionally...if she ended up living in the city. But she was getting ahead of herself.

Vater says to make sure you honor your Mutter's memory since your family is not present to chaperone.

Charlotte misses you terribly. She sleeps with us on the coldest nights. Helmuth is growing into a content, fat little fellow. Matt's clothes don't hang on him anymore, now that he's been eating all the good food you stored in the cellar. I'll always be grateful. Our lives would be very different if we'd stayed out east.

I wish I had some baked goods to send you, but I must bake later today since the men have gobbled everything up. We hope to see you soon.

Your loving sister, Dora.

Annika felt like dancing around the shop but realized Frau Engel was watching her. She glanced at the clock. It showed two minutes until eight, so she tucked the letters into her reticule.

"Go ahead and read them, child. Perhaps you'll drop fewer pins today."

"Danke. I'll just take a few minutes. I'm already feeling much more settled." Anna withdrew the two unopened letters and ripped open the one from the unknown sender. Her eyes darted to the bottom. It was signed Gustav.

Annika,

My journey to see your Vater was most satisfactory. He and your brother Matt and I partook of Kaffee and Kuchen while they interrogated me about my family connections and prospects in life. Your Vater has given his consent to my courtship of you with the stipulation that there is no understanding between us, as of yet. This period is to determine if we might be compatible.

Both he and your brother said they will hunt me down if I behave in an ungentlemanly way. They assure me you are the most beautiful, eligible woman in Braunfels and are to be treated like nobility. I hereby pledge to treat you with the utmost respect.

Would you like to join the Weber clan for an afternoon of games and music on Sunday? I know you enjoy your meal with the Kellers, so I could call for you at two o'clock. I will stop by the shop later this week for your answer.

Gustav.

Annika pressed the missive to her chest. She could hardly wait for Sunday.

Chapter 19

One morning toward the end of March, Annika noticed a few of the yellow spindle bushes blooming in the garden behind the Kellers' house. Spring had arrived.

After Gustav had begun courting her, February and March had flown. Gustav secured tickets to a Mozart opera and a Beethoven concert. On other Saturday nights, they went to the Gasthaus and danced.

Gustav's aunt, reveling in her role as family matriarch, welcomed Annika warmly, inviting her into the spacious kitchen to work alongside her three daughters. Annika felt closest to Ella since they were nearest in age and both unmarried. Paula and Klara were friendly but had other concerns with their husbands and children.

This weekend she and Gustav might be able to walk some of the fields surrounding Wetzlar. She would be able to smell the spring perfume of the linden trees, instead of the stench of the printer and other city businesses. Annika hurried inside Engel's to escape the odor of the shop next door. She usually didn't mind, but today she longed to smell earth and growing things.

Throughout the morning, the bell on the shop's door chimed frequently, admitting women inspired to choose warm-weather gowns. Annika stayed bent over a difficult bodice at the sunny window. This was a new pattern for her, and she wanted to please Frau Engel.

When the bell rang three times in a row, Olga set aside the sleeve she was tacking to a linen bodice and went to the front room. When someone bustled into the room a few minutes later, Annika didn't look up until a shadow blocked the light.

"Lucie!" Annika jumped up to hug her friend. "What are you doing here? It's so good to see you."

"It was warm enough to ride up with Paul for supplies today. Fritz is starting to plow, so I'll be busy next month. Frau Engel is with several ladies in the showroom, so she told me to come back and chat with you, as long as you can keep working."

"Annika's told us so much about you," Greta interrupted. "You do have hair like mine."

At Lucie's confused look, Annika explained, "Lucie, this is Greta Engel. Greta and I attended a dance together, so I styled her hair. I told her how you and I used to get ready for dances together."

"Of course." Lucie smiled at Greta. "I'm sure your hair looked lovely when Annika was done."

"It did. I received lots of compliments."

Annika picked up a pink dress that needed hemming. "I'll stitch something simpler while we catch up. How is Fritz?"

"He's well. So is your family. I brought you a basket of goodies from Dora and my mom. Tell me what's been going on in the big city."

Aware of the listening ears of the other seamstresses, Annika gave her friend a rundown of activities without revealing much about her relationship with Gustav.

When Annika finished the hem, Lucie stood reluctantly. "I'd better go so I don't take up too much of your morning."

Greta bounced off her chair. "It's late enough to have lunch. Do you want to join us, Lucie?"

Annika turned to look at the clock. "Greta's right. The morning's flown by, and you're welcome to eat with us."

"I planned to meet Paul at the Gasthaus. Would you be able to join us, Annika?"

"Let me check with Frau Engel."

After receiving permission, the two women hurried out the door. "Is Gustav treating you well? Matt wants to know."

"He's been the perfect gentleman."

"Do you think you'll marry?"

"He's a good prospect, but it's too early to say." Occasionally, Annika still woke from dreams of Ehrich.

Paul was lounging at a table with a beer when they arrived and ordered bratwurst.

Annika ate quickly. "Thank you for bringing Lucie, Paul."

"When do you think you'll be able to come home for a visit?" Lucie asked.

"I'm hoping to come for May Day."

"If you come a few days early, you'll be home for your birthday."

"I'd like that, but I haven't asked Frau Engel yet. I haven't worked for her very long, and no one's missed a full day of work except for illness."

"We're so fortunate our family owns a business. We can make our own hours."

"As long as we work longer hours another day, little sister." Paul paid their bill. "Whenever you arrive, Annika, come to the bakery and I'll give you a ride out to the farm."

"Danke. I've got to get back to Engel's. Give Dora, Charlotte, and Helmuth hugs for me, Lucie." As Annika walked the short distance back to the shop, she turned Paul's words over in her mind. He'd said the farm, not home. Was the farm not her home anymore? She had only been gone for three months.

She sighed. With Matt's family living there and Dora

organizing the household, it probably would feel less like home, but her bedroom at the Kellers' wasn't home either. When she closed her eyes at night and thought of home, she was back at the farm with her parents and brothers when she was growing up. A sense of loss gnawed at her.

Melancholy clung to her all week. On Sunday, instead of feeling the accustomed warmth of belonging, she felt like an outsider at the Kellers' family dinner. Excusing herself as soon as good manners allowed, she changed into older clothes she could get muddy and watched from her bedroom window for Gustav.

A phaeton drawn by an older horse pulled up on the narrow street in front of the Kellers'. Gustav jumped down from the driver's seat. Annika hurried down the stairs, wrapping herself in a wool shawl. She slipped out the door while Gustav was still winding the reins around a hitching ring.

"She's marvelous! How did you get hold of a horse and carriage?" Annika stroked the bay's muzzle.

"Guten Tag," Gustav said dryly.

Annika's hand flew to her face. "I'm sorry. Guten Tag. It's been so long since I've seen my family's horses. I miss them more than I realized."

Gustav relaxed. "I can see that. Be forewarned, Britta is rather slow, but I thought a carriage ride would be a nice change."

"It's a magnificent idea! Danke." Annika resumed petting the mare.

"Let's not give her too much appreciation before she gets us to our destination. Then you can give her a carrot."

"You brought treats for her? You thought of everything." Annika spied a basket tucked into the carriage. "Should I bring anything?"

"No, we're all set." Gustav helped her navigate over the wheel and into the seat. He handed her the reins while he climbed in on the other side.

"Can I drive?"

"Have you ever driven a phaeton? They're very light, not like a farm wagon."

"No." Disappointment tinged Annika's voice.

"Let me drive for now. I had to call in a favor to get hold of this rig. You can take over when we get out of the city." Gustav spread a lap rug over their legs and claimed the reins. "Sit back and enjoy."

Annika reveled in the view from the carriage seat. Although they traveled the same streets they'd walked, the buildings looked different from their higher perch.

Gustav soon had her laughing over his nephews' antics. Sun peeked through the clouds and lifted her spirits. True to his word, Gustav handed her the reins as soon as they left Wetzlar. Britta moved slowly but steadily and was responsive to the reins.

Gustav directed her to a side road that passed over a stream. "This is my favorite picnic spot outside the city. Let's stop here." He laid an old blanket on the grass and anchored it with the basket. "Would you like to walk before we eat the treats Aunt Hertha baked yesterday?"

They strolled to the top of a rise where they could admire the view of the stone bridge over the Lahn River and Wetzlar's cathedral rising behind it. Gustav gestured grandly. "The ugliest cathedral in Hessen."

"It is a hodge podge of styles, isn't it?"

"It was never finished, and when the Gothic part was built, the older part in the Roman style wasn't torn down. It is a hodge podge, but whenever I'm returning from a trip, its towers are my first glimpse of home."

"I know what you mean. The *Schloss* in Braunfels is the first building you can see from a distance. I'll be looking for it when I walk home."

"Are you very homesick?"

"Ja." Annika gazed at the cathedral's towers. "But I'm longing for something that doesn't exist anymore—the home my Mutter created." She brushed away a tear.

"I miss my Mutter, too, and it's been ten years. The house seems emptier without her, even though we've kept things in the same places."

"Since my brother and his family moved back in, furniture and things have been rearranged. It will be even more different when I visit."

"Home's where the people you care about are."

"Ja. I've just been feeling a little displaced. I've never been away like this."

Gustav took her hand on their way back down the hill. "I hope you'll become attached to your life in Wetzlar too. Maybe someday this will feel like home."

Annika smiled at him. "I think it could."

Chapter 20

Four days at home! Annika could hardly believe it. A banker acquaintance of Herr Keller was driving to Albshausen for business and had agreed to take her. She would be halfway to Braunfels before she needed to walk.

Frau Engel told her to return refreshed to deal with extra sewing since daylight would lengthen their hours. Annika pushed the thought of being indoors all summer aside and clutched the seat as the portly banker put his team in motion with a shake of the reins.

Annika reveled in the spring sunshine, careful to note passing landmarks so she could find her way back to Wetzlar. Gustav had warned her the road took several forks. She remembered their last conversation with a smile.

"No one's driving you back to Wetzlar? Are you sure you can make it by yourself?"

"Gustav! I am not five years old. Matt will bring me if he can, but I'm perfectly capable of walking."

"They don't know you're coming?"

"I sent word to Dora through Paul Becker, but I want it to be a surprise for the rest of them."

"Just make sure you come back."

Annika thought she heard him whisper "to me" as he left her at the Kellers' door.

The buggy stopped in front of a large farm. The banker frowned. "No one's waiting for you?"

"Nein. I'll walk to Becker's Bakery. Someone will take me home from there. Danke for the ride. It's saved me a lot of time."

"You're welcome. Enjoy your family visit."

Annika picked up her carpet bag and swung it jauntily as she headed to Becker's, devouring the familiar sights along the way. She shifted hands when it got heavy and was perspiring before she reached the center of Braunfels.

As Annika passed Dora's parents' modest, one-story house, Charlotte tumbled out the door and buried herself in Annika's chocolate brown skirt.

"Have you been waiting for me?" Annika hugged her niece.

"I've been watching out the window since we got here. It took you a long time."

Dora appeared with Helmuth in her arms. "Welcome home, Anna. Charlotte, it's only been a half hour, but you did a very good job. Now go in and see what Oma has for you." The little girl skipped back inside. "She was too excited to have a cookie earlier. She didn't want to miss you." Dora gave Annika a one-armed hug. Helmuth stared at her solemnly.

"Do you remember me, little fellow? I'm your Tante Anna."

Helmuth clung to his mother.

"I'm sure you'll be the best of friends by the time you leave. Are you eager to get out to the farm or could we visit with my Mutter a spell?"

"You have time. I'll pop in and say hello, but I need to go to Becker's since Paul had offered me a ride. I'll let him know you're here."

"Take your time. We haven't seen Oma since last week, have we, Helmuth?"

Annika stowed her bag in the wagon and greeted Dora's mother. Promising Charlotte to return soon, she headed to

Becker's.

Inhaling the scent of fresh bread, Annika burst through the door, eager to see Frau Becker. She stopped dead when she saw Margarete and Elsa standing in front of the glass display case.

Margarete arched an eyebrow. "Guten Tag, Annika. What a surprise! Are you done with your city job?"

"Guten Tag, Margarete, Elsa. Nein, I've come for a short visit."

"How nice!" Margarete purred.

Elsa ran over to hug Annika as Frau Becker reappeared from the back. "I'm afraid we don't have any macaroons today. I have to bake more. We'll have them tomorrow." Spying Annika, she said, "It's lovely to see you. I'll be right with you, dear."

"I'm sure Ehrich will come into town and pick them up for me. I'm feeling a little under the weather some mornings." Margarete gave Annika a sidelong glance.

"I'm going to be a Tante, Anna, just like you." Elsa beamed.

Annika felt the color drain from her face but tried to focus on Elsa. "You're going to make a wonderful Tante." She turned to Margarete. "Congratulations." She glimpsed Frau Becker's concerned face.

As Margarete handed some change to the baker, Lina entered. "Annika, what a treat to see you here." She studied her friend. "Are you feeling all right?"

Annika pasted on a smile. "I'm quite well, thank you."

Lina discerned the tension in the shop. "Annika, I'd love to catch up, but I need to get right home. I promised Mutter. Come, Elsa." She turned and left the shop with her younger sister in tow.

"Enjoy your visit." With a hand resting on her stomach, Margarete sailed by Annika.

"Don't mind her." Frau Becker bustled over to hug Annika. "Come sit with me and have a cup of Kaffee and some Kuchen."

Anna allowed herself to be guided to the Becker's kitchen table. The coziness started to thaw her distress as Frau Becker chatted about Lucie and the goings-on of the town. "Paul should be back shortly to take you home."

"I almost forgot. I came to tell you Dora and the children are here to fetch me. They're visiting with her Mutter."

"I'm glad Dora was able to do that." Frau Becker patted Annika's hand. "Don't let Margarete disturb you. Even if things haven't worked out how you've wanted, God has a good plan for you. We just can't see it yet." A frown darkened her pleasant features. "It's wrong of that girl to flaunt what she has."

A tear slipped down Annika's face. "I feel so lost since Mutter died. She saw me as special. I thought Ehrich did too, but obviously..." She swallowed hard. "Vater withdrew from everyone, and now with Dora running the house, I'm not sure it will even feel like home. I don't know where I belong."

Frau Becker hugged her tightly. "You have a place in God's family. You're precious to Him."

"It feels like He's forgotten me."

"There are times in life it feels like that, but you can't trust your feelings. They change." Frau Becker looked at her window box bursting with pink and yellow blooms. "The flowers come back to life after lying dormant all winter. God does amazing things after seasons that feel like nothing will be beautiful again. God has a plan for your life. In some seasons, you'll feel like hopes and dreams have died, but you'll have seasons of growth and joy again."

The shop's bell rang. "I have to get that, but you finish up, dear. And no matter how busy I am, say good-bye on your way out."

Chapter 21

Annika plodded along. She'd been walking for well over an hour and was sweating in spite of the spring breeze. She regretted every single item she'd stowed in her carpet bag, including Dora's deliciously light bread.

Deciding to rest on a hill that commanded a sweeping view, she realized she couldn't see the towers of Schloss Braunfels anymore. She peered into the distance for a glimpse of Wetzlar Cathedral. Nothing yet.

She tore off a chunk of bread and washed it down with water from a flask. Black-faced lambs were gamboling next to their ewes in the green meadows, but the sun was lowering. If she didn't get moving, she wouldn't reach the Kellers' before dark. Feeling revived, she reached for her bag.

"Hallo."

Relief flooded Annika when she spied Gustav hurrying up the road. "I'm glad to see you."

"And I you." He grabbed her bag and grinned at her. "I couldn't borrow a buggy, but I wanted to meet you. How was your trip?"

"It was good. My family's doing well. The goat had twins, and our cow is ready to calve." Annika flung her arms out to embrace the meadow. "Spring is definitely in the air."

"It's late. I thought I'd meet you closer to town."

"I stayed for morning chores. Then Charlotte and I hunted greens for their supper. I played with Helmuth while Dora baked bread. We washed the sheets."

"Whoa! No wonder you're worn out."

Annika laughed. "I guess you're right. I'm used to doing all those tasks, but I don't walk to Wetzlar too."

"Are you going to be able to work tomorrow?"

"I have to be."

"Maybe someday you'll be part of a family business so you have more control over your schedule."

Annika peeked at him through lowered lashes. "That would be nice."

Gustav filled her in on his weekend over the next half hour until they entered Wetzlar. "Could I take you for a bite to eat before I escort you to the Kellers'?"

"I'd like that."

They passed up a Biergarten for a cozy Gasthaus. Gustav found a small table with a wildflower bouquet in a blue pitcher.

While Gustav found a spot for her bag, Annika seated herself. "This is such a pretty place!"

"Sometimes our buyers stay in this inn, so I know they serve good food. They're serving *Wiener Schnitzel* tonight."

"One of my favorites." Annika dropped her eyes to her hands folded in her lap. "You're going to spoil me."

"You could use a little spoiling. Consider it your birthday celebration. Did you celebrate with your family?"

"Dora and Charlotte baked me a cake while I slept in. I spent the afternoon with Lucie. She gave me a handkerchief she embroidered with flowers." Annika showed it to Gustav.

"Very nice. Do you embroider?"

"No, sewing and knitting keep me busy. Dora gave me some more yarn, so I can start a new project." Annika tucked the handkerchief away.

Their meal arrived, and the couple focused on the hearty portions of veal, potatoes, and stewed apples.

Annika took a bite of the elderberry pie Gustav had insisted on ordering. "This is delicious. Thank you for dinner."

"Thank you for accompanying me. You must be tired, so let's get you home."

Folks were out strolling in the spring air when the couple exited the inn. They navigated through a residential neighborhood with tall homes overlooking the Dill, which was crowded with cargo barges and smaller pleasure boats, lights twinkling at their bows and sterns.

"The river's even prettier by night." Annika tightened her shawl as the air cooled.

"I'll take you out in a boat one of these weekends," Gustav promised. They headed toward the *Kornmarkt* with its communal pump. The buzz of women gossiping as they collected water drifted down the street. Gustav gestured up *Engelsgasse* to a four-story, half-timbered home. "I know the family who lives there. We'll visit sometime when you're not so tired."

Glancing up the street at the handsome house, Annika felt a wave of fatigue wash over her. By the time they reached the Kellers', she was clinging to Gustav's arm after having stumbled twice. Wishing him a Gute Nacht, she greeted the Kellers briefly, dragged herself up the stairs, and fell into bed.

Chapter 22

The week passed quickly as Annika worked late every night, including Saturday. On Sunday morning, she stretched luxuriously in bed, reluctant to rise. The long week had caught up with her. She would have to eat a cold breakfast and rush to get ready for church.

At least she had an afternoon outing with Gustav to look forward to. He had stopped by the shop and arranged to pick her up after Sunday lunch. He wouldn't share his plans.

She smiled as she got out of bed and hurried through her toilette.

Surrounded by the Keller family, Annika enjoyed singing the hymns but daydreamed during the sermon about a worldwide flood. The reverend was making a lot of noise about the sinfulness of men and their impending judgement. Pastor Brandt preached more uplifting topics like love and forgiveness. Annika tried not to fidget or appear overeager to leave, even when the Kellers greeted many of their fellow parishioners before heading home.

After a hearty meal of roast chicken and vegetables, Annika changed into clothes suitable for an outdoor activity. That was the only hint Gustav had given her. They usually walked in the fields or woods on Sundays, so he must have arranged a different excursion. Maybe another ride? She would like to pet Britta again and drive the phaeton.

But Gustav arrived on foot and steered her along familiar streets toward the Lahn River. He recounted his latest trip to find flax suppliers as they strolled along the river.

Gustav pointed to a skiff on the bank ahead of them. "We're going boating today." He pushed the little boat halfway into the water and helped Annika board.

Annika wobbled to the seat near the prow and sat down, settling her skirts out of the water puddling in the bottom of the boat. Hoping it wasn't leaking, she offered Gustav a weak smile.

He was settling the oars into metal hooks on the skiff's sides. "Here we go." He pushed off, and the skiff caught in the current.

Annika tried to concentrate on the sights lining the river, but her attention kept creeping back to Gustav's muscled arms as he rowed. It was a little disorienting to be traveling backwards. The shady coolness under a bridge crept up on her. After they passed through, she admired the gray arches.

Gustav hummed as he let the current carry them outside of town to a landing surrounded by trees. Annika cautiously turned around to watch a family of ducks feed in the cool shallows and laughed at the ducks' antics as they went bottoms up to search for lunch.

Gustav cleared his throat. "Anna, I have something to ask you."

She peered over her shoulder. He was leaning forward with something in his hand. "Would you do me the honor—"

A scow crewed by rowdy drunks turned into the landing, headed straight into their little skiff. Gustav half rose to push off the bow of the bigger boat, sending theirs into a tailspin and himself splashing into the water. Annika hunkered down, clinging to the sides.

"Sorry, Mate," yelled one of the drunken sailors.

Gustav stood up, spluttering, and shook his fist, eliciting laughter and catcalls. The revelers floated away with the current.

"Annika, are you all right?"

"Yes. A little wet, but I'm fine, in much better shape than you are."

Gustav looked down at his dripping torso. "I can't believe—" He dove back into the water.

When he re-emerged, he shook his head. "I'll never find it. Anna, I had something for you."

Annika smiled at him. "You mean this?" She held up a delicate gold ring etched with vines and flowers. "It's beautiful."

"But how did you—"

"It was in the boat. I knew you had something in your hand when that boat nearly hit us. I figured that's what you were looking for in the water, so I checked the boat. I was glad we didn't capsize before. Now I'm even more glad." She quirked an eyebrow at him. "You had something to ask me?"

"This wasn't what I pictured." Gustav took the ring. "Anna, you're an amazing woman. Would you do me the honor of becoming my wife?"

"Ja!"

Gustav slipped the circlet on Annika's finger and gave her a chaste kiss. He beached the boat and stepped back in.

"We're never going to forget this day," Annika said as Gustav grabbed the oars.

"Maybe you could highlight the romantic boat ride and downplay the drenching I got? And the misplaced ring?"

"Everyone will love the story just the way it happened. This was a lot more entertaining than a simple boat ride."

"I suppose." Gustav looked put out.

"And we'll tell our children the story every year in the spring."

Gustav brightened. "Children, ja. We'll have one on the way by this time next year."

Surprised, Annika asked, "When do you want to get married?"

"Is next month too soon?"

Thrilled to begin married life sooner rather than later, Annika calculated when haying and other farm crops would need tended. "I think the middle of the month might work. I'd need to ask Vater. Would we have the wedding in Wetzlar or Braunfels?"

"How would you like to be married in Wetzlar Cathedral?"

The idea stole Annika's breath. Never had she dreamed she'd be married in a cathedral. "Absolutely!"

"My family will inquire about availability. Vater and Onkel will get all the permissions from the Bürgermeisters. If we marry here, we can host a dinner at our shop, like the dance you came to."

Annika's mind whirred with the possibilities. Her family and friends could bring food and flowers. Candles and draped cloth would make the workspace magical as the sun set. "Could we have our ceremony in the late afternoon or early evening?"

"As long as the cathedral is available."

Stunned, Annika admired the ring in her lap as the shore slipped by.

"Your smile is more lovely than your ring."

Catching Gustav's eye, Annika blushed. He wasn't studying her hands or face. Resisting the urge to readjust her bodice, she searched for a way to divert him. She plucked a discarded sock from the bottom of the boat where he had thrown his wet shoes and socks. She stuck her fingers through two large holes. "I'll start knitting you some new socks."

"Danke. Most of mine have holes. If I give them to my Tante

or cousins, they'll darn them for me, but they're already busy keeping the children in clothes." He sighed. "Getting soaked interferes with the rest of my plans for the day."

Annika quirked an eyebrow. "There's more?"

"I wanted to take you by that house I pointed out to you after we ate at the Gasthaus. The family who lives there is renting out their top floor. It's not very big, but I thought it would be a good place to live until we can get our own place."

"We can see it another day."

"We have to get there quick if we want it. Could I take you tomorrow after work?"

"Ja. I worked late all last week, so I should be able to leave right at six."

"Good. After we look at the property, I'll bring you back to the shop for dinner. You have a lot of planning to do, and Tante Hertha will be thrilled to help."

Annika's head spun. She'd sit down and write to her family tonight. And Lucie. Maybe Paul could bring her hope chest next time he came for bakery supplies. It was full of linens and even a few dishes and pieces of crockery that had belonged to her Oma.

Chapter 23

The next Sunday Gustav surprised her by renting a horse and carriage and taking her to visit her family.

"We can't stay long," he warned her as Schloss Braunfels came into sight. "But I thought we should talk over our plans, especially the date. The cathedral is already booked the first two weeks of June. Vater reserved the third Saturday in June at half past three. We need to reschedule right away if that doesn't suit your family."

Vater and Matt kept Gustav occupied out at the barn with their best beer while Annika chatted with Dora.

"I can't believe you're marrying so soon. So much to do!" Dora set Helmuth on the rug. He crawled toward Annika and pulled himself up.

Annika hugged her nephew, who plopped back down and headed toward the cold hearth. "It's a dream come true. I always wanted to get married the summer after I turned eighteen."

"I was a June bride."

"I remember. It was a beautiful wedding." Annika paused. "And Mutter was still alive."

"I'll never forget how she welcomed me into your family. I always felt comfortable with her."

"Mutter had that knack." A tear slipped down Annika's cheek. "I wish she were here now."

Dora clasped Annika's hand. "I'm here for you, Anna. Always."

"I know. I couldn't have asked for a better sister-in-law. And if you weren't caring for Vater, I would never have gotten to work in Wetzlar. You were a godsend."

Dora looked around the neat cottage, Charlotte playing with a rag doll while Helmuth chewed on a block. "I do believe the Almighty sent us here. I don't think Helmuth would have survived in Prussia. I might not have either."

"It was the best arrangement for everyone. Vater is so much...lighter now."

"He dotes on his grandchildren. What is Gustav's family like?"

Annika leaned back in her chair. "They're industrious. They all work together in their weaving business. Gustav has his Vater and a younger brother, but his mother died ten years ago. His Tante Hertha is the matriarch of the family. She's been very good to me. She, her husband, and daughter Ella live over the workshop.

"Her older three children are married. There are three grandchildren so far. Most of them come for Sunday dinner. It's a loud bunch. They seem to care about each other."

"Sounds like a good family to belong to."

"I think so." Annika shifted in her chair. "Speaking of children, I have a few questions...about my wedding night."

Frau Engel gifted her a shimmering black silk when she heard Annika planned to wear her red dress for the wedding. "You should have something special for your wedding day."

When she shared her employer's generous gift with Gustav, he roared. "You're marrying into the Webers, producers of the finest linen in Hessen. You'll be wearing our linen for the wedding."

Stunned, Annika froze. Gustav's father and aunt heard his

outburst and hurried down to the workroom where the couple had been talking.

Herr Weber sent his son upstairs to fetch some drinks. "This was an oversight on our part, Annika. We should have realized you would require a new gown for the wedding. As kind as Frau Engel's offer is, you understand why you need to wear our cloth, no? You can choose from any of our linen."

He brought out lengths for her to peruse. "Did you have a certain color in mind?"

Annika fingered navy, pink, and white linen but couldn't decide. Gustav's aunt sent both men back upstairs and convinced Annika to take a drink of the ale Gustav had brought.

"The Weber men can be quite...volatile, dear, but that doesn't mean they don't love their women. A big part of our business is perception. Your wedding clothes are a testament to our skill. Gustav's suit is well underway. It was assumed that, as the talented seamstress you are, you would handle your dress, but we overlooked giving you the cloth. With so many details to attend to, it's hard to believe we left that one out, but there you have it.

"While I'm thinking of it, you understand our fellow guild members and others associated with our weaving will be invited to the ceremony and dinner afterwards? We have an important position in the cloth community in Hessen. Many of the same people you met at our winter dance. You'll charm them all, I'm sure."

Annika gulped down her ale.

"Feeling better?" Aunt Hertha studied her face.

Annika took a deep breath and nodded.

"Now let's decide on a fabric. I hear Queen Victoria wore white when she married, making white gowns the newest trend for weddings. Would you fancy a white gown?"

Although white linen seemed impractical, Annika went along with the suggestion. It felt a little glamorous. She'd only be able to wear such a dress to church, but why not? As a Weber, she would have access to all the cloth she could use. "Sounds lovely."

Gustav's aunt cut an ample piece of their white linen. "This will make a stunning dress."

Gustav strode down the stairs. "Let's get you home, Annika." He set out at a fast pace for the Kellers. "Are you happy with your selection?"

"Ja. Danke."

"Listen. I know I didn't handle that well. If you ever need anything, tell me. I don't know what's going on in that pretty head of yours unless you tell me."

"I will," Annika promised.

The next day Annika showed the other seamstresses the white linen. "There's enough for the style I'd chosen. I already told Frau Engel that the Webers want my dress to be linen."

Johanna gave her a sideways glance. "How'd that go?"

"I was afraid of offending her, but she seemed to take it well."

Olga shook out the fabric. "She should have let you select Weber linen, instead of offering silk."

Annika shrugged. "Her reasoning was sound. Silk is a luxury, and I don't own anything silk." She sighed. "It would have been nice. She told me to hold onto it."

"We've already cut it to your measurements." Olga swiftly pinned the black pieces to the white fabric. "We're going to have to sew even faster than we thought."

Greta joined the group after her morning chores. "Why are the pieces of your black gown pinned down to this fabric?"

"The Webers would like me to wear their linen."

Greta's eyes popped. "White will be much better than black. Mutter's fashion magazines say white is the new color for wedding dresses, because of Queen Victoria."

"It's not very practical, if you ask me." Johanna began carefully cutting out the new skirt.

"Queens don't have to be frugal," Greta said. "Neither does Annika, at least not with linen. She's marrying into a family of weavers."

Johanna snorted. "Every piece the family uses will cut into their profits."

"I suppose, but it also displays their wares. At least that's the kind of thing Mutter tells me when she or I have a new dress." Greta appraised Annika. "And Annika is so pretty, she'll make their product look even better."

Olga looked up from cutting the bodice. "You're going to make a fine mistress of this dress shop one day, Greta."

Greta blushed at the compliment. "I'll hem this for you if you'd like, Annika."

"I'd appreciate that." They would be rushed to finish, so Annika was grateful for all the help she could get.

When she was feeling the pinch of all that remained to be done the week before the wedding, Frau Engel swept into the shop with Lucie and Frau Becker in her wake. "Annika, your friends are here. I'm giving you the afternoon off after we all have a bite to eat together. It's not every day one of my seamstresses gets married."

Olga and Johanna cleared off the sewing tables while Greta fetched sausage and ale from the upstairs apartment. Lucie brought cheese she had made and fresh strawberries from the farm. Her mother brought pastries and bread from the bakery.

The women polished off the feast and shared marital advice with Annika.

After they ate, Frau Engel brought out Annika's wedding dress. It had short sleeves, a fan bodice that came to a V at the waistline, and a full skirt. Annika tried it on, and Olga pinned the hem for Greta to stitch.

"Oh, Annika, it's exquisite," Lucie breathed.

"I'll work on it this afternoon," Greta promised.

Frau Becker and Lucie accompanied Annika to inspect the two rooms of her snug attic apartment. When she and Gustav looked at the rooms in his friend's home, they had seemed small but perfect for newlyweds. A door on the third floor opened to a narrow stairway to the attic.

Gustav had found a horsehair sofa to set alongside the unrailed stairs. A dropleaf table filled the other side of the room where a double fireplace on the interior wall would provide heat for both rooms. The groom's family had gifted them a double bed and a cherry wardrobe designed by the Roths. As their gift, Hans and Max had crafted a matching washstand.

Frau Becker gave an approving nod, running a hand over Annika's quilt. "I've never seen a finer wedding quilt." Her eyes twinkled. "You need a few more bits and pieces for your new home."

"I know I need pots and such, but since we'll be taking our meals above the Webers' shop for at least a few months, we don't need them right now."

Paul emerged at the top of the stairs. "You might want to sit at your table before then." He hauled two wooden chairs with woven seats into the room. "Your Vater and Matt made these. Matt wanted to deliver these today, but the two of them are working like Trojans to have everything ready for the weekend."

Lucie scurried down the steps. Before Annika could blink, she returned with a wooden crate. "The Vogels sent you gifts. I held them the whole way here so they wouldn't break."

Annika unfolded a dish towel to reveal a hurricane lamp. "I had planned to use candles. This will be much better."

Lucie nudged the box. "Keep looking."

Annika unwrapped a smaller, matching lamp.

"For your bedroom." Lucie carried it into the next room and set it next to the pitcher on the washstand.

Paul reappeared with a large crate. Annika lifted out a cast iron frying pan and two pots. A flatiron and four pewter dinner plates rested in the bottom of the crate.

"You can keep the pots and pan packed away in the crate over there." Frau Becker pointed to an empty corner. "And stack dishes and utensils on top."

Annika laughed. "I don't have any utensils yet, but that's a good idea."

"There will be more gifts on your big day. I'm sure someone will think of tableware." Lucie took one end of the crate and helped Annika set it in the corner.

Paul returned with a basket. "This is the last one."

Frau Becker took the basket and set it on the table. "Dora sent this to you, Annika. She wished she could come, but she's baking for the wedding."

Annika flipped up the cloth covering the basket. Tears filled her eyes. "This was my Mutter's." She lifted out a bright-green cabbage sugar bowl and fingered a ridge where a leaf had broken off. "Matt and I broke this when I was four. I was riding him like a horse. Was she mad! He took all the blame and saved me from a switching."

Frau Becker put an arm around Annika. "Dora has one she received as a wedding present. She and your Vater agreed you should keep this one, along with everything else in this basket."

Annika wiped her eyes and removed a lace tablecloth her mother had used for holidays and special occasions. Underneath were nestled six Dresden plates. Annika ran her hand over them reverently. "I hope I have a proper kitchen soon. You'll have to be our guests once we do. Thank you so much for bringing all of this."

Lucie squeezed her. "We were happy to do it. There's one more thing we came to do with you. Have you bought your wedding shoes yet?"

"No. I was planning to go this afternoon. I have the coins in my pocket."

"We're taking you in the wagon," Paul said. "I've asked around for the best establishment to buy shoes at. It's on the other side of town."

The women followed him down the stairs and were driven to a mercantile Annika had never visited before. She was delighted by the selection of shoes. Paul winked at her. "I can see this may take a while. I'm going to keep an eye on my wagon since it's full of supplies."

"We won't be long," his mother assured him.

"Do you know what color you want?" Lucie asked.

"They need to be white to go with my dress. There must be ten pairs of white shoes here!"

Frau Becker sorted through the shoes, setting the fancier pairs that would be suitable for a wedding on the counter in front of Annika.

Annika tried one on. "Too tight."

"These are pretty." Lucie held up a pair of leather shoes

lined with pink silk.

Annika slipped her feet into them. "They fit perfectly, and I think they'll be comfortable for dancing."

"Good. They're a fine, soft leather." Frau Becker motioned to the shop owner, and Annika paid with the coins she'd saved.

"I'm sorry we need to leave, but we have to get back to the bakery," Frau Becker said. "Your wedding cake's not going to bake itself. I'm experimenting with a new batter tonight. We'll see if it's better than my Oma's secret recipe."

"Your Oma's recipe is delectable." Annika closed her eyes as she imagined the cinnamon-flavored cake. "Please don't go to any more trouble on my account. We already appreciate your baking the Kuchen and bringing it all this way."

Frau Becker patted her cheek. "It's my pleasure, child. Let an old woman fuss. There aren't enough happy occasions in life."

"I'm just sad you're not going to live closer." Lucie adjusted her bonnet. "Otherwise, things are perfect. I can't believe you're getting married in a cathedral!"

Annika flushed with pleasure. "Things have turned out almost perfect, haven't they?"

Chapter 24

Concerto music from a magnificent pipe organ soared past stained glass windows to the apex of the vaulted ceiling. Annika tipped her head back to admire flowers painted on the tallest cream-colored dome which was ribbed with red stone.

Her attention shifted to the wildflowers in her right hand. Blue cornflowers and pink love-in-a-mist dominated the bouquet. The cornflowers reminded her of Gustav's eyes. She searched for him at the altar. Handsome beyond words in his black linen suit, he stood with the pastor, eyes riveted on her.

Annika floated down the aisle on her father's arm. She glimpsed the Kellers in a middle pew. The Roth family sat in front of them with Lina Stein. Beside Greta, Frau Engel looked less stern than usual. Lucie and Franz beamed at her.

On the other side of the aisle sat an ocean of Webers. Ella gave Annika a discreet wave. Gustav's Vater and Erwin gazed at their newest family member without emotion while Gustav's Tante Hertha wiped tears from her eyes.

Dora and Matt sat in the front pew. Charlotte's mouth dropped open when she saw her aunt. "So pretty!"

The churchgoers suppressed chuckles. Annika's Vater leaned in close. "She's right. You're the picture of your beautiful mother." He solemnly transferred her to Gustav.

Gustav remained serious, but Annika couldn't suppress her smile. She had trouble focusing on the pastor's words but repeated dutifully. "I, Annika Louise Lange, take you, Gustav Peter Weber, to be my husband from this day forward, to join with you and share all that is to come, and I promise to be faithful to you until death parts us."

Gustav slipped the gold ring that had been baptized in the river onto her left hand.

"I now pronounce you man and wife."

Even Gustav smiled as they walked sedately down the long aisle and out into the sunshine, followed by all their family and friends.

The workshop looked even more lovely than Annika thought it could. The spinning wheels had been banished to a small storage room. The looms were draped with cloth and flowers. Gustav's Tante had set up candelabra. Flowers clustered in barrels and baskets on the floor. Tables had been borrowed and set up along the length of the room for the wedding feast.

Gustav's cousin Klara had stayed behind with her youngest child to continue meal preparations. She led Annika and Gustav to the center of the table where the Becker's confection towered in three layers. When Gustav moved to swipe a bit of icing, she swatted his hand. "Be a good example for your niece. You're going to have quite the time getting this one to behave, Annika."

Gustav tried to look wounded. "I'd be a good example. I'd share with her."

The three-year-old lit up.

"Not now," Klara told her. "You can both have some *after* you have eaten."

The Webers, Langes, and Beckers poured in through the front door. Gustav's Vater and Onkel stationed themselves by the door to welcome guests and seat the most important at the tables. The rest would have to find benches or chairs scattered around the room. Annika's Vater and Matt stood with them to introduce the guests from Braunfels.

Dora sat next to Annika with Helmuth in her lap. "It was the most beautiful wedding I've ever seen."

"Because Annika made the most beautiful bride," Lucie chimed in.

"It was a most auspicious beginning for a marriage." Gustav's Tante placed full steins at the bride and groom's places.

"Can I help you?" Lucie offered.

"Danke. You can make sure everyone has a drink. Milk is in the kitchen for the children." Hertha bustled off to direct her daughters in the final preparations.

Herr and Frau Keller claimed places near Annika. "We're so happy for you, but I'm going to miss you." Frau Keller dabbed at her eyes with a handkerchief.

"Maybe you'll take in another boarder." She looked around the room. Lina Stein and Frieda Roth were talking with Erwin and two other young weavers. "If there are jobs available, I have some friends who might be interested."

Having returned with a stein for Dora, Lucie asked, "Won't there be an open position at Engel's?"

"I'll still be working there for the time being."

Lucie looked confused. "Oh, I thought—"

"We'll teach Annika how to spin linen thread, of course, but Frau Engel has need of her expertise right now," Gustav interrupted.

Lucie nodded pleasantly. "Of course."

Annika knew Lucie didn't understand why a wife wouldn't work with her husband's family. In truth, Annika didn't understand either, but she liked the work at Engel's, so she wouldn't complain.

She turned her attention to the plate of food Ella was setting in front of her. "Danke."

Ella delivered a heaping plate of roast pork, sausage, sauerkraut, and vegetables to Gustav. "Mutter said to remind you to dance with everyone, even though your bride outshines them all."

Gustav grunted as he took a large bite. Ella sent Annika a look she couldn't decipher.

"Don't worry. I'll dance with every old Hausfrau." Gustav muttered in a low voice. He brightened. "But not until I've danced with my bride, and I expect you to save a dance for your old cousin too."

"Of course, but not until you've charmed all our customers."

"Ja, ja. I know. Get on with you." Gustav took a bite of bread. "You understand duty calls even today, Annika. All the old men will want a dance with the prettiest woman in the room. Try to forgive their clumsy feet. Many of them will drink too much, so better to dance with them early in the evening. I've had a word with Matt, and he'll look after you toward the end of our celebration. Once I finish the rounds we can go."

Annika nodded. Gustav got up in search of more beer.

Having heard part of the conversation, Lucie leaned over to Annika. "Sounds like a handsy crowd. I'll tell Paul and Fritz to claim dances at the end, too."

Relieved, Annika clasped Lucie's hand.

"Are you nervous about your wedding night?"

"Ja, and now I'm concerned about the evening, too. I usually love to dance."

"Relax and enjoy the food and dancing. Being with Gustav will be wonderful. Until then you have your family and friends to look after you." Lucie savored a bite of cinnamon apples.

140

"Eat up so you can try my mother's new Kuchen."

"She developed a new recipe for me?"

Lucie licked her lips like a tabby with a dish of cream. "She did. It's even better than Oma's."

Annika tucked into a sausage. "I have the best friends."

"Don't you forget it. We're always here for you."

When the musicians began to play, Gustav escorted Annika to the middle of the floor. He wasn't as good a dancer as Werner, but Annika had never felt happier as he gazed at her. Her stomach flipped, and she wished she could dance with him the rest of the evening, but after a waltz and a folk dance, he passed her to Herr Keller while he danced with Frau Keller and a string of older women Annika didn't know. Annika danced with their husbands and other male guests.

Just as one old man's hand started to wander too low, Paul cut in. "It's my turn with the bride, sir."

Annika sighed in relief. "Danke. You would think on a girl's wedding day the men would be more respectful."

"They've been drinking, and you're a sight to tempt any man." Paul twirled her gently. "Would you like to sit down when the dance ends?"

"That sounds good. I can hold Helmuth for Dora so she can dance with Matt. That will give me a good excuse for a rest."

When the accordion sounded the last notes of the folk dance, Paul led Annika to the head table. He disappeared long enough to procure drinks for both of them while Annika settled Helmuth in her lap. The little fellow was beating his hands to the music.

"I think we have a musician on our hands," Dora said.

Charlotte snuggled up at Annika's side and fingered her dress.

"And a seamstress." Annika stroked the girl's fair hair. "Do you like my gown?"

"I want one, too."

Dora shook her head. "White's not a good color, dear. It would get dirty too fast and need washed all the time."

Charlotte's bottom lip jutted out.

"How about pink, or red like my other dress? I almost wore the red one today," Annika suggested.

"Red would be pretty," Dora said. "She's all set for now, but I'm sure she'll need a bigger dress this winter."

Charlotte clapped her hands. "Pretty red dress." Harbin ran up and tagged her. She ran off in pursuit.

Matt appeared at his wife's side. "May I have this dance?"

"Certainly." Dora gave him her hand, and the couple joined those waltzing on the dance floor.

"Dora looks like she's back to full health." Annika kissed the top of Helmuth's head. "I'm so glad."

Paul grunted. "Hunger breaks a person's health quick. I pray the blight doesn't spread further, but I fear we haven't seen the end of food shortages. That's why I want to go to Texas where there's plenty of land to grow crops."

"Ach," Frau Becker said, coming up behind him and catching his last remark. "This is a wedding! No more talk of hunger and emigration."

Paul looked at Annika sheepishly. "Sorry, Annika."

Annika jerked her head toward the dancers where a hapless young woman was being groped by Annika's former partner. "You saved me from that, Paul. You can talk about any topic you wish. I like hearing your thoughts." She turned to Frau Becker. "This continues a conversation we had a few months ago."

Frau Becker nailed Paul with a steely look. "Save it for another time."

"Ja, Mutter."

"That fellow is headed toward Lina, Paul. Looks like you have another rescue to make." Annika rocked Helmuth. As her nephew's eyes fluttered closed, Annika smiled to think she could be holding her own baby next year.

Chapter 25

Feeling treasured and safe, Annika woke slowly on her first morning of married life. Peeking over at Gustav's side of the bed, she found him studying her.

"Guten Morgen." He kissed her soundly. After a repeat of the previous night's activity, he nibbled on her ear. "I'm rather hungry."

Annika laughed and pushed him away. "We have Kuchen or bread and ham."

He watched her put on a petticoat. "I wish we could stay here all day."

"But we're expected at church and family dinner. I'm sure you'll be hungry again by then, and we don't have much to eat here."

Gustav bounded out of bed and pulled on his clothes before she could finish tying her bodice.

"Just this once I'll go down and get water so we won't be too late." He disappeared into the other room and clomped down the stairs.

Annika finished dressing and started to brush her tangled hair. She was still brushing when Gustav returned. She paused to cut bread and ham while he poured water into two pewter cups.

"Where are the forks?"

Annika picked up a bundle by the door. They had been given four sets of pewter utensils. It was the only gift she had brought from the wedding last night. They would bring their other presents home today.

Gustav attacked his food with gusto.

Annika took a drink of water and bite of bread and resumed brushing her hair. By the time it was neatly coiled atop her head, church bells were ringing, warning them they would be late if they didn't leave immediately.

Gustav thrust some ham and bread into her hand, and they hustled down the steps and out into the street, which was empty except for a few latecomers like themselves. Annika chewed hurriedly, but it was difficult to keep up with Gustav's long strides. As they rounded the corner to the cathedral, she held up the food crumbling in her hand. "Gustav..."

"I wondered if that would be too much for you." He bent and bit off most of the remainder, gesturing for her to finish the rest.

When they were greeted at the door, they tried to nod in a friendly way, mouths still full. Now Annika was choking back giggles too.

Gustav escorted her to sit with his family. Once seated, Annika surreptitiously wiped her hands on a handkerchief. The altar boys were proceeding up the aisle followed by the pastor. She fought to quiet her thoughts, but as the service droned on, all she could think about was the man beside her and the life they'd begun together.

"'The Lord bless you and keep you. The Lord make His face shine on you and be gracious to you. The Lord lift up His countenance on you and give you peace.'" As the pastor's blessing faded, the organ music swelled. Families began to rise and stream down the aisles and out the grand portal.

Annika wished she and Gustav could be alone, but they had eaten all the food in their apartment for breakfast. Since husbands needed to eat, she followed Gustav's Tante and sisters to the kitchen above the workshop and cut vegetables while Paula, Klara, and Ella performed their accustomed weekly tasks.

The men lounged in front of the workshop, chatting with the neighbors and passersby until the meal was ready. Annika usually enjoyed meals with the Weber clan, but she barely tasted the chicken and potatoes as she longed for privacy with her new husband. He sat beside her and occasionally laid a hand on her knee or winked at her, causing her to blush. Fortunately, Erwin was eating elsewhere this Sunday afternoon so he couldn't tease them.

As they finished with pastries left over from the wedding, Hertha stood. "Just clear the table today, Annika. You can wash or dry dishes next week."

"Danke, Tante." Gustav gave her a peck on the cheek. "After I load some presents, we'll be ready to go."

"I'll give you a hand." Paula's husband and Alfons trailed Gustav downstairs.

After Annika and Ella finished bringing the dishes to Paula to wash, Hertha handed Annika a basket. "I daresay you'll not be wanting to join a family meal tonight. Here's enough food to get you through until tomorrow."

"Danke." Annika gave her a hug. "Thank you for understanding."

"You only get one wedding weekend."

When Annika emerged from the workshop, she caught sight of Britta and the phaeton. "First a stop to unload, then a nice drive with my wife." Gustav handed her up before giving her a glass bowl and tucking a stone crock at her feet and fitting the basket of food in its mouth. The back was stuffed with a washboard, broom, rug, and other gifts. "I should be able to carry the rest home over the course of the next week. Our friends were generous."

"Ja, it's a good start."

While Annika stayed with Britta, Gustav made several trips up the stairs with their gifts. When only the rug and hamper of food were left, he climbed back into the phaeton and took the reins. "We can have a picnic if we want." He drew her closer to him on the seat.

"Gustav, people will see us!"

"What can they say? We're married now." He placed a hand on her knee. "Maybe I can find a secluded spot, and we can..."

Annika blushed furiously. She wanted to be with him again, but outside?

The couple drove out of town into the fields of hay and other crops. Copses of trees bordered some of the fields. Gustav examined each one until he found some linden trees near a stream. He pulled Britta up and listened. "I don't hear any voices. Do you?"

All Annika heard was the babbling of the water. Gustav lifted her out of the buggy, letting his hands wander low. His touch melted something inside Annika. He grabbed the rug and snapped it out flat over miniature pine and linden trees in the shade of the mother trees. He resumed touching and kissing Annika until she found herself underneath him on the rug, longing for more. He went slowly, bringing her pleasure she hadn't felt the night before. "My angel," he whispered in her ear, spooning her close.

It was nearly dusk when Britta snorted, waking them. Gustav kissed the nape of her neck. "I'm hungry, but we've got to return Britta before my friend gets nervous. It won't take long if we go straight there." Gustav pulled her up and shook off the rug. She held one end while he rolled it toward her. As he took it from her, he kissed her.

Annika tugged her bodice up a modest distance and smoothed her skirts.

Gustav groaned. "If it weren't for this horse..."

Annika brushed her lips against his ear. "I can hardly wait."

"Don't tempt me, Frau Weber."

Annika laughed saucily and leaped into the seat without his aid.

He threw the rug in the back and hopped into the driver's seat. "Eager to get home, are you?" He encircled her waist and crushed her to his side as he held the reins in his other hand. "Giddy up, Britta. You've had a good rest. Now step lively."

The moon lit their way back to Wetzlar. When they reached his friend's, he unhitched the buggy while Annika unbridled Britta.

As they worked, the owner entered the barn. "You're back. Did you have a good afternoon?"

"Ja, danke. The horse and buggy were much appreciated." Gustav shook his hand.

The man grabbed a brush and started currying. "I'll take care of things from here. Consider it a wedding gift."

After collecting the rug and hamper, Gustav offered Annika his arm, and they strolled in contented silence back to their cozy home.

Chapter 26

Those early days of marriage seemed perfect. By day, Annika worked on gowns for the well-to-do of Wetzlar society. At night, Gustav loved her tenderly in their feather bed. No disagreeable farm work woke her before dawn.

It was easy to keep two rooms clean. They ate most of their meals with the Webers, so Annika had little shopping, cooking, or baking to accomplish. Laundry was challenging since she had to make at least two trips to the fountain with the wooden yoke for the buckets. Then she heated the water in the fireplace and hung the wet clothes across the tiny apartment.

The days and nights melded together until one October morning they woke up to cold floors. Annika added a wool blanket to their bed as she smoothed the linen sheets and wedding quilt.

When Gustav escorted her from the dress shop to family dinner that evening, he said, "It can't be put off any longer. I have to go to Limburg on business."

Annika's heart sank. He used to travel but hadn't gone anywhere since their wedding.

"The good news is you can go with me."

"Really?"

"Yes. We need to take our surplus cloth and sell it for the best prices we can get. We'll leave next week. Can you complete your navy linen dress by then?"

Annika considered the finish work that still needed to be done. "I think so."

"Frau Engel knew I might need your assistance on my trips. I'll talk with her tomorrow about what days she can spare you. It will take a day to get there by boat and two days to return by coach. Plus at least a day to sell the material. The Seidels have offered to host us while we're in Limburg. You met them at the wedding. They're old friends who own a haberdashery."

"I remember them. His suit was one of the finest in the room." Annika shifted her reticule to her other hand. "I've never been to Limburg."

"You'll enjoy it. There's a cathedral and a castle...and a church with stained-glass windows. I'm sure Frau Seidel or one of her daughters can take you to see the town while I'm conducting business."

The next day Gustav arrived with a delivery of cloth just as the shop was closing. Greta locked up the storefront while Annika continued sewing a bodice to a skirt.

When Gustav arrived in the workroom to fetch her, she wrapped herself in a shawl and took his proffered arm.

"We'll leave next Tuesday. Vater was able to secure passage for us and our wares on a barge, and Frau Engel can spare you. Luckily, she knows a dressmaker in Limburg and will give you a letter of introduction. I want you to try to sell some of our linen and get an order for the future. You can wear your navy linen dress to showcase our cloth."

Annika's heart sped up. "I'm honored to be part of your family business, Gustav. Surely I can help you sell such fine cloth."

"A beautiful woman like you will have no trouble sweet-talking dressmakers into buying from you." Gustav covered her hand with his. "That's why I married you."

Did I hear him right? Annika sneaked a peek at Gustav's face. He didn't seem to think anything was amiss. *He married me to sell* cloth?

The comment nibbled away at Annika's happiness over the next week. On the morning of their departure, she woke to peruse his sleeping features. *I thought you married me for love.*

Quietly, she rose and heated porridge for their breakfast. For the first time, she noticed how cramped their living quarters were. Of course, the carpet bags by the door took up a fair amount of space. She took six steps from the hearth and rifled through her bag to make sure she had packed all the necessities. She brushed, braided, and looped her hair before tucking her brush in with her red and navy dresses. Today she would wear an older gray gown for traveling, along with a stunning green cape Tante Hertha had given her.

Gustav entered the room with a yawn. Wordlessly, he thumped down at the table. Annika brought him a bowl of porridge and sat to eat with him.

"We need to be at the dock by half past seven."

"I'll be ready." Annika hurried into the bedroom and donned a wool petticoat and the gray dress. She glanced at the bed but didn't have time to smooth the coverings into place. It was more important to wash their bowls and spoons so the food didn't harden on them.

She poured water heated in a pot over the fire into a basin and washed her face. Then she made quick work of the bowls, porridge pot, spoons, and last night's beer steins.

"Time to go." Gustav exited the bedroom in an old suit and shrugged into an overcoat.

Annika swung the cape around her shoulders, grabbed a hamper of food provided by Tante Hertha, and followed her husband down the steps. Wincing as he thumped the bags into the walls, she hoped the Hoffmann children were already awake. It was a good thing the cloth was already warehoused at the dock and didn't need to be lugged across Wetzlar at this early hour.

Although chilly at first, the barge trip was enjoyable. Annika took out her knitting and watched the shore slip by. The trees were still holding onto their brilliant leaves, so the scenery was a feast for the eyes and soul. Gustav spent most of the morning conversing with the lightermen who steered the barge and used their poles to avoid collisions. At lunchtime, Gustav joined her for bread and cheese from their hamper.

As they watched a lighterman use his pike pole to push away from a nearby boat, Annika said, "Too bad that scow didn't use a pole the day you gave me this ring." She raised her left hand.

Gustav scowled, but then he grinned. "You're quite right." He kissed her palm. "I'm going to lie down for a bit." He made himself comfortable against a sack of their linen, set his cap over his face, and promptly fell asleep.

Finished knitting, Annika sat idly, soaking up the warmth of the sun. She dreaded the coming days of being cooped up inside. She, too, dozed. Shouts from a nearby skiff wakened her. The small craft was trying to cross the river but was having difficulty navigating between the stream of barges traveling downstream. The lighterman of another barge screamed at them to get out of the way. The tiny boat barely made it out of the heavy barge's path. "Use the bridge!" the exasperated worker bellowed.

The skiff's oarsman shook his fist.

The commotion also woke Gustav, who sat up and raised his eyebrows at Annika in such a comical fashion she had to laugh. "Maybe the Lahn is too busy for small boats."

"Remind me to stick to the Dill next time I take you out on a Sunday."

Annika nodded and took out her knitting to start another sock as Gustav went to the front of the barge. The sock was half finished when Gustav told her they'd be docking after the next bridge. "St. George's Cathedral, also called Limburg Cathedral, will be in view soon."

Curious, Annika stowed her knitting in the carpetbag and studied the town coming into view. A gorgeous, spired cathedral rose from a small hill. The red and white façade with its points and arches was more harmonious than the *Dom* where she had married Gustav.

The barge bumped against the dock, and Gustav tied it up. After procuring a horse and wagon, he oversaw the transfer of their cloth. Giving the driver the Seidels' address, he climbed into the back with their cargo and carpet bags.

As they headed to the west of St. George's, their driver pointed out various landmarks. From her vantage point at his side, Annika was thrilled to view a rose window in the church's western wall and determined to find an opportunity to visit the Catholic Dom.

After a brisk drive of twenty minutes, the Seidels' home came into view. It was in a row of charming, half-timbered houses. Evidently, the haberdashery made them a good living judging by the room they were ushered into by a servant. A large canopy bed only took half the space. A wardrobe sat between two tall windows, and a pair of chairs flanked a fireplace with colorful tiles.

After the wooden benches in the barge and wagon, Annika sank gratefully into the upholstered chair. Gustav took his suits from the carpetbag and hung them on pegs in the wardrobe. "Can you iron these for me?"

Annika rose to shake out her wrinkled dresses. "Ja. Let's go down to the kitchen to accept the servant's offer of refreshments. I can ask about an iron while we're there."

After a sample of the pumpkin soup simmering for dinner, Gustav left Annika to iron while he got his bearings in the town. Disappointed to be left behind, Annika slapped the flatirons around so vigorously the cook finally said, "Frau Weber, me table's taking a beating."

Annika stopped with the iron in mid-air. "I'm sorry. I wanted so much to see St. George's."

The plump woman grinned. "It's an amazing sight and stays open quite late for evening vespers. The mistress told me you'll be here until Thursday morning. We'll make sure you get a good look at it. You could always come to early morning mass with me."

"Danke."

"Your husband is just finding his contacts' addresses anyway. Wouldn't have time to pause and look around."

"You're right. It was silly of me."

"Not silly, my dear. Husbands don't always understand what women need, especially in the early days."

"Do they figure it out?"

"Sometimes. Hints don't always work. You might have to speak plain. I know because I've been married and widowed twice, God rest their souls." She crossed herself. "And I've almost got a third husband, and him a butcher. With me being a cook, it's a match made in Heaven.

"Being a cook, I have a wee bit of advice for you. When you're angry with your man, knead bread. Leave the ironing for another time. There might be innocent victims, like me poor table."

Annika's silvery laugh rang out. "You're absolutely right, but these clothes need pressed now. I promise to stop abusing your table. Tell me about this butcher of yours."

The woman pinkened with pleasure. "Where should I start? He owns his own shop. Was his Vater's before him. He's a strong man with powerful arms..."

The cook's lively monologue restored Annika's good humor. She completed her ironing before the Seidels and Gustav returned.

As the two couples ate, they discussed the next day's plans.

"Annika can come to the haberdashery with us. The dressmaker's is the next street over." Herr Seidel sopped up the juices on his plate with a piece of bread.

"We know them well, and I'll take her round and introduce her." Frau Seidel passed a dessert platter to Gustav. "We close a little later on Wednesdays, so dinner won't be served until seven thirty."

"Excellent. We appreciate your hospitality. If all goes well tomorrow, we'll leave on the eight o'clock diligence Thursday morning. That way we can be home by Friday evening." Gustav took a bite of plum dumpling. "Your cook is exceptional."

The Seidels beamed.

"She was quite a find." Frau Seidel wiped her lips with a linen napkin. "And our eldest son has a plum tree, so we get a lot of these little treats."

Annika and Gustav sat with their hosts around a fire in the formal parlor before retiring early. In spite of feeling nervous about becoming a saleslady, Annika sank into the feather mattress and was soon asleep.

Chapter 27

As they ate a hearty breakfast of eggs and sausage, Gustav said, "I engaged the wagon we used yesterday to haul our cloth to my contacts."

"How many places are you going?" Herr Seidel buttered a thick slice of bread.

"I have six possible buyers."

Frau Seidel passed the plate of sausage. "How will Annika transport cloth to the dressmaker's?"

"The wagon can take us all to your business this morning, so she'll just have the short walk to the dressmaker's. She's a strong farm lass, so it shouldn't be a problem." Gustav winked at Annika.

Blushing, Annika stared at her plate, hoping she wouldn't let him down.

After straightening a few displays and waiting on early customers, Frau Seidel put on her cloak. Annika followed her example and picked up the large carpet bag Gustav had left her. It was heavy, but she could manage.

"Are you all right, dear?" Frau Seidel held the dark wooden door for her.

"If it's not far."

"It's just a few blocks. Let me know if you need to stop for a breather."

Annika's arm was aching when Frau Seidel gestured to

an elegant shop ahead of them. "We're almost there. After I introduce you, I'll leave you to conduct your business."

Annika's nerves settled as they entered the well-appointed dress shop. Silks and satins in every color she could imagine tantalized her. She stroked a forest green silk, imagining a winter gown with a pelerine.

When she looked up, an angular woman in a lilac gown was inspecting her.

Frau Seidel stepped forward. "Frau Hahn, this is Frau Weber."

When the older woman didn't respond, Annika said, "Pleased to meet you. I work for Frau Engel in Wetzlar. She's written me a letter of introduction." Annika removed it from the reticule that looked shabby in the luxurious shop.

Frau Hahn tapped the letter on her palm. "I'm pleased to meet you too. Did you design and sew your gown?"

"I sewed it. The head dressmaker Olga Schumacher recommended the cut."

"It's stunning on you. Shows off your assets, though since you're young, I don't suppose you have many physical shortcomings." The proprietress motioned for her to twirl so she could see the sloping shoulders and bell-shaped skirt from the back.

Annika complied, holding out her arms to show off the cuffs with their velvet ribbon trim.

Frau Hahn slowly circled her to examine the cut from every angle. "Did someone fit it for you?"

"The head seamstress pinned it. I did the work."

"You're both fine seamstresses, Frau Weber."

"Danke. I enjoy the work."

Frau Hahn turned her attention to the missive. "Let's

discuss our business in the back."

Frau Seidel cleared her throat. "I need to return to the haberdashery. Frau Weber, can you find your way back?"

"I'll send one of my girls with her. It won't take but ten minutes." Frau Hahn led Annika through a spacious workroom. Passing half a dozen women cutting and sewing, they retreated to a storeroom where cloth was stacked along three walls. A dropleaf table was pushed up against the fourth. A huge orange tabby was curled up on the tabletop.

Frau Hahn shooed the tabby away. "Go catch some mice!" She flicked a rag over the table. "Now, what did you bring to show me?"

"My husband's family weaves linen." Annika draped the white linen over the table.

The dressmaker fingered it appreciatively. "This is fine enough for a dress."

"Since Queen Victoria married her Prussian prince, white is favored for weddings. I wore a white dress of this fabric."

Frau Hahn sniffed. "Not too practical."

"I wear it to church and special occasions."

"Were you wed recently?"

"Four, almost five months ago."

"Congratulations."

"Danke."

"Do you have a cambric suitable for undergarments?"

Annika showed her the requested cloth.

"I can use twenty ells of this."

"I brought ten. The Webers can produce more."

Frau Hahn frowned. "When could I expect it?"

Gustav hadn't mentioned how quickly orders could be

filled. Annika scrambled, trying to recall what she'd seen on the looms before they left. "Next month."

Frau Hahn's eyebrows raised. "That soon?"

"Ja," Annika promised. After all, Gustav had said to get an order. "I also have a finely woven black."

"Black's always in demand." Frau Hahn checked her watch. "I have a fitting in fifteen minutes, so we need to finish up."

Annika removed the black from her carpet bag.

"I'll take the black. I suppose it can't hurt to purchase the white for weddings. I'm sure there will be several this winter. I definitely need the cambric for petticoats and such." Frau Hahn whisked around and studied the cloth on her shelves. "I have some navy wool but not much linen, so I'll take the navy also.

"If you'll return to the front of the shop, I'll get your payment."

Annika drank in the shades and textures until Frau Hahn appeared with a bag of coins. Annika transferred them to her reticule. "Would you like to order any cloth besides the white? My sister-in-law has developed a champagne pink. It sells so fast we didn't have any to show you."

"That sounds like it would please my clients. How soon would it be ready?"

"In time for spring."

"Let's say the beginning of February for the pink along with twenty ells of black. If this material sells like I think it will, we can discuss another order."

"Excellent."

"Margot, please take Frau Weber to Seidel's Haberdashery and then return immediately."

The red-haired girl ran to get her cloak. Annika retrieved

her empty carpet bag.

"I hope you'll return in February and show me another of your dresses," Frau Hahn said.

Annika smiled. "I'd like that. We'll ship the white linen next month."

"Very good. Have a pleasant day."

Annika spent the rest of the day arranging silk cravats and ties for the Seidels. When it was quiet, she sat in a back room and penned a letter to Werner about her trip down the Lahn and her sales efforts with Frau Hahn. Frau Seidel helped her post it to Berlin on their way home.

Chapter 28

When Annika entered their bedchamber, Gustav was pacing in front of the fireplace like a caged wolf. "We'll have to stay tomorrow. I could only sell half the blasted cloth."

"Is there anything I can do to help?" Annika tidied loose strands of hair in front of a large mirror.

"Did you sell all the cloth you had?"

"Ja."

Annika caught a glimmer of appreciation on Gustav's face in the mirror's reflection. "You can accompany me in your white dress. It can't hurt for them to see a product finished with our finest material."

Annika sucked in a breath. "I didn't bring my white gown. I only wear it on special occasions."

Gustav glared at her. "And a trip with your husband isn't an occasion worthy of that dress?"

"I've never been to Limburg so I didn't know what the streets would be like. If I dirty the hem, it will be impossible to wash out."

Gustav sighed. "The navy will have to do again."

Annika smoothed the navy linen. "My gown seemed to impress Frau Hahn. She complimented me and requested I return in February in a new dress when we deliver twenty-two ells of black and twelve of pink."

"That's not a very big order."

"She said we could discuss more cloth at that time. She also ordered cambric to be delivered next month."

"That will work out well since Erwin's already weaving more."

Annika relaxed a little. "Are we finishing up with your list of contacts tomorrow?"

"Just one that I didn't reach today. I also heard of two new places to try. Merchants are switching over to cotton cloth. It's cheaper." Gustav slammed his fist into his hand. "Looks cheaper too."

There was a knock at the door. "Dinner will be served in just a few minutes."

"Danke." Gustav stood and straightened his hair in the mirror. "Act like today was successful, and we simply ended up with extra business."

Annika nodded, and the two went downstairs to the dining room.

The first merchant they visited didn't purchase any cloth. He was the last one on Gustav's original list.

The next showed them a storage room brimming with cloth unpurchased by his patrons. He complimented the quality of their linen but wasn't selling enough clothing.

On their way to the third, Annika spied a dress shop tucked beside a mercantile. "Would you like me to try there, Gustav?"

"We don't have an introduction."

"True, but I'm wearing a sample of what can be done with our cloth. Is there any navy linen left?"

"Ja. Thirty-two ells."

"Enough for three dresses. I think I can sell some of it."

Gustav told the driver to pull over and helped Annika

descend.

"What other colors do we need to sell?"

"A lot of black. Eleven ells of red."

Annika adjusted her bodice, straightened her skirts, and sailed into the dressmaker's. The shop was comparable to Frau Engel's, so she felt at ease and examined a sample day dress. The silk gown featured a pleated fan bodice, a shirred panel at its waist, and a full bell-shaped skirt. Patrons of this shop could afford fine clothes.

When the owner finished discussing winter dresses with a teen girl and her mother, she greeted Annika.

"This is a lovely design." Annika pointed to the dress she had been admiring.

"It is. I like the dress you're wearing. Where did you have it done?"

"At Engel's dress shop in Wetzlar. I'm a seamstress there."

The woman's forehead creased. "Engel's. Engel's. I've heard of Frau Engel. She's a widow, isn't she?"

"Ja. She and her husband established the shop, but he's been gone for years."

"You've done excellent work. What brings you to Limburg?"

"My husband's family, the Webers, weave fine cloth, including the linen I'm wearing today. We're looking to expand our business. Frau Hahn, as well as several other merchants, have purchased some material, but we have a little left, including navy linen."

The woman studied Annika from collar to hem. "We could use some dark colors. Do you have anything available besides navy?"

"I believe we might be able to spare some black, although

my husband might have promised it to the next shopkeeper. I'll see if I can persuade him."

"I'm in desperate need of black linen, Frau Weber. I can pay you well."

"Let me consult my husband. I'll be right back." Annika hid her smile. She returned with Gustav carrying ninety ells of linen.

"I definitely need thirty each of navy and black," the proprietress said.

"How about this red linen? A dress of this design..." Annika gestured to the sample, "would look stunning in red."

The proprietress pursed her lips as she studied the dress form. "If we can work out a good price, I'll take the red also."

Annika watched as Gustav and the elegant woman haggled over price.

Gustav was smiling when they emerged with their payment and only twenty ells of cloth. "We should be done with business by lunchtime. We'll go out for a nice meal and then I want to look at the wool in the marketplace."

When they visited Gustav's final contact, they sold the last ells of black linen. Gustav directed the driver to drop them off at the wool market and ushered Annika into a nearby Gasthaus. "Good work, Annika. What would you like to eat?"

"I'm not terribly hungry after our big breakfast, but I would like some bread and cheese."

"Sounds good. I'll order sausage, too. Beer?"

"Kaffee, please."

The couple watched the bustle in the market while they ate. Then they examined the wool yarn and cloth. Annika purchased yellow yarn to knit a hat and mittens.

"We have a few more hours before the Seidels finish at the

haberdashery. Is there something you want to do?"

"Ja. I'd like to visit the cathedral."

"Anything for my little merchant." He asked for directions from one of the wool merchants, and the couple headed for the church.

St. George's Cathedral was stunning with its multicolored façade and cream interior. Gazing at the frescoes, Annika walked slowly from the narthex to the altar while Gustav hurried ahead and examined the altar cloths.

Annika explored the transepts and paused to admire paintings and stained-glass windows. Overflowing with the church's beauty and tranquility, she exited to find Gustav on a stone bench staring at the rose window above the clover entrance. She tried to imprint the twin western towers and spire in her mind.

Gustav's hand closed around her arm. "We could weave better cloth for them. Too bad we're not Catholic."

Annika gaped at him. She had tiptoed past the women lighting candles, unsure what to think of praying in such a fashion.

"Close your mouth, Annika. It's not blasphemy. If God's not going to provide for us while we're Lutheran, why not convert?"

Annika's thoughts became as slippery as fish.

"I know He's up there, but I doubt he cares much about us." Gustav glanced back. "I have to say this cathedral is much more impressive than our Dom in Wetzlar. I don't think it will ever be completed."

Annika stumbled along beside her husband, sneaking a look at his hardened face. Was it possible God didn't care?

Chapter 29

Despite the successful trip to Limburg, it was difficult to make ends meet over the winter. The price of wheat, potatoes, and other food rose after another poor harvest. Fortunately, Dora was able to put up plenty of vegetables on the farm and repaid Annika's previous generosity. The beets and cabbage didn't go far for all the mouths at the Webers' table, but they helped.

Gustav's Vater and Onkel feared customers wouldn't buy much linen in 1843. Rosa, who was expecting her first baby, wasn't needed to spin thread anymore. Erwin started hanging around with steam mechanics. He was fascinated by the engines they were developing to power ships and trains.

At Engel's, the same clients came in, but they purchased fewer dresses. Annika was only working half days.

"How can we meet our rent with only half your pay?" Gustav pounded the table with his fists.

"Can your family pay you something?"

"The money from our cloth sales is almost gone. Aunt Hertha is hoarding what's left to feed all of us. Frau Hahn's order is almost ready, but that will only bring in a little." Gustav rose. "We're already late with the rent. I have to go speak with the Hoffmanns."

His shoulders were drooping when he returned. "I was able to pay them half of what we owe. I can bring a load of wood to make up the rest. Would your Vater let me take some wood from his land if I can get a wagon?"

"I think so. We always had plenty of firewood. If we walk out to the farm, we can probably use Vater's wagon."

"It will be late by the time we've hauled it back here. How will we return the wagon?"

"If Matt's not too busy, he'll drive to Wetzlar with us. He can take the wagon back to Braunfels as soon as it's unloaded."

Gustav ran his hands through his hair. "How can we find out ahead of time if your Vater will go along with our plans? I'd hate to spend the whole day going out there only to come back empty-handed."

"I'll leave a note for my family at the mercantile where Paul Becker picks up supplies. He comes at least once a month."

"Let's hope he comes soon. If this doesn't work out, we may have to sell something to meet the rent."

A pall hung over the pair for the next week. Annika was slogging her way through the laundry when there was a knock at the door. "Come in," she called as she wiped her wet, soapy hands on her apron. "Matt." She enfolded her brother in a hug. "I never expected to see you today. Is everything all right?"

"Everything is fine with us. I came in response to your note." He handed her a sack. "Dora sent applesauce, and Frau Becker sent pumpernickel bread and a few pastries." He looked around at the small space. "I'm glad you mentioned working half days so I didn't waste time going to the dress shop."

"Ja, business is slow."

"I can't stay long, but Vater said for you to come this Saturday or next. You can use his wagon. One of us will ride back with you to bring it home."

Annika clasped her hands. "That's such a relief." She pulled a pot over the embers on the hearth. "You must be cold. How about some Kaffee to warm you up?"

"Sounds good, but I can't stay long. I have to pick up some

hardware and get back home."

After a quick mug of Kaffee, Matt stood. "I'm sorry I have to go, but we'll see you soon."

"I can't wait. Give my love to Dora and the Kinder. And Vater, of course."

When Annika told Gustav the news, he brightened. "If the weather's good, we'll go this Saturday."

Annika tried to quell her excitement about visiting her family. She hadn't seen any of them besides Matt since the wedding. Paul had brought a few Weihnachten gifts from her family. She had sent Stollen and woolen sweaters for the children.

The appointed Saturday dawned brisk, but the sun promised a mild day for January. Annika flew out of bed and served Gustav a hearty breakfast.

Gustav seemed morose on the long walk, but Annika listened to the birdsong, which sparked an answering melody in her heart. She could hardly wait to see how big Helmuth had gotten.

When they reached the outskirts of Braunfels, she pointed out her friends' farms and gave Gustav a running commentary on the folks who lived there. One of Fritz's nephews waved to her from the Huber property.

Not many farmers were outside. Unless there was a problem with stock or fencing, this was the time of year to mend equipment and carve furniture in the warm barns. There was even time for reading or checkers in the evenings after dinner.

When Hans Roth caught up with them in his farm wagon, they climbed into the back and rode the rest of the way to the Lange farm. Bruno was waiting at the entrance to the drive and barked as he kept pace alongside them. By the time

Gustav assisted Annika out of the wagon, the entire family had gathered at the front door.

Even Vater looked pleased to see them. "Wilkommen." He gave Annika a one-armed hug and shook Gustav's hand. Hans declined an invitation to stay, saying Frieda wouldn't feed him for a month of Sundays if he didn't go get her first. "We'll give you folks a chance to catch up, and we'll come over later."

"We'd welcome help filling our wagon with firewood. Gustav needs it in the city." Vater swung Charlotte up into his arms.

"I'll be back in an hour." Hans chirruped to his horses and disappeared down the drive.

"Come in for a drink and some Kuchen before you work." Dora enveloped Annika in a hug. Annika was glad to feel some flesh on her bones.

Helmuth studied her with big blue eyes.

"Do you remember Tante Anna?" Annika held out her hands to the one-and-a-half-year-old. He clung to his mother.

"Show Tante Anna how you can walk." Dora set him down, and he toddled over to his toys on the rag rug in front of the fireplace.

After the men filled up and left, Annika sliced Kuchen for herself and Dora. "He's changed so much, and you look happy and healthy."

"Fourteen months makes a huge difference."

"I know. I barely knew Gustav then, and here I am married and…" Annika paused dramatically. She put a finger to her lips and nodded toward the children playing with wooden blocks on the rug.

Dora dropped her voice to a whisper. "You're expecting?"

"I think so. I've missed two bleedings."

Dora clasped her hand. "You'll know for sure when you feel the baby move."

"How soon can I expect that?"

"Sometime in the next two months. It's very slight at first, like a fluttering."

Annika sucked in a breath. "I haven't told Gustav yet since I'm not entirely sure."

"That's a good idea. Have you been sick in the mornings, or extra tired?"

"Just a little nauseous if I eat something like sausage. Bread or porridge settles fine. I have needed a few naps. It's a good thing I only work half days now."

"God had it all planned."

"Maybe." Annika toyed with a sugar spoon. "It's hard to meet our rent without my full pay."

"God will provide."

Annika brightened. "It *is* easy to get a wagonload of wood to make up the rest of this month's rent, and I get to see all of you. Gustav wouldn't have come if we hadn't needed the wood."

"Matt was talking about a trip to Wetzlar as soon as it warmed up enough in March, before the plowing begins." Dora stood to clear dishes.

"I'll wash," Annika offered, moving to the sink.

"Danke." Dora poured hot water onto the dirty cups and plates.

"Mutter, someone's here." Charlotte tugged the door open in response to a knock.

"Lucie!" Annika squealed upon seeing her friend. "I'm so glad you came. How'd you know?"

"Word travels fast in Braunfels." Lucie hugged Annika. "Fritz's nephew told us you passed the house, so I convinced

Fritz I needed to see you. He took our horse out to the barn." She took off her cape and turned to the side.

Annika squealed again. "You're in the family way?"

"There should be a little Fritzie or Lucie in late June."

Annika checked on the children, who were badgering their mother for Kuchen. She dropped her voice, "I think I'm expecting in late August, but it's still a secret. Only you and Dora know."

"My lips are sealed. Mutter says better not to say much until you feel the baby move."

Fritz came through the front door. "Where'd the men all go?"

"They're loading wood." Dora handed him a stein of Kaffee.

"Danke. I'll go find them after I finish this."

Charlotte darted over. "Mutter, more people coming!"

"It's the Roths, Liebling. Watch Helmuth for me."

In no time, Frieda had joined the women in the cottage, and Hans and Fritz drove a second wagon out to gather firewood.

"Annika, it's wunderbar to see you." Frieda took a sip of Kaffee.

"I know. It seems like the wedding was so long ago. I'm glad to be back for a visit."

"Have any jobs opened up in Wetzlar?"

Annika shook her head. "No, in fact I only work half days right now."

Frieda looked glum. "Oh well! Vater has me busy painting furniture anyway. I earn a few thalers here and there to spend on dresses or ribbons."

"Try to save a bit for married life," Dora said. "Money can be tight at the beginning. It's good to have a reserve."

"Don't I know it!" Annika let Charlotte crawl into her lap. "I wish I'd been able to save more before I married."

"Thalers are hard to come by right now. Hans says more than half our customers pay in foodstuffs or livestock. We've never had so many goats."

"Do you know how to make goat cheese?" Dora rocked Helmuth until his eyes began to flutter.

"Nein."

"I could show you. It's delicious on bread." Dora walked into the downstairs bedroom and laid Helmuth on the bed.

"That's a good idea. I could sell extra to Vogel's and earn a little."

"I'd like to learn too," Lucie chimed in. "We have plenty of goats. I try to keep some coins set aside, but farmers aren't paid in coins like bakers are. We end up bartering for most of our purchases at Vogel's."

Frieda studied her chipped nails. "I need to figure something out because I need a new dress…in case anyone ever wants to court me."

Lucie looked surprised. "Of course someone's going to court you." Frieda wasn't the belle of Braunfels, but she was a hard-working lass from a solid family.

"Green or yellow would look nice." Annika snuggled Charlotte on her lap.

Frieda swirled the Kaffee in her mug. "How much would green linen for a dress cost?"

"I'm not sure. I can look in the surplus at both Webers' and the dress shop to see what I can find for you."

"Danke. Set it aside for me, and I'll come in with Hans or Paul on one of their trips to Wetzlar when I've earned a little more."

"Since I'm only working half days, we could walk around the city, if it's warm enough."

"I'll wait for a warm day. It will probably be at least April before I have enough coin."

"Perfect. I can't wait. I've missed you all so much."

Another knock sounded on the door. Before anyone could respond, Elsa poked her head into the room.

"Elsa, you should at least wait for an invitation," Lina scolded from the porch.

Annika laughed. "Come in! I was just thinking my homecoming would be complete if you two were here."

Elsa engulfed Annika and Charlotte in a hug. "I'm so sorry I missed your wedding. Mutter's so mean she wouldn't let me go, but Lina brought me Kuchen. I want Frau Becker to make the same kind for my wedding. It was much better than Ehrich and Margarete's, wasn't it, Lina?"

"Ja, much, but the Schäfers knew better than to ask Annika's best friends to bake for Margarete's wedding. They tried to bake it themselves, and it turned out dry. Serves them right." Lina caught her breath. "Sorry. Elsa and I are having a hard time. Margarete's expecting again. Since she lost her first pregnancy, Mutter won't let her do anything. We have to wait on her hand and foot."

"She's sleeping right now, or we never would have escaped." Elsa took the mug of milk Dora offered. She sighed like an adult. "She's a trial for sure."

Annika smothered a laugh. "It *is* tiring to be pregnant." Realizing her slip, she rushed on, "Isn't it, Lucie?"

"Absolutely. Mutter comes out to the farm once a week to give me a rest. I'd rather visit with her, but when I sit down, my eyes won't stay open."

Dora topped up Annika's Kaffee. "Do you think it's a boy or a girl, Lucie?"

"Mutter says it's a girl because I'm craving sweets more than usual. She says she was like that when she had me but not my brothers."

"Sounds right to me," Dora said. "I wanted sugary foods when I was expecting Charlotte and salted meat with Helmuth."

"I don't care whether Margarete has a boy or girl as long as she has it, sooner rather than later. Especially since Lina's gonna leave us soon." Elsa held her hands out pleadingly to her sister. "Take me with you."

Lina blushed beet-red. "Hush, Elsa Stein."

"Where are you going?" Annika asked.

"Nowhere." Lina gulped her coffee.

"Hans is just waiting until you're eighteen," Frieda said. "But he's only fixing up a one-room cabin, so I'm not sure where you'd stay, Elsa."

"I'll sleep in the workshop if it means I can get away from Mutter and Margarete. There's a fireplace out there, isn't there?"

"Ja, but the shop's full of sawdust and paint fumes." Frieda chewed a bite of Kuchen. "Would your Mutter let you go?"

"We're hoping she'll think the house is too crowded with Margarete's babies and Frank coming back from the army." Elsa looked determined.

"Wait! Hold on." Annika waved her hands. "*Hans* is courting you, Lina, and no one told me?"

"We haven't seen you since your wedding," Lina said apologetically. "He started seeking me out at the fall dance."

"True enough, but you could have sent word. I've seen Paul."

Lucie shook her head. "You know Paul, Anna. He might not even realize Hans is seeing Lina. He doesn't care who's courting."

Lina looked like she expected a thorough scolding.

She gets enough of those from her mother. Although a little hurt, Annika tried to come to terms with the idea of her two neighbors marrying. "He's a wonderful man, Lina. Congratulations! I hope to dance at your wedding."

"I don't care what Mutter says, you and Gustav will be invited."

"Lina turns eighteen in March," Elsa piped up.

Annika nodded her head. "Then I can expect to see all of you again very soon. And for heaven's sake, write to me if something big is going on!"

The sound of men at the back door halted the conversation.

"We'd better go," Lina said. "Before we're missed too much and have to explain ourselves."

"I wanna talk to Annika more. I haven't told her about school or the dress we're making you." Elsa pouted.

"I have to leave soon. We'll have a long chat at the wedding, I promise." As Annika hugged Elsa goodbye, the men came in the back door.

Hans' eyes lit up at the sight of Lina, who had already donned her cape. "Let me drive you home, ladies. Gustav and Matt are emptying my wagon as we speak. Won't take but a few more minutes." He guided the Steins out the back door.

"Hans, I thought you wanted some Kaffee to warm up?" Vater called after them.

"I think he's plenty warm," Fritz teased.

"Humpf, boy needs to marry so he'll get his head back on straight." Vater accepted a mug from Annika. "We only have a few minutes, daughter. Matt needs to get on the road so he'll be home at a decent hour."

After Fritz and Lucie said their goodbyes, Annika told Vater and Dora all about the trip to Limburg and how she had helped sell linen.

All too soon, Matt and Gustav were ready to go, so she donned her warm cape, took some bricks heated on the hearth to warm their feet, and climbed up between her husband and brother for the ride to Wetzlar.

Chapter 30

Herr Hoffmann was bellowing in the courtyard. "What kind of junk did you bring me, Gustav? My boy can't split it, and the pine he can split doesn't warm the house."

Annika couldn't catch Gustav's answer, but she hurried to put a bowl of soup at his place. It was only beets in broth, but it should warm him. Maybe it would even sweeten his temper. He'd been like a bear since they'd returned from Braunfels. At least it was Friday. With the slowdown in business, he probably wouldn't have to work tomorrow.

She would work for a few hours until Frau Zeigler's new gown was finished. Perhaps Adele would commission some dresses if her aunt's dress was fetching enough. Although Annika disliked the girl, she prayed it would be so. If Engel's didn't acquire more orders for gowns, Frau Engel would be forced to let a seamstress go. When orders dwindled off last autumn, Annika's job had been saved only because Johanna's family emigrated to Australia.

Annika shuddered. The stories circulating about Australia were worrisome. Huge creepy crawlies. Poisonous snakes. A British colony populated primarily by convicts. She hoped Johanna's husband knew what he was doing. At least they were traveling with his brother's family. As coopers, the two men should find plenty of work. Her heart felt heavy for Johanna, who was worried about her two boys. Her mother-in-law was also emigrating, so when Johanna worked, at least someone would be watching them.

Gustav burst through the door, face red. "Why didn't your Vater give me some good oak?"

"Oak has to season. I'm sure he would have given you some if he'd had any." She gestured to the soup. "Have something to warm you up."

"What'd I do to be saddled with such in-laws?" Gustav roared. "Never mind soup. I'm going out. Don't wait up."

Gustav stormed out.

Had Hertha sent any bread home with him since they didn't eat nighttime meals with the Webers anymore? She would probably never know. Well then, she would just eat his soup.

When Gustav fell into bed in the early morning hours, Annika roused only enough to register the stench of ale. In the morning, she left for work while he was still snoring.

Over the next few weeks, it became the pattern for Gustav to disappear on Friday and Saturday nights. He stopped attending church. Annika stayed home the first Sunday morning, but there wasn't much to do in the small apartment. She started leaving her Sunday dress in the outer room so she could get ready without waking him.

He always caught up with her as she walked with the family to the workshop for Sunday dinner. The meal was becoming more and more scanty until finally there were no roasts, only soups to stretch a few pieces of meat with root vegetables. Conversations were strained. Aunt Hertha had a pinched look about her as she tried to divvy up the food. Annika was desperate to get more nourishment since she had felt the baby move. She was determined not to grow as thin as Dora had been. If she told the Weber women about the baby, she knew she would get more food, but she hadn't told Gustav yet. He'd been moody and unpredictable.

When Paul appeared at the shop as she was leaving on

Wednesday, Annika had never been so happy to see anyone.

"Hallo," he greeted her. "I have news."

"Is it Lina?"

"It is. Her wedding date has been set for Sunday, April 16th."

Annika clapped her hands. "Marvelous! I could use a trip home."

Paul looked at her sharply. "Is everything all right?"

"We're low on coins and food like everybody else," Annika admitted.

"Mutter sent bread and pastries."

Since it was far too cool to eat outside, Annika said, "Let's go back to my apartment and have lunch."

Annika dug into her share, licking honey from her fingers as she finished. Finally sated, she turned her attention to Paul, who was staring at her.

She flushed. "Sorry. I was pretty hungry."

"I'll say. I've never seen a girl eat like that except..." He blushed. "Are you in the family way?"

"Ja. Not very good timing."

Paul struggled to compose himself. Finally, he said, "You and Lucie will have little ones around the same age."

"I hope they'll be able to see each other. How is Lucie?"

"She's glowing. The goats are kidding well, so Fritz and his Vater butchered a couple of older ones so there'd be meat to keep her strength up. Mutter goes out once or twice a week to make sure she's well."

Annika nodded, missing her own Mutter. When she felt tears welling up, she changed the subject. "Has the Adelsverein found land in Texas yet?"

"Not yet. Prince Solms leaves soon to buy land. They're

building a brig in Bremen to sail settlers to the New World as soon as there's a place to settle." Paul's voice vibrated with excitement.

"Will you be on it?"

"Maybe not the first one, but definitely by the end of the year. You and Gustav should consider emigrating."

"We don't have the money."

"The Adelsverein is paying the way for some. They want to ease poverty and lack of land."

"We qualify on both those counts."

"As we get established in Texas, we'll send for more family to come. It takes three years of developing the land to earn it, but the Adelsverein supplies the seed, tools, and food to get through the first year. I'm going to bring Jaeger and buy chickens and plow animals. I'll be prince of my own property. I'll be able to work my land or hire men to work it while I open a bakery, whatever I want."

"Sounds wonderful."

Paul rose to leave. "When I return for supplies in two weeks, I'll bring you some eggs. Lucie says the hens are starting to lay better."

"I'd appreciate it, Paul. Danke."

"I must be on my way. Why don't you take a nap?"

With her stomach full for the first time in days, she did feel drowsy. "Good advice. Give everyone my love."

Paul tromped down the stairs. Annika curled up under her wedding quilt and fell asleep.

Gustav's heavy tread woke her. She was stretching when he crashed through the bedroom door, wild-eyed. "Slut! What man was up here with you?"

Annika froze. "Paul...Paul brought us some food from the

bakery. He left a long time ago."

Gustav's eyes raked over the rumpled bed. "Why are you in bed in the middle of the day?"

"I...I..." Annika fought back a wave of nausea.

"You what?" Gustav demanded.

This wasn't how she wanted to tell him, but he was angrier than she'd ever seen him. "I'm pregnant. I get more tired than usual, and since there's not much work, sometimes I take a nap."

He rubbed his head. "We can't afford to have a baby right now!"

"I know. I'm sorry."

"And why would you bring a man up to our rooms?"

"Paul came just as I was leaving Engel's. He's been here before, with Lucie and Frau Becker. He's like my brother, and I was so hungry when he showed me the food, I didn't think what it could look like. I'm sorry, Gustav." She held her breath.

The anger seeped out of Gustav's face. "You haven't been getting enough to eat, have you?"

"I'm more hungry lately."

"I'll have a word with Hertha."

"Danke." She looked out the window to judge how high the sun was. "Is it late?"

Gustav sank down on the bed. "Nein. We don't have many orders, so I came home early."

"Frau Becker sent food."

"I had lunch. We can wait until suppertime."

Annika smoothed the quilt back over the bed. "I have some wash to do."

"I'm going to find Erwin. He's been hanging around the

machine shops learning about engines. Sometimes they give him small jobs to do."

When Gustav left, Annika hauled water up the three flights of stairs to heat over the fireplace. She sank down onto the chair made by the Roths and tried to figure out a present she could bring Lina and Hans. It would have to be something she already owned. Even though it was cut into dress pieces, the black silk given her by Frau Engel would have to do. Gustav wouldn't ever let her wear silk, and Lina was close to her size. She wished she had thought to send the silk with Paul in case Lina wanted to use it for a wedding dress.

Dragging out the washboard, she scrubbed petticoats, a shirt, and a pair of trousers. There was still a nightgown and a dress, but she was too tired to tackle them. She set the clean clothes in another tub and trudged back to the fountain for rinse water. After rinsing, she wrung them out and hung them on a rope line. She threw the wash water out the window along with the contents of the chamber pot.

While they ate dinner, Annika told Gustav about the wedding.

"I have some things going on here, so I'm not going to be able to make it."

He was still sulking about the wood. Annika had hoped he would borrow Britta and the buggy, but now she would have to walk. "Would you mind if I go a day early to visit my family? Walking there and back might be too much for one day." She glanced at her stomach.

"Sure. We need to take good care of this little one." Gustav tried to infuse his words with some warmth. "As long as you don't miss any work at Engel's."

"I'll stay late the other days to make up for it."

As they lay down to sleep, Annika curled up and faced the window. Gustav stared at the opposite wall.

Chapter 31

Gustav began coming home in the afternoons with something for Annika to eat. Then he disappeared to shadow Erwin or drink in a Gasthaus with friends. Annika didn't care as long as he wasn't home brooding or getting underfoot.

She indulged in a nap and knitted or did laundry until it was time to warm their small suppers. Since Hertha wasn't sending much food, she borrowed Frau Hoffmann's oven one afternoon to bake her own pumpernickel bread. As well as using her own charcoal, she left a small loaf for the Hoffmanns as payment.

The pumpernickel bread lasted for several days, giving her more energy. She wished she had a plot of land for a vegetable garden. Dora would be planting any day with Charlotte's help. It had taken Annika four days to plant their huge garden the year before Matt came home. Since it was feeding more mouths, it would be even bigger this year.

When Annika spoke with Frau Engel about the wedding, the shopkeeper said, "There's not enough work to keep you on for six full mornings a week. I only need you for twenty hours a week. If you want to go to Braunfels a day or two early, you can make up the hours before or after your trip." She sighed. "Let's pray it's a good harvest this year so there's more trade in the fall."

Since she could go for a longer visit, Annika realized she might even be able to secure a ride.

True to his word, Paul returned with eight eggs for

183

Annika as well as the usual bread and pastries from Becker's. Shamefaced, she said, "I can't invite you in to share a meal. Gustav was angry when you came up the other day."

"I'm the one who needs to apologize. It never occurred to me that it could be a problem. I'll explain to Gustav at the wedding."

"Oh for the days at Kellers when the maid was around to keep things proper!" Annika teased. She sobered. "You won't see Gustav at the wedding. He's not coming. But I have plenty of time to come for a visit since work is slow."

"What day were you thinking of coming?"

"Thursday, if that suits Dora and Vater. Could you ask them to send me a message if that doesn't work?"

"I'll drive out there to make sure. I have a delivery next Thursday in Albshausen. Would you like to meet me there?"

"That would be wunderbar."

"Will it cause a problem with Gustav?"

"I don't see how it could. We'll be out in the open in a wagon. I'll tell him about it beforehand, so it won't seem underhanded."

Paul shook his head. "You're too good for him, Annika."

Annika remained silent. She was starting to think so too.

The next Thursday Paul handed Annika up into the Beckers' wagon. All her plans were running like clockwork. Gustav had merely grunted when she told him the arrangements. He was spending less and less time at home. He did bring home a few coins now and then, so Annika was able to buy a little food at the market.

She planned to ask Dora about working in the garden for a share of the food. She couldn't wait to see what new antics Helmuth and Charlotte were up to, and she should have time for a long heart-to-heart with Lucie.

As though Paul had read her mind, he turned down the lane to the Huber farm. "Lucie insisted I bring you here first." He grinned. "She bribed me with custard. Said she'd have it waiting for us."

"I was just thinking of Lucie, so I'm glad we're stopping here first. When I get out to our farm, I plan to work. I want to help Dora with the garden. Food's becoming more and more dear in the city while work becomes more and more scarce. Everyone's praying for a good harvest this year."

"We bakers hope so too. The price of flour keeps rising."

"It's getting tough for everyone."

"That's why I'm planning to emigrate to America. I'm saving up for the voyage."

"I can't imagine Braunfels without you, but I hope it works out for you, Paul."

He brought Tilli to a stop. "It will."

Lucie waddled out to greet them. "Annika!"

"Lucie!"

"Don't even think about trying to get down without my help." Paul set the brake and came around the wagon to assist Annika. "I'll be right in after I take care of Tilli."

"We'll all have custard and then you can go find the men so Anna and I can have a real chat." Lucie steered Annika into her cozy home. It was smaller than the Lange cottage but plenty big enough for a family. The single room had a hearth in the center of one wall and a large back window which opened to spring-green fields. A horsehair couch sat in front of the fireplace while a table and four chairs sat to the right of the front door. A large hutch crowded with dishes filled the rest of the back wall.

"It's lovely," Annika said with a touch of envy.

"It's a mess." Lucie surveyed the dirty dishes and a floor littered with crumbs. "I'm having trouble moving around, and my back aches if I stand for more than ten minutes. I've been trying to get those dishes done all day."

"Never mind. You're bringing a new life into the world."

"So are you."

"This little one will be at least two months younger than yours."

"You've always been tall and thin. I don't think you'll ever get this round."

"Maybe not, but as long as the baby's healthy it will be worth it, don't you think?"

"Of course. I'm just more bothered by things than usual. Aren't you more emotional?"

Annika paused to consider. "I don't think so."

Lucie rolled her eyes. "We can talk more about that later. Come sit down and try this custard. It turned out just right, even though I keep dropping ingredients and pans."

Paul heard the last comment as he came through the front door. "I'll carry the custard—to make sure it arrives safely." He lifted the pot from its arm over the hearth.

Annika sat where Lucie indicated. Spoons and blue stoneware bowls were already set on the table. She closed her eyes as she savored the smooth dessert. "Heavenly!"

Lucie beamed. "At least I can still do something right!"

Paul had already finished. "It's the best you've ever made. I'd love more, but I'll save the rest for Fritz. Where is he?"

"Out plowing in the far field. Can you take him the jug of water near the pump?"

"Sure. I'll return soon. I need to get back to the bakery."

"I could walk the rest of the way." Annika spooned up the

last of her dessert.

"Absolutely not. You've walked far enough in your...um... condition." Paul flushed.

"Walking won't hurt me, or the baby."

"Nevertheless, I'm driving you the rest of the way." Paul headed out the door.

"I'll be ready when you want to go," Annika promised, licking her spoon.

"Hungry?" Lucie asked in amusement.

"Always. Aren't you?"

"Not anymore. I get indigestion a lot. Mutter says that's normal. She told me to eat small meals more often."

"Does that help?"

"Ja. What other symptoms do you have?"

"I have to nap almost every day. Since I only work half days, I have plenty of time to rest."

"Hmm. I was never that tired. I think you need more meat and eggs."

Annika shrugged. "I'd love to eat better, but you know how things are."

"We have more eggs than we can use. I'm going to start sending them every time Paul picks up supplies."

"Lucie, you can't do that! You could trade them at Vogel's for Kaffee and such."

"I can spare the eggs. I care for the hens, and two are raising chicks right now, so I'll have more hens soon."

"It will be a while before the chicks are old enough to lay."

Lucie looked at her friend in exasperation. "You can do some sewing for me or the baby if you want it to be a trade."

"That would work. I can get some small remnants from

Engel's or the Webers, especially baby-sized ones."

"Deal."

Annika stood. "For now, I'm going to wash some of these dishes while you put your feet up."

Lucie stretched out on the couch. Annika thought she was dozing until she whispered, "Are you scared, Anna?"

Annika broke out in a sweat. How did Lucie know about Gustav?

Lucie didn't wait long for an answer. "I worry about giving birth. Some women have an awful time. Gretchen didn't make it." Paul's wife Gretchen had died in childbirth along with her baby seven years ago.

Annika wiped her hands on a towel and sank down on a footrest next to her friend. Taking Lucie's hands, she said, "You're going to be just fine. Paul's a big man who fathered a big baby, and Gretchen was long past her due date."

"On Paul's birthdays, Mutter always used to say Paul was nearly the death of her with his big head. She was joking, but..."

"She was fine. You will be too. The Hubers are much smaller than the Beckers."

Annika was glad the front door opened because she didn't have any more comfort to share even though Lucie still didn't look convinced.

"Hallo, Annika." Fritz entered the house with Paul on his heels. "I heard there's custard."

Lucie sat up. "Help yourself, dear."

They all laughed as Fritz started eating it out of the pot.

"What? I'm saving dishes."

"So thoughtful!" Annika walked back to the sink. "I just have a couple more to wash if you have a few minutes, Paul."

"Ja, but as soon as you're done, we'll be on our way."

Annika's welcome home was chaotic. When Bruno's barking alerted the children, Charlotte flung the door open, and Helmuth tripped down the front stairs, resulting in a bumped head and loud cries. Annika was still sitting in the wagon, so Paul scooped the toddler up until Dora bustled out the front door. She welcomed Annika over her son's screams while Paul ran to the pump and wet a handkerchief for the little boy's head. Then he handed Annika down and departed amidst the barking and screaming.

The whole afternoon and evening continued with Helmuth's peevishness and the men getting in from the fields late. Halfway through being milked, the cow kicked the bucket, splashing Annika and wasting the milk. At the same time, Dora burned the rolls while trying to appease Helmuth. Thankfully, both children were already in bed when the men returned tired and grimy. They each gave Annika a pat on the shoulder and ate without talking while Annika and Dora served them. After the men retired, the women brewed tea and sat on the couch.

"You'd never know from today, but we're all doing really well." Dora pulled her feet up under her skirts. "Helmuth's usually an easy little guy. Charlotte's good at keeping an eye on him, so he doesn't get into much trouble while I do the cleaning and gardening."

"How is the garden coming?"

"The lettuce and peas are in. I need to plant the carrots and cabbage."

"Could we plant them together tomorrow?"

"They can wait until next week so you can have a pleasant, restful visit."

Annika shifted. "I'd really like to help. From the looks of

things, we're going to rely on your garden again this coming year. I want to feel like I put some work into it."

"Anna, we lived off your labor the first winter we were here. I can repay your kindness."

Annika's eyes welled with tears. "Danke, but if we work together, don't you think we can grow more?"

Dora tapped her chin. "Ja. There might be space for Matt to plow up a new patch next to the pasture. I'll speak to him in the morning."

"I can come for some visits this summer and weed and pick, maybe even preserve. My sewing work is slowing down. At some point, I may not even have a job." Annika picked at a loose thread on her dress. "I don't know how we'll pay the rent if that happens."

"God will provide. He always does."

"I suppose." Annika yawned. "I'd better turn in."

"Sleep as long as you can in the morning. I'm sure the little one is making you tired."

"That's the truth!" Annika put her mug in the sink and climbed the stairs. As she undressed, she admired Charlotte's innocent face in the moonlight. Gustav might want a son, but she wanted a little girl. Oh the dresses she would sew for her little one! She carefully eased into bed. Her niece's light breathing lulled Annika into sweet dreams.

Chapter 32

A pair of bright blue eyes greeted Annika when she woke the next morning. "Hey, you!" She smiled at Charlotte. "I've been lying here still as I could. I didn't wake you up, did I?"

"Nein." Annika stretched.

Charlotte grinned in relief. "Can we get up now?"

"Ja. I hear your Mutter making breakfast downstairs."

Annika and Charlotte smoothed the bed and dressed before Annika plaited Charlotte's hair as well as her own.

"Guten Morgen." Dora handed Annika a mug of coffee. "I'm glad you got to sleep in."

"Are Vater and Matt already gone?"

"Ja. Matt said he'd plow for us before he went out to seed with Vater. They're working hard to get one last field of barley in."

"What should we plant in the new plot?"

"The soil's not going to be very good. Let's leave it until Matt can add manure. We can put in beans next month. Today we should plant cabbage in the big garden."

"How's Helmuth?"

"I'll check on him. He was up once last night but went right back to sleep."

Dora returned with a smiling Helmuth and set him in his highchair. Annika put some scrambled egg on the tray, and he happily began stuffing his mouth.

"Whew! I think our boy is back to his usual cheerful self." Dora took a long drink of Kaffee and dug into her own eggs.

"He has quite the bump." Annika sat down.

Dora studied her son. "Charlotte, you have to be careful not to touch Helmuth's sore spot today while you're watching him. It will hurt, and he'll start to cry. Can you be a big girl and keep him busy while Tante and I work in the garden?"

Charlotte sat up straighter. "Can we play outside?"

"Ja."

"I'll play ball with him. That will keep him out of trouble."

"Good idea." Dora smiled at her daughter.

"You're a great big sister." Annika poured her some more milk. "You're going to be a great cousin too."

"What's a cousin?"

"A cousin is your aunt or uncle's child. Tante Annika is having a baby," Dora said.

"Like Helmuth?" Charlotte wrinkled her nose.

"What's wrong?" her mother asked.

"I'd really like another girl to play with. Helmuth doesn't like my doll."

The two women laughed.

Annika patted her protruding stomach. "We won't know whether it's a boy or a girl until he or she is born."

"How long until then?"

"Four months."

"That's a long time. I'd like a girl to play with now."

"It will be a while before the baby can play." Dora stood to clear dishes from the table. "Remember Helmuth didn't play when he was born."

"Neither did I. I didn't feel like it."

Dora and Annika looked at each other in shocked surprise.

"You didn't?" her mother asked.

"I sat or laid on the bed."

Dora tried to think back. She'd been so worn out after Helmuth was born.

"Now I feel like playing all day," Charlotte hopped off her chair, "until I get tired at night." She picked up some food Helmuth had dropped on the floor and popped it into her mouth. "Can I go get the eggs?"

Wordless, Dora handed her the egg basket. Charlotte skipped out the back door.

"Well…" Dora finally said, sliding the plates into the sink. "I didn't even notice." Her shoulders slumped.

"You were trying to keep Helmuth alive, Dora, trying to survive yourself. I was afraid for you when you first came home. You were skin and bones." Annika caught her breath. "I hope things don't get that desperate for me and Gustav."

Dora attacked the plates with a rag. "Let's get to that garden. It should help."

Annika wiped Helmuth's face and hands. "I hope so, Dora. I hope so."

Chapter 33

Contentment flooded Annika as Matt drove her home late Sunday afternoon. The wedding had been beautiful. Annika's contribution had been arranging Lina's hair in intricate braids.

After the short ceremony, the guests converged on the Roths' workshop, which had been scrubbed free of sawdust. The abundance of chairs, benches, and tables was one of the benefits of marrying into a furniture maker's family. After the meal, furniture was removed to make space for dancing. Annika accepted dances with Hans, Max, and Matt but sat with Lucie most of the afternoon.

The only dark spot was poor Elsa, who was despondent at being left with her mother and Margarete and spent most of the day scowling. Relieved she'd escaped living with Frau Stein, Annika's heart went out to the twelve-year-old.

The spring sunshine made her drowsy, and she was nearly asleep by the time Matt arrived at the Hoffmanns'. He handed her down from the old farm wagon, gathered her carpet bag, and followed her up the stairs. Gustav wasn't home.

"Danke." Annika hugged her brother.

"Take good care of yourself." Matt disappeared down the stairs.

Annika set a crock of preserved apples on the table and lay down in the other room. Gustav's arrival woke her. He burst through the door. "This is all you brought me from the wedding meal?"

Confused, Annika sat up and blinked at him like a barn owl.

"Answer me, woman!"

Gustav had clearly indulged in too many steins of beer.

"I had to leave before the celebration was over. Guests were still eating when I left so I couldn't take food." Annika's mind raced. "Hans said you were sorely missed and many thanks for the gift."

"Eh," Gustav snarled. "And what did we give them for a gift? We don't have enough to feed ourselves."

"I took Lina the silk Frau Engel gave me last year. I knew you didn't want me to wear it."

"We could have sold it."

She could hardly have attended a wedding with no gift or sold cut cloth for a good price.

"Äpfel aren't enough for a meal. I'm going out." Gustav slammed the door.

Annika lay back down. She'd eaten plenty at the wedding. Apples would tide her over until breakfast.

Gustav didn't return home that night. Sick with worry, Annika choked down a piece of toasted bread and hurried to the Webers'. Through the window, she glimpsed him sitting at his loom. Afraid to cause a kerfuffle and already late to work, Annika headed to Engel's. She stayed a few extra hours to offset the time she'd been away before returning to their home. Gustav wasn't there.

Annika hoped he'd bring some dinner when he came. After arranging a bread-baking session for the next afternoon, she made dough and set it to rise.

Gustav didn't appear for supper. Annika ate a heel of bread and more preserved apples. At least there was only one dish to deal with after such a scanty meal. She washed it and settled down to knit a wool soaker for the baby.

When Gustav arrived home late, it was obvious he'd been drinking. "What's for dinner?"

"All we have is Äpfel."

"Stupid Hausfrau! Why didn't you go to the market today?"

"I don't have any money."

"See! I told you we needed that silk to sell."

"It was already cut into dress pieces. It wouldn't have been worth much."

"Don't talk back, woman. Now I have to think of something else to sell off." He glared at her while she continued knitting. "Your ring will bring the most money. Give it to me."

Annika reluctantly laid her knitting in her lap and tugged on the ring. "It's stuck, Gustav."

"Try harder. How can you already have gotten fat?"

"I'm not fat, Gustav. I'm pregnant, and it's warm. Fingers swell."

Gustav stood over her. "Let me try."

Annika held out her hand and winced as he pulled. "Ow! Maybe if I run some cold water over my hand, it will slide off. I'll go up to the fountain."

Gustav jerked her to her feet. The knitting fell from her lap and tangled her bare feet.

"Gustav, wait! My knitting." But Gustav pushed her toward the stairs.

Annika scrambled for her footing, but she didn't connect with the top step. She screamed as she tumbled down the steep stairs, hitting her head as she landed.

When she woke, she was in the Hoffmanns' bed with a sharp pain in her abdomen.

"Lie still, child," Frau Hoffmann soothed her.

Annika grabbed her hand. "It hurts so much. Is my baby all right?"

"Time will tell." Frau Hoffmann put a cold cloth on Annika's throbbing forehead. "You just rest." She spooned something into Annika's mouth.

The next time Annika woke it was dark. She shifted and felt a rush of blood.

"I'm so sorry." Frau Hoffmann smoothed her hair back. "The baby's coming."

Tears seeped from Annika's eyes. "Could someone go get Dora, my brother's wife?"

"I'll see what I can do." Frau Hoffmann left the room. A band of pain gripped Annika.

"Gustav is going to borrow a horse and ride to your family's farm."

Annika nodded at Frau Hoffmann's words. The next hours were exhausting as she miscarried a tiny baby girl.

In the end, Annika had an empty womb and a massive headache. A doctor called by the Hoffmanns when Annika kept losing consciousness gave her a sleeping draught.

The last thing she heard was Gustav's oath when he returned just in time to receive the doctor's bill. Dora hurried to her side and squeezed her hand as Annika sank into oblivion.

Chapter 34

Annika begged Dora and Matt to take the tiny body back to the farm and bury her beside Mutter. Dora smoothed the quilt over Annika. "Come out to the farm as soon as you're able. The food and fresh air will be good for you."

"I won't let her get up until she's ready," Frau Hoffmann promised. "And I'll send word if she needs anything."

Annika barely registered their departure through her haze. When the doctor's medicine ran out two days later, her mind cleared enough for a flood of grief to engulf her. She crept back up to her own bed. Tante Hertha or Paula visited every day with broth or bread. They said Gustav was sleeping in the workshop so he wouldn't disturb her.

"Thank God you didn't break your neck." Frau Hoffmann brought pumpernickel bread baked from the dough Annika had kneaded before the accident.

Annika wasn't feeling thankful in the least. She had a large egg on her forehead where she had hit the floor. The only thing that hurt more than her head was her battered heart.

At the end of the week, Tante Hertha got Annika up for a bath. "You'll feel much better once you're cleaned up."

Annika began sitting by the window each day, brushing her hair. Her knitting had disappeared, so her hands lay idle until Olga arrived before suppertime on Saturday.

"We all miss you, Annika. Frau Engel sent some sausage for

your dinner and a bodice and sleeves to line, if you're up to it. I have a packet of tea that should help with the healing."

"I suppose." Annika sighed. "I can't afford to lose my job."

"It's going to be all right." Olga poured her some tea. "We all lose babies. Myself, I lost two. I'm so sorry it was your first, but you'll get through this."

Annika wished she could lose her husband, but that would mean no more babies. "I'll come back to work next week. I don't know which day."

"Nein. I'll bring your work next week. If you're feeling up to it, you can come the week after."

"Danke, Olga." Annika didn't try to hide her tears.

"I'm praying for you."

"I need it."

After Olga left to tend her own family, Annika cleared off the top of the crate. She took all the little clothes she had lovingly stitched and shoved them into the crate's darkest corner. She restacked the dishes, ate the sausage, and side-stepped down the stairs. Sitting on the stoop, she watched the dusk deepen until she felt the night's chill. She crept back up the stairs to her apartment.

She was sewing in a chair by the window the next day when Gustav arrived.

"Tante Hertha says you're better. It's good to see you out of bed."

"Ja." Annika kept her eyes on the dress, though her trembling hands wouldn't allow her to add any stitches.

"We got a few orders for linen from the merchants in Limburg."

"That's good."

"Annika, I'm sorry about what happened. I never meant…"

Annika refused to look at him.

Gustav cleared his throat. "It was a terrible accident."

Silence stretched between them.

"Tante Hertha sent this." He set a bowl on the table. "You don't look very comfortable. Would you like me to push the couch in front of the window?"

Annika nodded and stood.

Gustav set her chair back at the table and pushed their horsehair sofa over to catch the light streaming in the single window.

"I'll stay at the shop a few more nights."

"That would be best." Annika sat down on the couch with her sewing.

"I see Engel's sent you some work."

"Ja. I'll work at home this week and go back next week."

"I could come tomorrow and help you down the stairs to get some fresh air."

"No need. I can manage on my own."

Gustav twisted his hat in his hands. "Well then, I'll be off."

It was a relief to return to work. She had walked a little farther each day in order to build up her strength, and on Saturday afternoon she had made it all the way to Engel's. On Monday morning, she rose at her usual time, ate some toasted bread and Kaffee, gathered the frock she had finished, and headed to work.

Olga explained the current orders. Seating herself by the open window, Annika started stitching a fan pattern into a bodice.

Greta burst into the room. "Isn't it a gorgeous morning? The birds are all singing today." She stopped abruptly when she saw Annika. "It's good to have you back." She sat down across from Annika and began hemming.

Annika was glad Greta reined in her chatter for once, but unable to be silent for long, Greta began humming, a strange off-key sound in contrast to the songbirds.

Annika gritted her teeth and moved to another seat. Olga smiled at her sympathetically.

Mid-morning Greta disappeared upstairs and returned with Frau Engel and a pot of tea.

"Annika, I'm so glad you're back." Frau Engel examined the dress pieces on the cutting table. "Take a break, girls, and have some tea."

Annika kneaded her lower back.

"Are you all right? You can leave whenever you need to."

"I'm still a little sore. I also get headaches, so I'll probably leave before noon today. If you'd allow me to take this bodice, I can work on it this afternoon."

"That sounds like an excellent plan. We have six dresses this month, including one for a wedding."

Greta handed Annika a cup of tea. "This should ease the headaches."

Annika's vision blurred, and she fumbled the delicate cup. "Sometimes I have double vision, but it's going away."

Greta poured another cup for Olga. "It's too bad pregnancy makes us clumsy." She blushed. "I mean...as the reason for your fall. It's just a shame, is all."

"What?" Annika speared Greta with a look.

"Gustav said you fell due to clumsiness. Mutter explained that women in the family way get off-balance."

"Clumsiness had nothing to do with it," Annika said icily.

"Oh..." Greta shot a look at her mother, who kept her eyes

on her teacup. "Beg your pardon." She hastily raised her teacup to her lips.

The nerve of that man! Annika knew Gustav wouldn't have admitted to his part in her fall, but to blame it on her was unconscionable. Tears pricked her eyes, but she sniffed them back and drained her teacup.

Chapter 35

Although an ache took up residence in Annika's heart, life slowly returned to normal. Gustav returned to their little apartment at night. He found a few odd jobs, and they were able to meet their rent as well as purchase flour, eggs, and vegetables at the market. Her ring was sold to pay the doctor's bill.

Frieda came to visit near the end of May. She chose a spring-green linen from Engel's and shared a meal of freshly baked bread with Annika. The two women wandered along the Lahn and through the markets until Hans had to head back to Braunfels after delivering several wardrobes.

Paul brought eggs and baked goods every other week on his supply runs. When he came in mid-June with news that Lucie's son had arrived, Annika decided it was time to visit. She wanted to see little Fritzie, and Dora would need help in the garden. Annika had recovered her strength and could wield a hoe.

Over the next fortnight, she worked extra hours at Engel's so she could be away for four or five days. Gustav grumbled, but he had just returned from a trip to Limburg. He finally stopped complaining when Annika promised to bring back fresh vegetables.

As Paul guided Tilli out of Wetzlar after his next supply trip, Annika basked in the sunshine and fresh air, feeling better than she had in a long time. The usually taciturn Paul entertained her with anecdotes about the bakery.

When there was a lull, Annika said, "I saw a map of Texas.

It's huge. Where will you emigrate to?"

"I don't know yet. The Adelsverein is still looking for the right land grant."

"You're very brave."

Paul grinned. "I want to own land. That's not possible in Hessen, or anywhere nearby."

"But you're a baker. What will you do with land?"

"I dunno. Grow my own grain, maybe? I have to wait and see what the land's suitable for. I can be anything I want in a new country. That's the charm of emigrating. You don't have to stay in the family business if you don't want." Paul turned to look at her. "What you've done—a farmer's daughter becoming a seamstress in a city—is unusual."

"I suppose so, although my husband's family is in a related trade." Annika was quiet for several miles. "Don't mention it to anyone, but the Webers' business isn't getting many orders. Erwin and Gustav don't work the full week anymore. They spend time at machine shops, learning and doing errands or small jobs."

"I've read in the papers that cotton cloth is pushing out linen."

"Ja, even though it's not as fine a fabric."

"Well, emigrating might be something for you and Gustav to consider."

"We don't have any money, and I can't imagine leaving everything I've ever known."

"You left Braunfels and went to Wetzlar. Everything was new there."

"But I can come back and see my family and friends. Once you leave for another country, there's no coming back."

"After I get settled, others in my family can come."

"I'm glad for you, Paul. I hope you find everything you want."

When they reached the Hubers' farmyard, Annika jumped down and reached into the wagon for the bag of little gowns she'd sewn for Fritzie from scraps of soft linen. A pang went through her at the thought of her lost daughter, but she pushed it away.

"Lucie says to go right in. Don't knock in case the baby's sleeping," Paul called as he drove to the barn.

Annika swung the door open to reveal Lucie nursing Fritzie. "Hallo," she whispered.

"Annika!" Lucie flushed. "I can't get up, but pour yourself a drink."

Annika poured herself a stein of milk and sat at the kitchen table while Fritzie finished with a loud burp.

The two friends laughed. Lucie stroked his downy head as his eyes drifted shut. "Do you want to hold him?"

Annika took the sleeping baby and cradled him in her arms. Her eyes filled with tears. "He's perfect."

Lucie's face beamed with motherly pride. Then regret sobered her features. "I'm so sorry, Anna, about your baby."

Annika took a deep breath. "I won't be a mother this year, but maybe next. Our Kinder will still be close in age."

"Should you see the midwife while you're here?"

"I have a doctor in Wetzlar. He says all is well."

"That's a relief to hear." Lucie heaved herself out of her chair. "You've had a long drive, and it's lunchtime. How about fried eggs and some of Mutter's honey wheat bread with goat cheese? Dora sent the cheese over. She's taught Frieda how to make it, but I've been too busy to join them."

Annika's stomach rumbled. "Sounds heavenly."

"You can put him down in his cradle if you want. It's in the bedroom." Lucie pointed to a door on one side of the fireplace.

Annika gently laid him on a wool blanket in the cradle and shut the door. "I brought Fritzie some things." She handed Lucie the sack.

Lucie pulled out a tiny yellow gown and ran her fingers over it. "Oh, Annika! It's the softest thing we have for him. Danke." After pulling out white and green gowns, she hugged her friend. "Sit and tell me what's happening with you."

Annika shook her head. "Not much. Let me wash these few dishes while you cook. I'd rather hear about you. How many new lambs are there?"

"There were ten, but one didn't make it."

"And pigs?"

"Seven piglets growing fast. My garden's doing as well as can be expected considering I couldn't bend over for two months and Fritz hasn't let me do any work since Fritzie came. He said maybe next week. He and his brothers have been keeping down the weeds."

"I expect to be hoeing in Dora's before the day's out." Annika wiped her hands on a rag and sat at the kitchen table.

"I'm sure she'll be happy for the help."

"I did talk her into enlarging it. We'll need the vegetables since money's been tight. Engel's did six dresses last month. Only five this month, and three of those are for weddings."

"I wish you lived closer."

"Me, too. I've realized there are some big advantages to living on a farm." Annika dug into the plateful of eggs Lucie placed in front of her. "Like eggs, even if the crops don't do well."

"It would be perfect if you could live somewhere with a little land so you could keep chickens and plant a garden."

"Ja, but the Webers still have their business, even though it's slow. Gustav has started spending time in the machine shops. They're building steam engines, the kind that pull trains. He says he's learning a lot."

"Isn't he the eldest son? Why wouldn't he inherit the weaving business?"

"Tante Hertha's family brought his Onkel into the business, so their son Conrad inherits it even though Gustav is older. Hertha's family lives in Alstaden. They get the flax and send it by barge down the Rhine to the Lahn."

Lucie filled Annika in on the village gossip while they ate. Annika made Lucie sit on the couch while she washed the frying pan and their dishes. By the time she finished, Lucie had fallen asleep, so Annika slipped out to the barn to find Paul, who was mucking out stalls with Fritz.

"Ready to go?" Paul hung the shovel on a nail.

"Ja. I should get out to Vater's." Annika turned to Fritz. "Fritzie is beautiful. Congratulations."

"Danke." He struggled to find words of comfort for Annika's loss.

"It's okay, Fritz. Next year, God-willing."

Fritz nodded.

Paul hitched Tilli back up to the wagon, and they trotted down the long drive past the lambs playing in the field.

Annika threw herself into farm chores. Although Dora and Charlotte had done their best, weeds were taking over the new garden. Annika attacked the weeds with a fury, venting her frustrations. Every night she sank into bed with Charlotte and slept deeply. Every morning she rose early to milk the cows.

Charlotte clung to her after morning chores on the fifth day. "I'll come back next month," Annika promised. "I have to walk back to Wetzlar today so I can work at Engel's tomorrow. Be a good helper for your Mutter."

Dora finished diapering Helmuth. "You were a godsend, Annika. I stopped looking at the second garden. It was too discouraging to be that far behind."

"I talked you into planting it. I'm sorry I don't live closer so I can do more."

"We'll make it work." Dora looked tired.

Annika felt guilty. "Hire Elsa to weed if you need more hands. She's a good worker. I'll find some scraps of cloth to repay her with."

"Her Mutter and Margarete run that poor little thing off her feet. When she comes over here, I let her play with Helmuth. I get more done, and she gets a break."

"I'm glad she came over on Sunday so I could see her. She's growing into a beautiful young woman."

"Inside and out, which is more than I can say for the women she lives with." Dora put her hand over her mouth. "I shouldn't have said that. Charlotte, there are some things that are true that shouldn't be said and certainly shouldn't be repeated."

"I can't say Elsa is beautiful?"

"No, you can say that as much as you like. We don't say other people aren't beautiful."

Charlotte looked confused. "Can I go play with the kittens in the barn?"

"Let's walk with Tante a little way. Then you can play."

Charlotte took Annika's hand. Dora picked up Helmuth, and they walked across Vater's fields to the road.

The closer Annika got to Wetzlar the more she felt weighted down. A mercantile supply wagon gave her a lift the last few miles, so she made it back to the apartment mid-afternoon. But the cramped space no longer seemed like home.

Chapter 36

Gustav's uncle pushed back his plate after Sunday dinner. "I have an announcement to make."

Tante Hertha paused from clearing dishes, placing her hand on her husband's shoulder.

"We won't be receiving a shipment of flax this year. We'll be moving to Alstaden when we've finished spinning the flax we have."

The family stared, thunderstruck.

"Why?" Ella asked with tears in her eyes.

"There aren't enough orders to continue doing business like this. We need to live closer to the flax fields. It's more cost effective to ship cloth rather than large bundles of flax."

Klara began to cry, and her mother rose to envelop her in a hug that soon included mother and all three daughters.

Erwin ignored the women. "I'm not going."

"I didn't think you'd want to. I know you're more interested in steam engines than linen," Oskar said. "I've had a word with Herr Keller. You can board with them if you're interested."

"What about me?" Gustav demanded.

"We're going to need a seller for this area. Right now, there's not enough space in the Alstaden workshop for anyone besides me, your Onkel, and Conrad. Your Onkel's looking to rent a house large enough so Hertha, Ella, and the other women can spin at home so our looms will fit in the existing workspace."

Gustav took a long draught of his beer.

Oskar sighed. "The two of you are young. You'll do better with the engines. I'm too old to learn a new trade."

Annika leaned forward. "Where will you live, Vater?"

"I'll board with someone, maybe my brother, if the house is large enough."

Annika dropped her voice. "Ella's a pretty girl. She'll be married before you know it, and there will be space for you."

"When do you think you'll leave?" Erwin took a bite of Kuchen.

"I plan to pay our rent until the middle of August. We think the flax will be spun by then, so it will be easy to transport as thread. Your Onkel will take the women and household goods first. Conrad and I will stay behind to pack the looms and close the business down."

"When do we need other jobs?" Gustav topped off his beer from the pitcher on the table.

"You'll both be paid until we finish weaving as much of our thread as possible before the move. We'll leave all our woven cloth with you to sell, Gustav. You keep twenty percent of the sales and put the rest in the Weber business bank account. We'll be able to draw the money in Alstaden since there's a branch there."

Gustav nodded glumly. "Do you think one of the shops will take us on, Erwin?"

"I'll find out first thing tomorrow."

On Monday afternoon, Annika borrowed the Hoffmanns' oven to bake fresh bread to soften any disappointment Gustav might be feeling. The rich pumpernickel with Dora's fresh butter did little to appease him.

"Of course, there's a steady job for Erwin. He's been hanging around, picking up on things for over a year. There are only odd jobs for me." Gustav grunted. "We're going to need a cheaper place to live."

"I'll keep my eyes and ears open."

"How much work is there at Engel's?"

"Three dresses so far for this month. We need orders for at least three more if I'm to continue sewing."

Gustav sat with his head in his hands.

Annika buttered a slice of bread for herself. "We'll be all right."

Gustav raised his head. "I'm going out tonight."

"Where?"

"To meet some of the boys at the Biergarten."

Annika tried to bite her tongue, but the thought of their dwindling coins loosened it. "Do you think it's a good idea to spend our coin on beer?"

Gustav's palm connected with her cheek.

"Oww!" Tears pricking her eyes, Annika stumbled back.

"They're contacts who might know of a good job for me." Gustav whirled toward the door. "Don't wait up for me."

Not likely. As Annika pressed a cold cloth to her face, she worried about Gustav's temper after an evening of drinking with his friends. Work was scarce. Since many of them didn't have jobs, they wouldn't be of any help to Gustav.

The next morning Annika arranged her hair loosely so it fell over her cheek. She put her bonnet on and studied herself in the mirror. The mark wasn't visible.

She toasted a slice of bread and ate the last egg. Gustav hadn't come home last night. He was probably at his family's workshop, though he could sleep outside for all she cared.

At the entrance of Engel's, she straightened her spine. *You have nothing to be ashamed of.* She marched in, removed her bonnet and sat with her sore cheek to the window. Engrossed in a difficult bodice, she missed Greta's entrance.

Greta gasped. "Annika, what happened?"

Olga paused mid-cut. The sewing room went silent.

"This is the *clumsiness* Gustav told you of." Annika's words cracked like a whip.

"But...but..."

Olga cut Greta off. "Could you start on the hem of the pink gown? I've already pinned it. The next fitting is tomorrow."

Greta shook out the voluminous gown and sat down. Annika could feel her scrutiny.

Annika concentrated on her stitches, blocking out the rest of the room. Finally, the tricky V-shaped bodice was smoothly attached to the pleated, silk skirt. She relaxed against the back of the chair.

"Greta went to make a pot of tea." Olga folded up the skirt she had finished cutting out and sat across from Annika. "Want to talk about it?"

"The Webers are closing their shop in Wetzlar. Gustav's Onkel's family is going back to Alstaden to spin and weave. Gustav's Vater is going with them, but there's no room for Gustav and Erwin." Annika hesitated. "Gustav needs a job, and we need a cheaper place to live."

Olga reached out gently. "That doesn't explain this."

"I should have kept quiet, but I suggested Gustav shouldn't spend our coins on beer with his friends."

Olga pursed her lips. "You're not to blame. No matter what you said, he shouldn't have struck you."

Annika focused on her hands, fighting back tears. "Danke. I

needed to hear that."

Frau Engel swept into the room with a teapot, followed by Greta with a tray laden with cups, sugar, and milk. "I have excellent news. Frau Zeigler and her niece have each ordered a dress. Greta also needs a new frock for fall, so we now have six orders this month."

She sat down and poured tea for each of the women.

Relief poured over Annika. Her job was secure for July.

Frau Engel set her teacup back on the tray. "We have a fitting tomorrow. Is the dress complete?"

Greta arranged the pink gown on a dress form, and Frau Engel examined every seam and flounce. "It's stunning. Good work."

After her mother left with the tea tray, Greta flew to the cloth cabinet. "Mutter said I can use any of the material in here. How about this red linen?"

"That's a good color for autumn." Olga pinned the pieces of a skirt. "I wouldn't be surprised if Fraülein Zeigler wants the same cloth."

Greta frowned. "There won't be enough for two gowns."

Annika ran her fingers over the material. "I can see if the Webers have some red linen if you'd like."

"If I use this fabric today and Fraülein Zeigler does want crimson like mine, she can fund the purchase from your family." Greta's eyes gleamed. "Everyone gains."

Olga tapped her temple with a finger. "Good thinking, Greta. You have a head for business."

When Gustav reappeared several days later, he brought wildflowers. Neither he nor Annika mentioned their last interaction. Apparently, none of his drinking buddies had been able to point him toward a job.

He brightened when Annika mentioned Engel's might need red linen. "We have twenty ells. We also have a lot of black, some yellow, and pink. There's blue and white on the looms."

"If it's all right with you, I'd like to go out to the farm next Thursday to work in the gardens. There should be lettuce and beans to bring back."

"When will you be back?"

"Wednesday afternoon or evening so I can still fit in two and a half days at Engel's."

"Try to get some eggs."

"I will." Annika turned her attention back to the soakers she was knitting for Fritzie in exchange for all the eggs they'd already been given. She wished she had something for Paul to thank him for the ride.

Chapter 37

The days at Vater's farm flew by with dew-soaked mornings and labor-filled days that melded into nights of deep sleep. All too soon, it was time for the walk back to Wetzlar.

Halfway back, Annika noticed a cottage that looked abandoned. No wash hung outside. No hens pecked bugs in the small, fenced yard. Sheep grazed on the pastureland surrounding it.

Curious, she pushed open the gate, which swung smoothly on oiled hinges. "Hallo."

When no one responded, she knocked on the door. Still nothing. She tried the latch and peeked inside. One room with a fireplace greeted her. The only furnishings were a sagging table and worn bench. She re-latched the door and sat down on the stoop.

She was an hour from Engel's. If they rented this place and had a horse, the distance would be manageable. But they didn't have a horse. Still, if she only walked to Wetzlar three days a week, it could work. But what about Gustav?

She stood up and scanned the countryside, finally spying a shepherd beside a brook. She backtracked and approached the man cautiously.

"Guten Tag. Do you know who owns the cottage?" She pointed to the small hut.

"The cottage belongs to Herr Martin. He owns all this land and its sheep." The shepherd flicked his hand in a circle.

"Do you know why it's empty?"

"They emigrated. Herr Martin wants to rent it. Are you interested?"

"I might be. Where would I find him?"

"Back a mile or so. Take the track next to the large rock."

"Danke." Annika paused, considering if she had time to backtrack.

"Don't wait long. Lots of families looking for a place."

"I know." Annika gave him a small wave and set off at a brisk pace for the Martin farmhouse.

Herr Martin was out in the fields. His wife was carding wool in the farmyard while two youngsters chased kittens. She informed Annika the cottage was available immediately for three thalers a month. The roof needed patched, which would fall to the tenants. Annika thanked her and headed home, wondering if she should tell Gustav. The rent was the same, but they'd be able to grow vegetables and keep hens. Would he consider it?

Gustav wasn't around when Annika reached the apartment. She heated water to wash the dishes that were crusted with food. She straightened the bed and snapped beans for supper.

He arrived at dinnertime, looking morose. "Finished my weaving today. We'll start dismantling the loom tomorrow. Onkel's headed out the end of next week."

Annika sank into a chair. "That was fast."

Gustav scrubbed his hands through his hair. "Erwin started at the steam engine shop this week, so I'll finish his cloth. I'll be working on that into next week, but after that…"

"There's still the linen to sell."

"But who's buying? Does Frau Engel want more?"

Annika shook her head. "There are barely any orders coming in, and the ladies have been choosing material that's in stock." She got up to stir the beans bubbling in their pot. "I brought beans, tomatoes, and lettuce as well as eggs and milk. What would you like for supper?"

"I'll have some beans. Hertha gave us a big lunch. Then I'm going out."

Annika tried to keep any sign of displeasure off her face. "Think I'll turn in early. It was a long walk."

Gustav grunted, and they ate in silence.

The Webers' last Sunday dinner was decidedly unpleasant.

Klara and Ella sniffled through most of the meal. Hertha looked like she'd aged five years and barely ate anything as she fussed over the three grandchildren she was leaving behind. Paula clung to Rosa's chubby baby boy until Rosa pried him away to visit with her family on their last Sunday in Wetzlar.

On the way home, Gustav led her down unfamiliar streets to a shabby row of half-timbered homes. "I heard about a room for let on this street. It's less than we pay now." He examined the doors. "I'm looking for a sun on the door."

When they finally spotted the yellow sun on a weathered door, Gustav knocked.

"Who's there?" a child's voice asked.

Gustav frowned. "Herr and Frau Weber to see the room for let."

A lad of about nine opened the door. "Follow me."

The smell of cabbage assaulted them as they entered a dirty kitchen. A toddler played near the hearth, but there were no signs of an adult.

"Pa's here, but he's feeling poorly." The young boy opened a door and scampered up a ladder staircase.

Annika took a deep breath and hiked up the skirts of her white dress, wishing Gustav had told her about this inspection so she could have chosen a different frock.

As her eyes came even with the grimy floor, Annika's foot slipped. Gustav supported her from behind. The boy took her hand and tugged her into the one-room attic apartment. There was room for a bed, wardrobe, table, and maybe her trunk, but nothing more. One window looked out to an even more decrepit half-timbered house with chunks missing from its plaster.

"It comes just as you see it, no furniture." The boy's face was thin, his arms skinny. "Just two thalers a month."

"My wife and I will discuss it." Gustav backed down the ladder, and Annika crept behind him. "Danke for showing it to us. I hope your Vater feels better soon."

The boy nodded and shut the door behind them.

Annika took a deep breath of fresh air. A headache pounded in her temples. She couldn't live there.

"That's not going to work." Gustav offered her his arm.

Relief coursed through Annika.

"September's rent is going to be a problem."

Annika peeked up at his worried face. "I saw a cottage on my way back from Braunfels."

"Why didn't you say something sooner?"

"It's an hour's walk and the same price as what we pay now."

"That doesn't help!"

"That's why I didn't mention it. The roof also needs repaired...but we'd be able to grow our own vegetables and keep some animals."

They walked in silence to their loft. Gustav poured himself a stein of beer. "We'll keep looking."

On August 11, 1843, Weber's closed permanently in Wetzlar. Gustav's Vater handed the keys of the shop over to the new owner and went to the Kellers for a few nights until the barge he'd arranged to take the looms and remaining furniture set off for Alstaden.

Annika, Gustav, and Erwin gathered early the morning he set out. He slipped both boys several thalers. "I'm sorry it's come to this. I'll try to see you when we ship cloth to Wetzlar."

Erwin shook his father's hand. "It's hard times everywhere. I'll be fine. I've got to go, or I'll be late to my new job." He loped away from the docks.

Annika handed Oskar a hunk of fresh pumpernickel bread. "Write and tell us how it's going."

"Ja." He blinked away the moisture in his eyes and clapped Gustav on the back. ""You're a smart man, son. You'll find work." At Conrad's call, he boarded the barge.

Annika waved half-heartedly until he was out of sight. "I'll be at Engel's this morning. I'd like to go out to the farm on Thursday. Dora should be harvesting some of the vegetables."

"That's fine." Gustav stared at the thalers in his hand. "At least we can pay September's rent."

"We have eight dress orders this month, so I should be able to work full days when I come back."

"Good. I'll go around to the engine shops today, see if there's some work, but first I'll walk you to Engel's. It's a little rough down here." He thrust the coins into his pocket.

When they reached Engel's, Gustav ushered her into the showroom. He put his hand in his pocket and withdrew three thalers. "I'm not sure when I'll be home tonight, so you settle the rent with Herr Hoffmann at a decent hour."

Annika stared at his retreating back. They never paid their

rent this early. Was Gustav removing the temptation to waste the money on drink? She hummed as she went into the back room to start sewing.

Chapter 38

The harvest was a dismal failure. Annika grieved over the straggly plants in Vater's fields. It would be another difficult winter. At least there would be enough work for her to continue sewing throughout September. Folks in the city had more money than farmers.

Wiping her forehead, she hoed weeds between the rows of beets. Later, she and Dora would pick beans. Tomorrow Lina and Frieda were coming to help snap them. They would be able to catch up on each other's lives while working together.

After hoeing a row, Annika crouched down in the dirt to weed close to the plants. When she breathed in the aroma of fresh dirt, peace settled over her like the sun on her shoulders. Her one regret in becoming a seamstress was the lack of time outdoors. She dug her hands into the soil to check on the beets. Almost big enough. Her mouth watered at the thought of pickled beets.

A little girl's singing drew her attention. Charlotte was crossing the farmyard with a stein. Annika stood up and brushed away the dirt clinging to her work dress and apron. Her niece walked slowly, focused on the stein, trying not to spill.

Annika met her at the edge of the garden.

"Mutter sent me with cold water." Charlotte handed the stein to Annika.

"Danke." Annika took a long drink. "Would you like some?"

Charlotte shook her head. "I'm supposed to take the weeds

to the pile for you."

"I'd appreciate that." Annika returned to weeding. By the time Charlotte had removed the weeds, it was time to get lunch.

After washing at the basin by the back door, they entered the kitchen to the smell of freshly baked bread.

"We're having bread with the butter you churned yesterday, Anna." Dora sliced thick slabs of warm barley bread.

"Sounds wunderbar."

The next day Lina and Frieda arrived shortly after the men departed for the fields.

"That's a lot of beans." Frieda's eyes bulged when she caught sight of four baskets lined up along the kitchen wall.

"There are more in the root cellar." Dora dumped a basket into a large pot of water and swished them around vigorously.

"Wouldn't it be easier to clean them out near the pump? Mutter always did it out there so she could rinse them twice without carrying as much water." Annika picked up another basket.

"Good idea."

Frieda, Lina, and Annika took the baskets out to the pump where Annika used a shallow pan to remove the worst of the dirt. Frieda rinsed them again, and Lina took the clean beans into the kitchen where she and Dora began snapping them.

"At least it's cool out here under the trees," Frieda said.

"Ja." Annika lifted her face to the breeze. "How did your green dress turn out?"

"I brought it to show you. It's almost finished, but it doesn't fit me quite right."

"I'll take a look. I'm sure we'll be able to figure it out."

It took a long time to rinse the dirt off six baskets of beans, but the cool water made the task bearable. Annika was glad her dress was damp when she entered the stuffy kitchen.

All four women sat down at the table, fingers flying as they snapped beans in pace with their conversation.

"How's married life, Lina?" Annika asked.

"Hans is great." Lina blushed. "We have some news. I'm expecting."

Annika's heart plunged, but she jumped up to give her friend a hug. "Congratulations!"

"Danke. I've been tired, and sick most mornings. That's why we didn't arrive earlier."

Dora shooed Helmuth back to his toys. "You were plenty early. Do you need a bite to eat?"

"I brought some bread since I couldn't eat this morning."

"Go ahead and eat. The rest of us already had breakfast." Annika brushed a pile of ends into the pail for the pigs.

"We appreciate all your help. Otherwise, this would take twice as long." Dora got up and brought Lina a cup of water.

"We appreciate your teaching us to make goats' cheese," Lina said.

"I was glad to. How many goats are you up to now?"

"A dozen. Hans said the next time we receive goats as payment, the men will slaughter two."

"At least goats aren't picky. They eat whatever we give them, and they keep the grass down." Frieda dropped beans into a crock. "And the cheese is real good."

Around noon, Helmuth toddled up to the table.

Dora picked him up and settled him in her lap. "Are you getting hungry?"

"I am." Charlotte jumped up.

"Have some beans." Annika handed her a long bean.

Charlotte wrinkled her nose. "I'm tired of beans." But she took a big bite.

Annika crunched on one, too. "These are good."

"But I want something to go with them." Juice dribbled down Charlotte's chin.

"When we're done, I'll make us some eggs and fried bread." Dora kneaded her back with both hands.

"Yum." Charlotte resumed snapping as fast as she could.

The women laughed and redoubled their efforts to keep up.

Annika's feet dragged as she climbed the narrow stairs to their attic. She hated these stairs. At least if they moved, she'd never need to climb them again. It was already late afternoon. Frieda's dress had needed a few alterations after lunch, which meant Annika had walked back in the heat of the day.

She set down her carpetbag and a basket overflowing with produce. Since she was worn out, she decided to sit and knit. She lifted the yellow yarn she'd chosen for a sweater into her lap. *Up, around, under, off, up, around...*

She jerked awake to the sound of footsteps at the top of the stairs. Stuffing her yarn and needles into a bag, she rose and smoothed her dress.

"No dinner?"

"Not just yet." She started to unload lettuce, cucumbers, and beans from the basket Dora had lent her. "I can make you some eggs real quick. How did things go around here while I was gone?"

Gustav grunted as he sank into her vacated chair. "One

day's work at Erwin's shop and a few errands for another. No one's taking on permanent workers. I'll write to Vater and see if it's different in Alstaden."

Annika's heart constricted. They couldn't move any farther from her family's farm. What would they eat? She infused cheer into her voice. "I have work for all of next month. Frau Engel told me right before I left."

"We may be able to meet the October rent even if we can't find a cheaper place." Gustav wiped his face with his hand.

"Dora sent a bottle of milk. Would you like to drink it, or shall I soak the old bread in it?"

Gustav sniffed at the small glass bottle. "That's all she could spare after all your work there?"

"It's all that would fit in the basket with everything else she sent."

Gustav shot out of his seat. "Don't talk back to me, woman."

Annika backed up into the wall. "I'll bring more next time." She could leave her work dress at the farm so she could carry more food. Her heart skittered in her chest.

Gustav returned to his chair and a day-old newspaper. "Hurry up with dinner. I'm going out."

Annika stole peeks at the news while she beat the eggs. In the early days of their marriage, Gustav read the news aloud to her. Maybe he'd leave the newspaper behind when he went out for the night. She used a little milk to soften the stale bread before frying it but poured most of the milk into a mug. Using a second pan, she fried eggs so dinner would be ready before he finished the paper. Just as he was folding it up, she set his filled plate on the table. "All set."

Without waiting for her, he shoveled food into his mouth. When had his last meal been? There was no food in the kitchen except what she'd brought from the farm and half a loaf of stale bread. If stretched, the eggs, butter, and produce would last a week. *If* she baked more bread. When could she bake it? She needed to work to make up the time she'd been gone. Ach! She'd go down and talk to Frau Hoffmann after Gustav left.

As the summer days slipped away, reports of the poor harvest flooded into Wetzlar. Prices rose.

Gustav couldn't find steady work.

They received a letter from his Vater that positions were also difficult to come by in Alstaden. His Vater encouraged them to stay near the Langes' farm. As it was, he slept on a sofa at Onkel's house to save on rent. Ella already had a bevy of beaus, so he expected her to marry by spring.

One piece of good news was the Catholic diocese in Limburg wanted the Webers' cloth for their altar and robes. Frau Hahn had secured them the job after the former linen supplier went out of business. The Webers had filled her February order and received another small order from her. She was sorry Annika hadn't delivered the cloth these last two times.

Gustav threw the missive into the fire and stormed down the stairs.

Annika sighed and stirred the vegetable soup she was making. He hadn't had so much as an odd job for the past week. There was no money for food. She would leave for the farm on Thursday. If she could convince him to come, at least he'd have something to eat besides porridge. They'd even have a ride with Paul, who had cut back on his supply trips to once a month. The Beckers were struggling like everyone else.

Gustav refused to go to the farm. Annika baked him a loaf of bread with the last of her flour and breathed a sigh of relief. The farm had become her refuge from Gustav's surliness. Although her Vater had once been almost as unpleasant, he wasn't the unhappy man he'd been after Mutter's death.

Charlotte and Helmuth had brought new joy into the house.

Chapter 39

Annika returned from the farm with a heavy sack of potatoes and a basket of eggs and vegetables. This needed to last for a month, except for bread. Arms aching, Annika put the foodstuffs away and surveyed the mess in the apartment. She needed to pump water and wash dishes. Every single plate and pan was dirty. At least nothing was stuck to the dishes. Gustav must have licked them clean.

Bone-tired from days of digging in the garden, topped off by the walk home, Annika took two pails down the flights of stairs. Frau Hoffmann was preparing dinner.

"Hallo, Annika. Have you been at the farm?"

"Ja, I've just returned."

"How's the harvest?"

"The vegetable garden's done well. The field crops were poor, but Vater thinks there's enough hay to get the livestock through the winter."

"That's something. How's work at the dress shop?"

"It's slow, but Frau Engel said there's five orders for next month, so I'll have work in the mornings."

Not every morning, but most. Perhaps more orders would come in.

"Dorothea's growing so fast she needs a new frock. I have some material to make over. Could you have a look?"

"I'd be happy to. Next week after I get caught up. You can't imagine the mess my husband's left."

Frau Hoffmann snorted. "He's been tromping up and down and banging pots the whole time you were gone."

Annika attached the buckets to the wooden yoke. She winced as she straightened.

"Ulrich!" Frau Hoffmann shouted. "Come help Frau Weber with the water."

Annika sent her a grateful look.

"You look done in. I'm baking bread Friday afternoon if you want to bring some dough down."

"Danke." Annika chatted with Frau Hoffmann while Ulrich went up the street to the town fountain.

When he returned and removed the yoke, she clutched a pail and struggled up the stairs behind him. Wiping sweat from her eyes, she turned to her next task but nearly cried when she realized there wasn't any kindling. She was too tired to retrace her steps and look for sticks. Then she spied a newspaper under the table. It was dated several days ago. If she lit it along with the straw cushioning the eggs in her basket, she might get the charcoal to light.

Kneeling, she breathed a prayer and managed to coax a spark to catch the paper, then the straw. She blew on it until the flame licked at the stick. If the wood was dry enough…

To her immense relief, it began to burn. She poured water into a cauldron and swung it over the fire. It would take a long while to heat. In the meantime, there weren't any clean dishes and the table was sticky. She washed a tomato, closed her eyes, and took a big juicy bite. Savoring the freshness, she sank into a chair.

She was halfway through the dishes when Gustav clattered up the stairs.

"I'm glad you're back. Is there something to eat besides porridge?"

Annika dried a bowl. "Would you like some eggs and potatoes? And there's milk to drink."

"I'd like Kaffee, but we haven't had beans for months."

"I miss it, too." Annika deftly broke four eggs and whipped them before pouring them into a heated pan.

Gustav filled a stein with milk and took a few gulps. Then he began looking for something on the table and chairs. "I'm sure I left a copy of the paper here. Have you seen it?"

Annika stiffened. "It was on the floor, so I thought it was trash. I used it to light the fire."

Gustav pounced on her, twisting her arms behind her back. "How could you be so stupid?" he yelled into her face. "Erwin gave it to me. I hadn't finished reading it."

Tears seeped from Annika's eyes. "I'm sorry. I didn't know."

Gustav gave her a vicious tug and released her. "Don't burn my dinner, woman."

Annika grabbed a long-handled spoon and stirred the eggs. She washed a potato and sliced it with unsteady hands. When the eggs finished, she put most on a plate in front of her husband, reserving a small mound on a second plate. Adding the potato and a slice of onion to the pan, she huddled by the hearth, keeping her distance from her husband.

She approached the table with the hot pan in her aproned grasp and scooped most of the potatoes onto Gustav's empty plate. Then she backed into the hearth's corner, watching him warily while she toyed with her small portion.

Gustav shoveled the hot food into his mouth, grunting as he finished. He mashed his cap onto his head and departed without a word or glance for Annika.

Annika's body relaxed. The lump in her throat melted, allowing her to finish her meal. After all, there were only eight eggs left. Tonight's meal was a feast. When every dish was washed and stacked neatly on the crate in the corner, she used a little hot water to bathe herself, put on a clean shift, and sank into bed.

The next day she rose before Gustav and dressed in the kitchen. She could count every one of Gustav's fingers on her tender arms. At least these purplish bruises were easy to hide.

Unwilling to wake him, she settled for eating another tomato. She took beans and a round of goat cheese to work. Perhaps if she shared, someone would reciprocate with bread. Otherwise, it would be a very strange lunch, but at least it would fill her.

"Did your sister-in-law make the cheese?" Olga asked as she spread it on half a piece of thick, rye bread.

Annika spread the rest of the cheese on the other half. "Ja."

"It's delicious." Olga patted Annika's arm in approval.

Annika winced.

"I'm sorry. What's wrong?"

Annika shifted. "Too much hoeing."

Olga quirked an eyebrow. "I'm not a farmer, but wouldn't it be your shoulders and back that would be sore?"

Annika dropped her eyes. "I...used Gustav's newspaper to light the fire last night. It was several days old, and I found it on the floor. Turns out he wasn't done with it."

Olga took Annika's hand between her plump ones. "Is it only your arms?"

"Ja. He grabbed me. It's not too bad, just a little tender."

"You don't deserve treatment like that, Annika. Has the man found any work?"

"Nein."

Olga's lips twisted. "Feeling like a failure can make a man mean. It's not an excuse, but it *is* a reason. Men turn to drink, too, to forget the frustration, for a little while."

"It just makes everything worse. Especially when he uses the few coins we have to drink."

Olga sighed. "They need something to do. If there's no work, drinking fills the time.

"My husband's not making many shoes these days either. We're going to move in with his mother above the cobbler's shop."

"Oh no! You're losing your home?"

Olga's eyes shone with tears. "Ja. It hurts, but we don't need all the space now that our children are grown. We've been renting all these years. Home is more than four walls."

From her one visit to Olga's, Annika pictured the bright kitchen with vines perfuming the air through the window. She squeezed Olga's hand. "How long have you lived there?"

"Nearly twenty years. I won't miss cleaning the place." Olga took another bite of bread. "I'm just glad we have a place to go. My husband's family has owned the cobbler's shop with the apartment above it for generations. It'll feel like home soon enough."

Chapter 40

During the fall, Gustav found enough work to buy barley flour and keep himself in beer. Annika sewed at Engel's and visited the farm for a week in both September and October to harvest and preserve food. She and Gustav were barely speaking to each other.

She looked forward to December when Matt and Vater would slaughter five hogs, which meant at least a taste of meat. Weihnachten would follow with presents for the children, tasty treats, and pine boughs draped around the farmhouse. She wished she could join her family in Braunfels for Christmas, but she was needed at Engel's.

Paul's supply trip fell early in the month, so Annika would be at the farm for the hog butchering. She dressed in wool petticoats and a wool shawl with her green cape. With a heavy riding blanket on her lap and a scarf wrapped over her bonnet, Annika stayed warm for the forty-five-minute ride but gave up on conversation after a couple attempts. Their voices were too muffled to understand each other.

When they reached the farm, Annika jumped out as Bruno barked a welcome. "Danke!"

"Have a good visit. See you later." Paul turned Tilli back down the drive.

Helmuth came barreling out of the house with only a sweater on. Annika scooped him up. "You need a coat. Let's get you back inside."

As she entered, Charlotte hugged her around the waist. "Kaffee's ready. Do you want some?"

"Absolutely! Do you think you could take my bag upstairs?" It was empty except for warm socks knitted for every member of the family for Weihnachten. She could fill it with food to take back to Wetzlar.

Dora took Helmuth from Annika. "If you're a good boy and play with your blocks for a bit, you can have some warm milk while Tante and I have Kaffee." She set him down, and he scampered over to the toys on the rug in front of the fireplace. "Are you frozen?"

"Nein. My feet are cold, but otherwise I'm quite toasty." Annika peeled off her scarf, bonnet, and cape.

"Pull up a chair to the hearth and warm your feet while I heat up the Kaffee." Dora pulled the pot over the hearth and prodded the embers underneath. "The men are planning to butcher tomorrow, so today we'll chop the onions and herbs and clean the sausage grinder so we'll be ready. Matt already got the salt from Vogel's."

Charlotte climbed into Annika's lap as soon as she returned from the loft. "I'll warm you up, Tante, and we can keep each other warm tonight."

Annika tickled her. "Is that so? We won't need any bricks heated by the fire?"

"We'll need them at the beginning. It's too cold to get into bed without them."

Annika smoothed back Charlotte's hair. "You're a wise little woman."

Dora brought Annika a mug of Kaffee. "Hop off now, Charlotte. Go sit at the table with your milk. Helmuth, you too."

The children scurried over to the table for their warm drinks.

Dora sank onto the couch next to Annika. "I'm glad you're

here for the butchering. I just finished making goat cheese. I've got a soup going for tonight."

"That will be perfect for a cold night."

"We can bake Äpfelkuchen this afternoon. The Steins gave us a bushel of apples for Matt's help with the harvest, and a jug of fresh cider."

"Pork and apples will be a welcome change."

Dora glanced toward the Kinder and lowered her voice. "Have you been eating enough?"

"Ja, but a lot of porridge. At least I have the honey Matt found at the edge of the pasture to give it some flavor. We have potatoes for dinner most nights."

"You can take some sausage home with you."

"I'd like that."

Dora stirred her Kaffee. "Elsa is coming tomorrow."

"Wunderbar. I can't wait to see her."

"She's not the only one Vater invited."

Annika's pleasure dissipated. "Don't tell me…"

"Ehrich is butchering with the men, and Margarete—"

"Oh, Dora, why?"

"Your Vater doesn't think of things like feelings."

Annika searched her sister-in-law's face. "Is it hard for you to live with him?"

"He's very blunt." Dora grimaced. "I'm not the best cook, and he's not patient with my efforts some nights."

"No. I love him, but…it was hard living here alone with him."

"I can imagine. Matt's talked to him, and he's gotten better. As far as I know, he's always good with the kids, but Matt and I don't let them go off alone with him. That won't always be the case as they get older, especially with Helmuth." Dora cast a worried glance at the toddler who'd finished his milk and was chasing the cat around the room.

Annika grasped Dora's hand. "Matt's one of the kindest men I know. I'm sure Helmuth will take after his dad."

"I hope so." Dora squeezed Annika's hand before letting go and taking the mugs for refills. "But about Margarete. I don't know if she'll come or not."

"Doesn't she have a baby now? She won't stay long if she does come, will she?"

Dora smiled conspiratorially. "We'll try to encourage her in that direction."

Butchering day dawned cool and sunny. Ehrich, Margarete, Elsa, and baby Georg arrived in their wagon shortly after breakfast.

Annika took a deep breath to steady herself and went out to greet them. "Thank you for coming to help. Ehrich, the men are out at the pigsty. Vater said to let your horse free in the south pasture.

"Margarete, Charlotte was sneezing this morning, so it might be best if everyone stayed out of the house. I'll be sharpening the knives over at the whetstone. You know how important that is."

When a look of consternation passed over Margarete's face, Annika knew she remembered giving Annika a dull knife to cut up cider apples. That had been two years ago when they were vying for Ehrich's attention and Frau Stein's approval.

"You can help the men clean the pigs."

Margarete grimaced but handed Georg to Elsa and marched off in the direction of the pump where the first hog lay on an oilskin.

"That job's not going to last long for five pigs." Elsa gave Annika a one-armed hug.

"Dora will come out after a while and suggest Margarete clean the intestines." Annika smirked. "How soon do you think she'll go home?"

Elsa laughed. "Not long after she's given that task. She always pawns the dirty tasks off on someone else." Elsa looked longingly at the house. "Do we really have to stay outside all day?"

"No. Charlotte *was* sneezing this morning, but only because she was helping her mother prepare the herb mixture for the sausages we'll make tomorrow. She inhaled some pepper."

Elsa giggled. "Oh, Annika, I've missed you so much."

"And I've missed you. You've gotten so tall, and even prettier if that's possible. I'll plait your hair before you go home if you'd like."

"I'd love it." When Georg pulled her hair, Elsa asked, "What should I do with this little one? We can't stand outside all morning until his mother decides to go home."

"Why don't you take him to the barn to see the animals? Keep him away from the black cat, but the gray one is friendly enough. I'll help Dora until the knives need resharpened."

It took about two hours to kill and clean five pigs. Annika was kept busy sharpening the butcher knives for the three men, so Dora enlisted Elsa's aid to take Kaffee to the workers while Margarete nursed Georg in the barn.

When Margarete emerged, Dora said, "The next task for us women is cleaning the intestines. We'll need them to make sausage tomorrow. Could you start on that, Margarete? I'll be out as soon as I take care of these dishes." She began gathering the steins onto a tray.

Vater stood up. "Well, men. Let's hang these hogs and get

as much meat out of them as possible. Where's the tub for the lard?"

"I saw it in the barn, Vater. I'll bring it out to you." Annika hurried to fetch the tin tub. She scrubbed it out before setting it near the hanging carcasses.

Margarete had just been given the first length of intestines and was removing the offal with a look of disgust on her pretty face. Annika took a dulled knife from Matt, washed it, and retreated to the whetstone in the barn.

Annika had sharpened two more knives and the men had carved another pig before Margarete came into the barn. "Elsa, it's not good to have Georg out in the cold for too long, so we're going home in the wagon. Ehrich will walk home later."

Neither Elsa nor Annika pointed out the barn was almost as warm as the house. Instead, Annika said, "Without your expertise, we really could use Elsa."

"And how am I going to get Georg home by myself?"

"I'll come with you. Then I'll bring the wagon back." Elsa handed the baby to Margarete and went to hitch up their horse.

The grinding of the whetstone filled the barn, but when Annika finished honing the knife, an awkward silence stretched between her and Margarete. "Well, I'll just take this out to the men and get started on the next pile of intestines. Thanks for your help today."

Margarete didn't bother to reply.

Annika was still chuckling when she handed Matt the knife.

"What's so funny, little sis?"

"Oh, that Georg. He's a cutie."

Ehrich beamed with pride. "He's our bright spot. That's for sure."

"Margarete and Elsa are going to take him home, so he doesn't get a chill. Charlotte was sneezing this morning, so I warned them away from the house. Elsa's planning to come back."

Vater sliced the pig belly. "Do you want ham and bacon as payment for your work today, Ehrich, or two hams?"

"I'm partial to bacon, so we'd appreciate some of both. Danke, Wolff."

"It's only right. We should be done before sunset if the women can keep up with the intestines and such. Ah, here comes Dora now."

Dora and Annika moved to tubs holding the pigs' innards.

"It worked," Annika whispered to Dora.

"I knew it would, but what about Elsa?"

"She said she'd drive the wagon back."

"Smart Fräulein. It's a shame she has to put up with so much. She watches Georg more than his own mother does."

"Maybe her good nature will rub off on that little boy."

"Annika, we need the knives sharpened," Vater called.

"Coming, Vater."

The rest of the day passed pleasantly. Elsa, Dora, and Annika worked together to clean the intestines, which would be used for covering crocks of preserved food as well as making sausage. Annika kept up with sharpening the knives. Even with a break for lunch, everything had been accomplished by four o'clock.

While Ehrich enjoyed a stein of beer with the men, Annika plaited Elsa's hair into intricate braids. "They should stay in overnight, if you don't toss and turn too much."

"I'm gonna try to make them last at least two more days. I

want Stan Vogel to see how pretty I am."

Annika looked at the twelve-year-old in concern. "Don't be in too much of a hurry to grow up."

"I want to make my own home…far away from Margarete."

"I sympathize, but don't settle for any man who comes along."

"If I were to marry Stan, I'd get to be a shopkeeper's wife instead of a farmer's. I think I'd like that."

"Make sure he's a good man, like your brother or Matt."

"I will." Elsa hopped off the sofa as Ehrich called her name. "I'll try to convince Mutter to let me come tomorrow to make sausage with you, but I don't think she'll let me."

"We would love to see you again, but Dora and I will be able to handle it if you can't come."

With Matt's help grinding the meat, Dora and Annika finished making all the sausage on Saturday, and Annika had a full basket to take back to Wetzlar, along with a slab of bacon. That night she passed out her simple Weihnachten gifts to her family, and they sang a few carols before retiring to bed.

After church on Sunday, Matt drove her back to Wetzlar.

Chapter 41

W hen Annika returned from Braunfels, her thoughts turned to Weihnachten. She was working on a scarf for Gustav, and she decided to send Herr Weber a card like she saw in the shop windows. She couldn't afford the luxury of buying one, but she could create one.

When the Weber business closed, Gustav had brought home odds and ends that included paper and pencils. Annika cut a square of paper and penciled some pine boughs with Frohe Weihnachten arching above. After practicing on scraps of newspaper, she drew a flying dove. A bird of peace seemed appropriate for Christmas.

She added her name and Gustav's in her most elegant handwriting. Satisfied, she fashioned an envelope, addressed it, and mailed it on Friday, December 15. Even if it didn't arrive in time for Weihnachten, it would arrive by the New Year, and he would know they were thinking of him.

Since several women expected their gowns by Christmas Eve, the shop hummed with activity for a full week. Frau Engel gave them Weihnachten off, but Annika sewed for full days the rest of the week to prepare another two evening gowns for New Year's. As she stitched, she wished for work for Gustav, a healthy baby, and a bountiful harvest in 1844.

Their clients appreciated the fit of their stylish new gowns. Frau Engel didn't allow them to take the gowns until they were paid in full. "Now I can buy new cloth. Annika, can you get word to the Webers that I'd like twelve ells of pink linen? I'm sure we'll need enough for at least one spring gown."

"I'm expecting a letter anytime from Herr Weber. I'll ask him in my reply."

"Very good." Frau Weber handed Annika her wages. "That was the good news. Now for the bad. We only have four dresses ordered for January. I won't need your skills until the middle of the month at the earliest. There are always fewer for January, but this is the worst I've ever seen."

Annika suspected she wouldn't be needed until the end of the month, if then. Although she clasped three thalers in her hand, more than she usually earned, they wouldn't sustain her little family for long. But at least she could pay the January rent.

"I'll be in touch as soon as enough orders come in."

"I understand." Annika donned her green cloak, bid Olga and Greta goodbye, and stepped out into the winter night.

Fighting back tears, she rushed through a snow shower, hoping Gustav had kept a fire going so she could cook their dinner of sausage and potatoes.

He was hunched in front of a banked fire when she dragged herself up the stairs. "What's wrong?" He set aside the newspaper.

"Frau Engel has no work for me for at least two weeks." Annika removed her cloak and bonnet.

"It's harder for me to find jobs in the cold weather. Did she pay you?"

Annika set the thalers on the table.

"We have enough to stay here for another month." Gustav scooped up the coins.

"But I don't see how we'll meet February's rent. We're going to need the last thaler for necessities like flour." Annika took a rope of sausage from the rafters and started slicing one.

Gustav noticed the few remaining links. "There aren't

many left."

"Next time I go out to the farm, the ham will be smoked."

Gustav brightened. Ham was his favorite. "When's Paul's next trip to Wetzlar?"

"It should be next Thursday if the weather's not too bad."

"Are you going back with him?"

"I might as well. I don't have any sewing here. There's always work to be done at the farm."

"And you can bring back ham and anything else you can get."

Annika pivoted to the pan she had heating on coals. Gustav's words made her feel guilty, like she was taking food out of her family's mouths, but she and Gustav desperately needed it. Overwhelmed, she whispered, "What are we going to do?"

Gustav looked at the thalers. "I'm going to pay Hoffmann now. That may earn us some goodwill if we can't find cheaper lodging and February's rent is late." He sent her an almost kind look. "We'll think of something."

The next morning Annika rose quietly to attend church. She was bone weary, but there was nothing to do in the apartment except stare at Gustav and imagine how many Pfennige he had spent on beer last night.

Annika slid into the Kellers' pew next to Erwin. As the pine boughs and candles delighted her senses, the choral music lifted her spirits. A peacefulness settled over her as the minister read Psalm 90. "'Lord, you have been our dwelling-place in all generations.'"

Annika's mind flitted back to Braunfels and Pastor Brandt's explanation of the verse. He had said a dwelling-place is a home, so the verse could read, "'Lord, you have been our home since the beginning.'" Home is the place we feel comfortable and safe. Annika had known exactly what the pastor was describing. It was her home before Mutter died. She'd never found that feeling again, except perhaps in the first days of her marriage.

Her attention returned to the minister who was expounding on God's view of the brevity of a thousand years. "It may seem like Hessen has been suffering for a long time with crop failures and food shortages, but it's the blink of an eye for the Almighty. He can send the right measures of rain and sunshine to grow abundant crops this year. But we need to examine ourselves for any sin that would block God's blessings.

"Verses seven and eight say that we are consumed by God's righteous anger for our iniquities and secret sins. We must repent so our days are not consumed by His anger. I call on you to repent now. Confess and turn from your sin. Not like the Catholics do in their confessionals. Simply name your sins to God and ask His forgiveness based on the blood of Jesus.

"'What sin?' you ask. 'I don't bow down to false idols or profane the Sabbath or murder or commit adultery.'

"How about the sin of pride? Or greed? Or laziness? Your sin may not be obvious to others. You may think it's secret, but our Almighty God knows all. You cannot hide any sin from Him, no matter how small."

The reverend closed his Bible. "Now we will take time for silent prayer. Beg God for His forgiveness so He will bless our land once again."

Annika bowed her head. Should she confess her angry feelings toward Gustav? No! He should be here confessing his violence, drunkenness, and wastefulness. Since God hated these sins and responded to them with righteous anger, surely she was allowed to be angry too.

Almighty Father, please change Gustav. He's spending money we need for food on beer, and you've seen how he treats me. Annika went on and on, listing Gustav's misdeeds. *Help me know what to do, Lord. Please continue to provide our daily bread and a roof over our heads.*

Prayer didn't make Annika feel any better. She was seething by the time she reached their apartment. Gustav might not be able to find work, but he could refrain from spending what she earned. She should have held back the last thaler. Determined to go through his pockets and regain some coins, she charged up the stairs.

Gustav was sitting by the hearth. He looked almost... hopeful.

He waved a sheet of paper in the air. "Vater wrote. He says there will be railroad work near Alstaden. Prussia approved a line from Cologne to Minden two weeks ago. I should go immediately. I can stay at Onkel's."

The anger seeped out of Annika like milk from a cracked pitcher. Had God heard her prayer? She sank down into a chair and struggled to collect herself. "If there's a chance for good work, ja."

Gustav stood. "Can you spare me some provisions?"

"We have bread. You can take the rest of the sausages and some potatoes."

Gustav stood and took coins out of his pocket. Annika was relieved there were so many. He'd exchanged her thaler for smaller coins like Silbergoschen and Pfennige, but it didn't look like he'd wasted many on drink last night.

Her heart sank as Gustav counted out ten Pfennige. "Can you get by with this until I can deposit money in the bank for you? I'll have a word with Erwin before I go. He can withdraw it for you."

246

"I'll try. Send word as soon as you know about a job."

"I will."

Annika swung a pot over the fire to heat water for tea. Dora had given her peppermint leaves from the garden. She needed something to calm her.

"Can you pack for me? I'm going to Kellers' to see Erwin." Gustav threw on a coat and hat.

Annika settled down with her tea, a piece of bread, and her knitting. Gazing around the little room, her heart lifted. Maybe they would be all right.

Chapter 42

Before dawn, Annika handed Gustav his blue scarf and gave him a quick hug.

"No doubt I'll find rides along the way. I just hope I make it in time to get a job." Gustav grabbed the carpet bag and rushed down the stairs.

Annika began to slowly wash the bowls and spoons. How could she keep busy until Thursday when Paul would arrive? She had a remnant of blue linen to make Fritzie a little jacket. Later today she could visit with Frau Hoffmann and ask if her family had any sewing needs. Maybe she could trade her skills for some meals so she wouldn't need to spend any of her Pfenninge at the market before she left for Braunfels.

Cheered by that thought, Annika spread out the linen on the scrubbed table. She was able to cut out a pair of short pants along with the coat.

In exchange for altering some of Herr Hoffmann's old clothes for Ulrich, Annika was allowed to share the Hoffmanns' soup and bread.

On Wednesday, Annika went to Olga's new home above the cobbler's. Olga's mother-in-law told them funny stories about her sons' growing-up antics. Annika's belly hurt from laughing over a story about their trimming the neighbor's poodle's hair.

When she stayed for dinner, they all bowed their heads and recited the obligatory prayer. "Come, Lord Jesus, be our guest, and let these Thy gifts to us be blessed."

Annika was surprised when Herr Schumacher continued.

"And please bring more work to Engel's."

All the Schumachers said "Amen" in unison.

Over cabbage soup, Olga's husband revealed his inherited talent for humorous anecdotes. Annika enjoyed herself immensely and fell into an untroubled sleep when she returned to her loft.

Dressing warmly and carrying her bag and Dora's food basket with Fritzie's new outfit, Annika arrived at the Becker's supplier as the eleven o'clock church bells tolled.

Paul paused from loading the wagon. "Hallo, Annika. We'll be ready soon."

Annika went inside to keep warm.

Within a half hour, the wagon was leaving the city center of Wetzlar with Paul and Annika bundled against the cold in hats, scarves, and lap robes. Once again conversation was difficult, so Annika studied their surroundings, squinting against the bright winter sun.

Halfway to the Lange farm, she pointed out a pile of rags in the middle of the road. Paul guided Tilli around the rubbish. When they were abreast of the ragged cloth, she noticed a boot and then a flickering hand.

Grabbing Paul's arm, Annika yelled, "Stop!"

Startled, Paul pulled Tilli up abruptly. The good-natured mare snorted in annoyance but came to a stop just beyond the obstruction.

Annika jumped down and grasped the cold hand. "Why are you in the road?"

A boy's pinched face rose from a coat with more patches than original material. "Ma sent me for help, but I fell."

Annika looked around and saw the cottage she'd inquired about in the fall. "Is your Mutter in there?"

"Ja, and my sister and brother. They're sick with fevers."

"Let's get you out of the road. Can you stand if I help you up?"

The little fellow nodded, so Annika tugged on his thin arms until he was standing. She removed a glove and touched his forehead. "No fever. Have you been sick?"

"A few days ago. I'm better now, but dizzy."

Paul moved the wagon off the road and hitched Tilli to the gatepost. He lifted the boy and led the way to the cottage which had a thin plume of smoke rising from the chimney. The stench of sickness in the cottage was overwhelming. Paul set the child down. "Can you go check on your Mutter for us? We don't want to startle her."

When the boy shuffled across the room to the single bed, Paul pushed Annika back out into the fresh air. "We don't know what we're dealing with here. Stay outside."

They hovered in the doorway as the boy whispered, "Ma, I found help."

The woman in the bed coughed, stroking her son's brown hair. "You're a good boy, Josef. Check on your brother."

Josef went to a pallet next to the hearth. "Wake up!" He shook his brother's shoulders before returning to his mother. "I'm sorry, Ma."

"It was his time. It's no fault of yours." Tears tracking down her cheeks, she patted his arm. "Your sister passed a little while ago." She showed him the still bundle beside her. Josef collapsed on the dirt floor and shook with sobs.

In two strides, Paul scooped him up and took him outside to Annika. "There's a blanket in the back of the wagon. He needs to have his clothes stripped off to leave this contagion here. You can wrap him up in the blanket. We'll take him to my Mutter."

Annika ran to fetch the wool blanket and assisted Josef in pulling off his boots and discarding his clothes. She wrapped his emaciated little body in the scratchy wool. Even before he sickened, he must have been starving. Sitting on a bench and leaning against the cottage, he closed his eyes.

Paul ducked out of the cottage and dropped his voice. "She's not long for this world. We'd best take care of the boy."

"Where's the father?"

"Died two weeks ago."

"We shouldn't leave her to die alone."

Paul shook his head. "Whatever she has is probably contagious. Josef seems to be over whatever it was. He needs broth and a warm place to sleep."

"Your Mutter will be able to take care of him." Annika thought for a moment. "I'll stay. The children's bodies need washed for burial. I can do that. As soon as the woman passes, I'll open the door and windows and air the place out."

Paul's brow furrowed. He blew out a breath. "All right. I'll come back for you." He gently lifted Josef into the front of the wagon.

Annika took two empty buckets from the front porch and filled them at the well. When she heard hens clucking, she freed them from their coop, scattered grain from a nearby bin, and filled an empty water dish.

She took a steadying breath and returned to the death-ridden cottage. "I'm going to stay with you and prepare the children for burial," she told the sick woman. "Would you like some water?"

"Ja, so thirsty."

Annika supported the woman so she could drink without choking.

"Danke. I'm Liza."

"You're welcome, Liza. My name is Annika Weber. Paul Becker has taken Josef to his family's bakery where he'll be well cared for." Annika poured the water into a large pot and added fuel to the fire. "Would you like anything else?"

"Could I have the blanket there by the fire? My Oma knitted it when I was a child."

Annika freed it from the dead child, who looked about nine, and took it to Liza.

"It'll be a comfort to me." Liza hugged it.

Annika retreated to the hearth and sat down. When the water was warm, she found a rag and began to wash the young boy. Unable to find a decent set of boys' clothes, she dressed him in a long shirt that must have belonged to his father.

"May I prepare your little girl?" The feverish mother didn't seem to hear, so Annika lifted the bundle from the straw mattress. The toddler's hollow cheeks and peach-fuzz blond hair brought tears to her eyes. *This little one deserved better.*

She glanced over at the mother struggling for breath. At least she wasn't awake to watch her children being prepared for burial.

Annika washed the little one's body. She looked in a trunk and found a blue dress trimmed with lace. It was slightly large, but she slipped it over the girl's head.

Just as she was finishing, Liza woke and held out her hands for her youngest. After sponging down Liza's feverish face, Annika laid the toddler in the crook of her mother's arm. Liza sighed and drifted off to sleep.

At dusk, Annika shut the chickens in their coop. She searched the small yard for wood and found some sticks and logs by the back door. Stoking the fire, she considered whether it would be safe to make herself a cup of tea. She decided to wait for Paul, but she did drink some fresh water from the well. Sitting in a chair by the fire, she dozed off.

When she woke, Liza was stirring. "You should take my Kate. You did such a good job cleaning her up. Lay her right there by her brother." Talking seemed to exhaust her, and she closed her eyes. A smile flickered across her lips. "Soon I'll be with them again."

About a half hour later, she whispered, "It's so beautiful, warm, and light. I'm goin' home." Her breathing became raspy, until it stilled altogether.

Annika opened the doors and windows before preparing the woman's body, mulling over her last words. What had she seen? It must have been Heaven. How could Liza call a place she'd never been home?

Maybe because her husband and children were there. Or maybe it was something else entirely.

Chapter 43

P aul returned shortly after Liza's death. Annika shed her clothes behind the cottage in exchange for clean ones brought by Paul. They put the chickens in the wagon and drove to Becker's.

The Beckers insisted she shouldn't expose her family to illness, so she spent the night in Lucie's former bed at the bakery. Josef slept in a warm lean-to usually stacked with supplies. Frau Becker had plied him with three bowls of chicken soup over the course of the afternoon until he sank into a deep sleep. "I think he's going to be just fine," she told Annika. As Annika ate soup and rye bread, she told Lucie's Mutter about the possibility of a railroad job for Gustav.

"I pray for you two every day, and now the good Lord's sent you here." Frau Becker washed the dinner dishes while Annika sipped chamomile tea. "I want you to stay in bed tomorrow and rest. No arguments. You can read one of the Dickens novels on Lucie's bookshelves."

Annika felt so tired she couldn't summon the strength to argue. Troubling dreams woke her repeatedly, nightmares of being tucked against her mother's side as her mother died. She woke sweaty and tossed the covers off. Later, she woke shaking with cold and burrowed under the soft quilts. Exhausted, she slept until the sun was high.

Finally, a tap at the door wakened her. "Anna, Liebling, are you all right?" Frau Becker cracked the door and peered in.

Annika licked her dry lips. "I think so." She reached for a cup of water on the nightstand.

"All right, dear. Go back to sleep."

Annika drifted back to sleep. When she woke up, she pulled on yesterday's borrowed dress and crept down to the kitchen for some food. The Beckers were waiting on customers in the storefront. While the thick slices of wheat bread toasted, she peeked into the lean-to where Josef snoozed on a straw ticking in the corner. When the toast was a perfect shade of brown, she slathered it with jam. Finished eating, she went back upstairs to read.

Tired of reading, she added embroidery to Fritzie's pants until it was time to start dinner. When she went downstairs, the kitchen was empty. Noticing a pile of potatoes, Annika finished scrubbing them just as Frau Becker bustled into the kitchen. "You're out of bed!"

"I was getting bored. I feel fit as a fiddle."

Lucie's Mutter touched her forehead. "You look rested and well. All right, if you could slice the potatoes and fry them with sausage and herbs, it would be a big help. The bakery's been busy all morning. Everyone's coming in to find out about Josef's family.

"The doctor stopped in to examine the little fellow. He doesn't think the family had anything that would require a quarantine. Josef was starving before he caught something minor. It sounds like it turned to pneumonia for the mother and siblings. Josef said they were all coughing.

"The doctor's seen this tragedy over and over already this winter. He says it's high time the Adelsverein helped some of the poor emigrate.

"Anyway, you can go home with your family after church if you're still feeling fine on Sunday. Until then you'll stay with us." She smiled fondly at Annika.

The shop bell announced another customer. "We may not have any bread left for our own dinner tonight." Frau Becker hurried back to the bakery.

While chopping herbs and sausages, Annika puzzled over Josef's future. Was there a relative who could take him in?

When the little boy entered the kitchen rubbing his eyes, Annika gave him a one-armed hug. "As soon as I get these in the pan, I'll pour you some milk. Go ahead and sit at the table so the grease doesn't pop and burn you."

Josef's eyes grew wide at the sight of the sausage and potatoes. How long had it been since the child tasted meat? "Would you like a cookie with your milk?"

Josef's blue eyes widened further when she set a gingersnap next to his milk. "Danke." Before she could even stir the sausage, he had gobbled down every last crumb.

"Dinner's coming soon. Try to eat slow so you don't upset your tummy."

He nodded solemnly.

"Do you have an Oma or Opa nearby?"

"Nein. They lived in the same place we used to, far away. When we moved, we had to sleep in the wagon two nights."

"Did you live in a big city?"

"Nein, it was a farm."

"When you traveled here in the wagon, was the sun in your eyes in the afternoon, or was it behind your back?"

Josef tilted his head. "In my eyes. I needed my hat."

This family may have been fleeing the same crop failures that brought Matt's family home just over a year ago.

Paul clomped into the kitchen. "Guten Abend. Dinner smells good, Annika. Doesn't it, Josef?"

"Ja, sehr."

Paul ruffled Josef's hair. "You look better today."

"I feel better."

Herr and Frau Becker soon joined them at the kitchen table. "Come, Lord Jesus, be our guest, and let these Thy gifts to us be blessed," they all prayed.

"I spoke with Pastor Brandt." Paul spooned food onto his and Josef's plates. "The funerals will be tomorrow at ten at the church. It's too cold to stand outside for long."

"Would you like to go, dear, while I tend the shop?" Herr Becker bit into a sausage.

"Ja, danke." Frau Becker patted Josef's knee. "I'll keep an eye on these two to ensure they don't overdo."

After dinner, the men engaged the boy with checkers while the women washed and dried the dishes. Content with the warmth from the fire and the good food and company, Annika sat in a rocker and continued embroidering before retiring early with the family.

"We have to be up at four to start the bread ovens." Herr Becker climbed the stairs behind his wife while Paul picked up Josef and laid him on his makeshift bed.

Annika pulled a quilt snugly over the sleeping boy. "I wonder what will happen to the little fellow?"

"Neither the doctor nor Pastor Brandt have found any relatives. When the cottage is cleared out, maybe they'll find an address."

"I wish he could stay with me, but I don't even know where I'm going to live."

"Even if you had the room, who would watch him while you work?"

"Right now, I don't have any work."

"You will soon, Anna. You're too good of a seamstress not to find work."

Warmed by his faith in her, Annika nodded.

"He'll be taken care of, one way or another. I'm sure of it."

Secure in Paul's assurances, Annika sank into Lucie's bed and drifted to sleep.

"'And if I go and prepare a place for you, I will come again and will take you to myself, so that where I am, there you may be also.'" Pastor Brandt lifted his eyes from his Bible to the three coffins crowding the front of the Kirche. "This is Jesus' promise to us in John 14 verse 3.

"Jesus came back for Liza Winter and her two children. We mourn because they're no longer with us, but there was rejoicing in Heaven over God's children coming home. Jesus has prepared a dwelling-place big enough for all of us in that perfect place. It will feel more like home than any home we've experienced on earth." His eyes roved over the crowd before settling on Josef huddled against Annika in the front pew. "And now let's pray 'The Lord is my Shepherd.'"

The funeral goers stood and recited the familiar words. It had been the prayer at Annika's mother's funeral. She squeezed Josef's shoulder. "'Even though I walk through the darkest valley, I fear no evil; for you are with me.'" Annika shuddered. Sometimes evil seemed much closer than at other times. Surely death was evil. It had separated this youngster from his entire family.

Her attention snapped back to the last line of the prayer, "'... and I shall dwell in the house of the Lord my whole life long.'" How could a person live in a church, unless he became a monk or a nun like the Catholics? She kept turning over the phrase in her mind. Was it possible King David hadn't been speaking of a building? After all, he was accustomed to pastures and caves.

Annika grasped Josef's hand and followed the coffins to the graveyard.

"Are we all God's children?" Josef asked as he scrambled into his bed.

Annika took her time shaking out his trousers and hanging them on a nail. "The Lord God made all of us, so in that sense we're all His children. Why do you ask?"

"The pastor said there's a place in Heaven for God's children. I wanna make sure I go there to see my ma and pa again." Josef's guileless eyes searched Annika's.

"Were you christened as a baby?"

"Ja. It's recorded in the family Bible. Ma said I cried the whole time."

Christening didn't seem like enough to get into Heaven. Annika desperately cast about in her memory for more. There was a verse somewhere about Jesus being the way.

"Do you believe Jesus is God's Son and the way to Heaven?"

"Ja. Of course, I learned that in church. We went every Sunday."

"You should be all set." Annika smoothed his hair. "Now let's hear you say your prayers."

Josef rattled off his prayer, ending with, "Please tell Mutter I miss her, but I'll see her soon."

Annika hoped Josef wouldn't join his mother too soon. Would she have answered his questions differently? Annika was dissatisfied with her own answers. How did a person know with certainty he would make it to Heaven?

Chapter 44

After two weeks, on a gloomy Thursday, Annika caught a ride with Hans back to Wetzlar and asked him to drop her off at Engel's. Frau Engel said there wouldn't be any work until the end of the month.

While Annika was warming up with a cup of tea, Olga tacked lace to a gown. "Business is so slow I have Monday afternoon off. Come see us and stay for dinner."

"I'd like that. Danke."

When Annika entered her cold attic apartment, it seemed cheerless and lonely. She decided to leave the door open to catch any heat and the sounds of the Hoffmann family. At least Gustav hadn't been here to leave a mess. She put her basket down and went to fetch water.

It was too cold to linger at the pump for gossip, so Annika was back home in a trice. She put away the ham, root vegetables, and two precious eggs from the farm and then sat in her chair to decide what to do next. She had socks to knit for Gustav, but she could accomplish that by candlelight. Daylight was precious in January.

Her eyes flitted around the room and landed on a few books that had been wedding presents. She read three chapters of a Goethe novel before opening the family Bible gifted to them by Oskar. She traced the names inscribed on the front pages, dreaming of adding her own children. With Gustav away, there was no hope of a pregnancy.

How long would it take to build a rail line? If it took a long time, maybe she should join him and look for sewing jobs in

Alstaden.

The weekend dragged. Annika slept in since there was little to do besides attending church on Sunday morning. When there was enough sunlight, she searched the Bible for chapters she was familiar with. She started with Psalm 23. It reminded her of the words in the funeral service about Jesus making a place for his followers, but she couldn't find that passage.

Closing the tome with a sigh, she heated ham for her dinner. She was tired of eating by herself. At least she would have company tomorrow night when she went to Olga's.

Annika arrived at Olga's mid-afternoon. Her husband was working at his cobbler's bench on the first floor. "Guten Abend, Frau Weber. Go right up."

Olga took Annika's cloak and hung it on a peg by the door. "We try to keep the house as warm as possible for Mutter. She's asleep right now. It's harder and harder for her to get up with this damp cold."

The warmth of the apartment enveloped Annika. "I like it. It's hard to keep my attic warm." She sank into a rocking chair near the fireplace.

"What have you been doing to keep yourself busy?" Olga handed Annika a cup of tea and sat down in a chair opposite her.

"Reading. *The Sorrows of Young Werther* is interesting. I've also been looking at some chapters in the Bible."

Olga gestured to a family Bible on a nearby trunk. "I try to read at least a few verses from the Good Book every day."

Annika leaned forward. "Do you know where the verses are about Jesus making a home for us in Heaven?"

"The one where He promises 'I go to prepare a place for you'?"

"That's it!" Annika's eyes lit up.

"John chapter fourteen."

Annika added honey to her tea. "The death of Josef's family has stirred up so many things. I've felt...like something's missing since my mother died. I couldn't wait to leave our farm. Now all I dream about is going back, but even when I'm there, it doesn't feel quite right."

"Losing a mom leaves a gaping hole in our lives." Olga rocked for a moment. "But tell me, when your Mutter was alive, did you feel like your life was complete?"

Annika searched through her memories of gardening, plucking chickens, and completing tasks in the kitchen with her mom. She often felt out-of-sorts and wished she were doing something else, maybe up at Schloss Braunfels instead of at a humble farm.

Although her mother had been patient, they occasionally exchanged sharp words. Mutter always soothed away the day's offenses at bedtime when she would talk with Annika for a few minutes and kiss her on the forehead. When Annika was younger, Mother would listen to her prayers. As Annika grew, sometimes they would pray together. Annika often chattered about the husband and home she would have one day. Her mother would say, "Don't grow up too fast, Liebling."

Tears came to Annika's eyes. "Not always."

"There's no place on earth we'll be completely comfortable and satisfied for long. That's because our true home is with God." Olga sipped her tea. "You asked me if I'd miss my old house. Sometimes I do, but I'm content here. My favorite Bible passage is a few chapters before the one you were asking about. It's John chapter ten and talks about how we belong to Jesus, like sheep belong to their shepherd."

Before Annika could respond, Olga's mother-in-law tottered out of the bedroom, hair askew. "Sheep? Sheep! Those rascally creatures. Let me tell you a story about when I lived on the farm as a little girl..."

Annika spent the evening laughing at the Schumachers' anecdotes and filling up on Olga's delicious soup. When she stepped out of the cobbler's shop, she shivered, not only from the icy wind but from the loss of something she couldn't name. Squaring her shoulders, she set out for her attic.

Chapter 45

Over the next week, Annika read John fourteen again and again. She also perused Olga's favorite passage. Didn't she already belong to God since she'd been baptized, confirmed, and married in the church? Jesus said he wanted his people to have abundant life, but Annika felt like she was hanging on by a thread. She sighed and set her Bible aside. It was time to fetch water and start a soup that needed to stretch until the end of the week.

She bundled up against the cold, grabbed the yoke, and braved the icy wind. As she was waiting her turn at the pump, the son of the Gasthaus proprietor ran up to her with a letter. "This came for you." The boy was gone before Annika could thank him. She examined the envelope. A letter from Gustav! Ignoring the curious looks from the Hausfrau in line behind her, she thrust it into her pocket and filled her buckets.

Descending the steep slope from the Kornplatz to her street, she set the yoke down and opened the Hoffmanns' door. Grasping a bucket in each hand, she maneuvered up the three flights of stairs and poured one into the pot hanging over the hearth. She blew the embers to life and fed the fire some small sticks. Throwing off her cloak, she yanked the letter from her pocket.

Dearest Annika,

I've been successful in obtaining a position with the railroad. I'm writing this from Onkel's home, but soon I will be sent somewhere north of Cologne where the first part of the track is to be laid. Vater and Onkel are well. They have some small orders to fill.

Ella has chosen a husband from all her beaus and will marry in the spring. Aunt Hertha is sad, but Vater will be glad to get Ella's room. He and I are sleeping in the main room, which is very inconvenient. I miss you and my bed.

I will put whatever I can save from my wages in the bank. Erwin will withdraw funds and pay the rent for you. I have deposited a thaler towards February's rent in case Engel's hasn't provided work for you. It's all I've been able to earn doing small jobs in Alstaden. If you don't have enough for the rent, tell the Hoffmanns there will be more by the middle of the month as I will start work on January 29. Or perhaps you can borrow from Erwin if he has the money.

Your devoted husband,

Gustav Weber

A weight slid off Annika's shoulders. She didn't need to find another place to live. Today was Monday, January 29, so Gustav had already started his job. She smoothed the page out and set it on the table. She would celebrate by adding a chunk of ham to her soup.

Tomorrow night she would go to Kellers' and speak with Erwin about withdrawing Gustav's thaler. Next Monday, she would return to work, so she would be caught up on rent by the middle of the month.

Unfortunately, she only had one Pfenning left for food, but she had plenty of potatoes and beets. She would ask Frau Hoffmann about baking bread with half the remaining flour. If she could bake on Saturday, she could stretch a small loaf out until Tuesday. Perhaps if she baked for Frau Hoffmann this week, Frau Hoffmann would bake for her next week. The flour would be gone, but she would be paid next Friday. She could do this. She had to.

Annika cut ham, potatoes, and carrots into small pieces to add to the broth. She would only eat a small bowl tonight. Tomorrow morning there were oats for porridge. She even had honey to add, and there was plenty of peppermint to make tea in this cold weather.

God must have been smiling on her because when she appeared at the Kellers' to talk with Erwin, they were lingering over Kuchen and Kaffee and invited her to join them.

Annika gratefully accepted Äpfelkuchen and the hot beverage. "Gustav secured work with the railroad. He started work near Cologne on Monday."

Erwin stirred his Kaffee. "I heard the line will extend all the way to Minden. That will take years to complete, even with all the men they're employing."

Annika was relieved, but a little worried. How long would she and Gustav be separated? She turned her focus back to Erwin. "How is work in the machine shop?"

"Interesting. I'm learning a lot."

The Kellers soon made excuses to leave the table so Annika could speak with Erwin privately.

"Gustav deposited money in the bank for me. Can you withdraw a thaler tomorrow or Thursday so I can put it toward February's rent?"

"Is that enough?"

"Nein, but I start working again on Monday, so I'll be all right."

Erwin ate his last bite of Kuchen. "I ripped a pair of my trousers at the shop. Could you mend them for me? I also need a pair of wool socks. I'll pay you half a thaler."

Annika couldn't accept an offer that felt like charity. "I'll knit you two pairs of socks and mend your trousers for that price."

After fetching his trousers, Erwin accompanied her through the dark streets to the Hoffmanns'.

"Danke for being so kind to me." Annika took the bundle of trousers.

"We're family, Annika. I was going out for a stein or two anyway. It was no problem to walk you home. I'll bring the money on the first."

Annika went up to her rooms, took out her knitting, and started a pair of blue woolen stockings before going to bed.

The next day she mended the trouser leg after breakfast. She would give Erwin the gray socks she'd knitted for Gustav. If she hurried, she could finish the blue pair by the time Erwin stopped by tomorrow night.

With occasional breaks to fetch water or kindling, Annika knitted furiously, staying up late on Wednesday and rising with the sun on Thursday. When Erwin arrived on Thursday evening, Annika had both pairs of socks wrapped up in the mended trousers.

"Have you eaten?" Erwin asked.

"Ja."

"The Hoffmanns are going up to the Gasthaus for a beer. Would you like to join them?"

Annika hesitated, reluctant to admit she didn't have a Pfennig to spare.

"It's my treat." Erwin laid the thaler from the bank as well as payment for the clothes on the table.

"I'll get my cape."

While Frau Hoffmann was giving Ulrich and Dorothea instructions about staying home, Annika gave Herr Hoffmann the partial rent payment. "I'll have the rest on the sixteenth. I start work again on Monday."

Hoffmann grunted. "I'll expect March's rent on time."

"It will be," Annika promised. She would have five and a

half thalers by the end of the month, besides whatever Gustav added to their bank account. She wouldn't need much for food, and Gustav wouldn't be using any of her wages for beer. She would start saving some coins for a rainy day. Her Mutter used to have a few coins hidden in a tin in the kitchen. Had Dora found them?

Frau Hoffmann finally joined them, and they set off for the Gasthaus.

Chapter 46

On Monday, Annika happily settled into a chair by the window at Engel's and began to stitch green satin sleeves to a velvet bodice. "This gown is fit for a princess."

"Fraülein Zeigler's going to wear it to a ball at Schloss Braunfels the beginning of March. Mutter says she needs to find a husband soon, or she'll end up an old maid." Greta was hemming a black linen dress for a new widow. "I wish I could go to a ball."

Annika couldn't be bothered with fine parties. She was just grateful for the warmth of the workroom. Frau Engel kept it a comfortable temperature so their hands didn't become too cold to sew properly.

"Isn't there a dance at the Gasthaus down near the cathedral this weekend?" Olga asked from the cutting table.

Greta brightened. "Ja. Minna and I are going. Annika, would you have time to do our hair? We could have dinner together here before we get ready."

"Sure." Annika hoped Frau Engel would visit both the butcher and the baker on Saturday. Whatever she offered would be more than Annika could scrounge up at home.

The week passed smoothly. On Saturday, Frau Engel served a hearty meal of lamb, root vegetables, and bread. For the first time in weeks, Annika ate until she was satisfied. Greta and Minna were too excited to eat much, so it was a short meal. Annika styled their hair in loops with small buns. Both girls hurried out the door when Minna's brother arrived to escort them.

Frau Engel was finishing the dishes when Annika entered the room to thank her.

"The girls were in such a hurry, I forgot about these macaroons." Frau Engel gestured to a plate on the table. "Would you like a cookie?"

Annika eyed the coconut treats. "Dinner was so delicious I shouldn't eat anymore."

"I'll wrap up a couple for you to take."

Annika strolled contentedly home, admiring the stars along the way.

The next week wasn't nearly as pleasant. Adele Zeigler arrived mid-week for a gown fitting. Although the emerald-green gown was lovely, she found fault with the cut of the neckline. Only Olga's skillful alterations and Greta's flattery spared them from having to remake the entire bodice.

"No wonder that Fraülein's not married off yet!" Olga mopped her brow with a handkerchief as soon as they heard the bells on the outer door announce the lady's departure.

"She's so pretty though," Greta said. "And her family has a fortune."

"Neither of those assets make a good marriage," Olga said. "I hope your mother required her to pay at least half. I'm afraid she's going to refuse the gown no matter how it turns out."

Annika's hands trembled as she picked up the bodice and began stitching the new neckline. If Adele refused to pay for the dress, Frau Engel might have to cut her hours. She took a deep breath and concentrated on the tiny stitches. At the end of the day, she held up her handiwork.

Frau Engel studied it critically. "It's better than the first design. Good work, Annika. Good idea, Olga."

Annika breathed easier.

"I don't know how Fraülein Zeigler could find fault." Greta ran her hands over the bodice. "It's the finest thing we've ever produced. I think we should duplicate it in a different fabric and display it in our window."

"It would be stunning in burgundy linen with velvet sleeves." Olga went to the storeroom and returned with a few fabrics to demonstrate her vision.

Frau Engel sighed. "I'm not sure we can afford to make a gown this expensive solely for display."

"We could display it after the ball. Other ladies might want a gown similar to Fraülein Zeigler's. We'll leave it up for a few months before selling it too." Greta's eyes shown.

Frau Engel fingered the cloth. "Well, we have the cloth. It's a clever idea. Let's try it."

Greta clapped her hands. Annika beamed.

"We won't start the new gown yet. If Fraülein Zeigler refuses this one, we'll put it in the window and sell it to someone else." A shrewd look passed over Frau Engel's face.

"That would serve her right. Let someone else wear the prettiest dress at the ball." Olga gathered up the burgundy fabric and set it aside.

The next day Annika had a very small bowl of porridge for breakfast. There were enough oats left for Friday. But she only had a potato and a beet left. She decided to skip lunch so she wouldn't go to bed hungry.

It was a dismal, gray day. As the day progressed, Annika felt light-headed. She paused to have peppermint tea when the others ate their midday bread and cheese.

"I have extra cheese, Annika." Olga passed her a hunk of cheese.

"Danke." Annika savored the cheese.

"This bread will go stale unless we finish it up." Greta gave Annika the heel of a rye loaf.

"Perfect." Annika layered the cheese on the bread.

She suspected her companions knew about her lack of food, but she was too hungry to care. Tomorrow she would ask Frau Engel for her wages at lunchtime so she could go to the baker's.

But on Friday morning, Annika started to feel more and more lightheaded. When she stood to go into the showroom to speak with Frau Engel, the room blackened, and she felt herself start to fall.

When she woke, she was lying on the workroom floor. Frau Engel was waving smelling salts near her face. "Ugh." Annika pushed them away as bile rose in her throat.

Olga's face came into view above her. "Does anything hurt?"

Annika tested her arms and legs. "Nein."

"You gave us a scare, but you're right as rain. Was there something you wanted to share?" Olga coaxed.

Annika blushed. Did Olga want her to admit how little food she'd had this week? "I'm...I'm not feeling well."

"Of course you aren't. How far along do you think you are?" Olga patted her hand.

What was Olga talking about?

"Let's sit you up nice and easy. Greta, could you make Annika some ginger tea?" Olga propped Annika up with a cushion. Annika's stomach gurgled.

"And a piece of toast," Frau Engel called after her daughter's retreating back.

"Do you want one too, Mutter?"

"Make a large pot of tea and toast for all of us." Frau Engel turned her attention back to Annika. Both older women watched her for several minutes.

"When was your last bleeding?" Olga finally asked.

Comprehension dawned on Annika. They thought she was pregnant. "Um..." She struggled to think. It was a good question. Last month had been stressful, and she wasn't always regular. "November or December?"

Frau Engel stood. "You're probably in the family way."

A wave of worry washed over Annika. She hadn't eaten well lately. Would that hurt the baby?

When Frau Engel left to help Greta, Olga whispered, "What's wrong?"

"There hasn't been much to eat. It's a good thing we get our wages today."

"How little?"

Annika averted her eyes from Olga's kind face. "At least something small three times a day. I wouldn't have had any lunch yesterday, but you and Greta shared. I had vegetables last night. The good news is spring is coming. The sheep and goats will be lambing soon. I'll be able to get fresh milk and butter."

"And God-willing a harvest of winter rye so bread won't be as expensive."

The two women smiled at each other.

"I prayed for a baby this year."

"And God heard." Olga's blue eyes twinkled. "Prayer's not hard. It's just telling God what's on your heart."

Chapter 47

Humming, Annika flipped over her bacon with a fork. She had splurged at the butcher's due to the tiny life growing inside her. She would make sure she ate well so the baby would be healthy and strong.

Tomorrow she should write to Gustav, acknowledging his job news and assuring him that February's rent was paid. Last evening, she had brought Herr Hoffmann the remainder of the month's rent as well as paying a thaler in advance for March. Then she had hidden an entire Silbergroschen, worth twelve Pfennige, deep in her trunk, pausing to finger the baby outfits. She could start knitting soakers after she finished a pair of socks for Gustav.

Annika decided not to include the news about the baby. Gustav hadn't been happy about the first one. No one knew except Olga and Frau Engel. She would keep it her secret until she was further along.

The day flew by. Frau Keller visited the shop and picked out cloth for a summer dress. She also invited Annika to Sunday dinner the next day. Annika gladly accepted.

Paul stopped by to drop off baked goods when he was in Wetzlar on the twenty-ninth of February. Annika left the shop to accompany him to the Gasthaus.

"Danke for the sausage and beer, Paul."

"Mutter told me to take you to get a bite to eat. Now I can tell her you're looking healthy and as beautiful as always." He blushed. "I mean..."

Annika amused herself with his discomfort for a moment before rescuing him. "Please give her my love. If I don't come home next month, I will in April."

"My next supply run will be the end of March."

Annika wrapped her hands around a stein of beer. "There's enough work right now to keep us busy. Speaking of which, I'll need to get back to the shop soon. You've caught me up on Lucie and Fritzie, but how is Josef?"

"All right. He's going to school. It's not his favorite thing, but he's learning to read and do sums. Pastor Brandt hasn't been able to trace any of his family. He still sleeps in our storage room. He makes himself useful, sweeping up and delivering bread."

"Not a permanent arrangement. The boy needs a family."

"I agree."

"Please tell him I said hello and want to hear him read next time I'm in Braunfels."

To the relief of all the staff at Engel's, Adele Zeigler paid in full for her dress without too much complaining. It did fit a bit snugly, although it had been perfect only three weeks earlier.

Too much Kuchen, Annika thought, although maybe... Was it possible Adele's dresses were tight for the same reason Annika's were? In that case, Adele had better catch a husband and become a spring bride.

Maybe Engel's could design her wedding gown.

Annika shook the thought from her mind and kept stitching the bodice of Frau Keller's yellow dress.

Olga was laying out the rest of the burgundy fabric for the sample dress that would grace the shop's window. "I hope this earns us more dress orders."

"Ja. At least we have seven orders this month."

"We used to have a dozen a month during the spring and fall. Kept us working until seven at night, every night, except the Lord's Day of course."

"I don't know if I want that much work. Ten dresses are all I can imagine handling."

"Then we'll pray for ten." Olga deftly cut out the skirt. "How are you feeling?"

"I feel great. I haven't felt the baby move yet, but it's still early."

"I never felt the fluttering before five months. Are you getting enough to eat?"

"I have more than enough. I'm even saving a little money for tough times."

"Very wise."

"It's easier with Gustav working for the railroad." In so many ways. He wasn't using her earnings on beer or flying into a temper and taking it out on her. "He deposits money into our bank account. His family business used to provide food and clothing for us, but they paid him very little."

"The Webers' business has been on the decline for a long time. When Gustav's mother was alive, his family owned a fine house, but cotton cloth started pushing out linen."

"Did you know Gustav's Mutter?"

"Ja, I knew Alma. She was a fine Christian woman. You would have liked her."

The two followed the threads of their own thoughts until Olga broke the silence. "How are things going for the Webers in Alstaden?"

"There's enough work for Gustav's Vater and Onkel. The pink cloth Frau Engel ordered should arrive next month."

"Excellent. This design in pink would be perfect on the

young ladies."

Their display gown drew new customers into the shop. Three well-to-do mothers ordered gowns for their marriageable daughters. Greta preened, proud her idea worked so well. Her mother allowed her to assist the young ladies in choosing material and trim.

"She'll make an excellent proprietress," her mother bragged to Annika and Olga. "Maybe I'll get a bit of rest in my old age."

"You deserve it." Olga tacked lace to the scooped collar of a blue gown.

"Annika, can you check on the pink linen from your in-laws? One of the girls ordered pink after Greta showed her a scrap. With her fair hair and blue eyes, it will look stunning. Maybe even bring in more orders." Frau Engel fanned herself. "I may need to hire a new seamstress."

It was on the tip of Annika's tongue to suggest Frieda.

"I can't hire anyone quite yet. Let's see what summer brings."

Annika could barely grasp what April was bringing. The shop had orders for ten gowns.

Chapter 48

Anxiety began to keep Annika from sleeping well at night. The Webers had been planning to ship the pink cloth by the end of March. By Annika's calculations, it should have already arrived.

April had flown by as the seamstresses cut out and stitched nine gowns. The tenth was delayed due to the lack of the pink fabric. Frau Engel was getting nervous.

"I've never known the Webers not to fill an order," Annika assured her employer.

Frau Engel's mouth pressed into a firm line. "We have less than two weeks to finish the gown, and we don't have the cloth to start it." She swept out of the room.

Annika was fighting to stay awake as she hemmed a yellow gown that reminded her of sunshine. Its auburn-haired owner would have her last fitting in the afternoon.

The bell on the door chimed as Annika was tying off the threads.

Frau Engel came into the back room. "You have visitors, Annika."

"I'll be right out." Annika fitted the gown onto a mannequin. Olga or Frau Engel would examine it before the new owner arrived. She glanced back to admire the V-neck, shirred waist, and tailored sleeves before going into the showroom.

"Paul! And Josef!" She hugged the little boy. He wasn't as skinny as he had been when she and Paul rescued him. "What a lovely surprise!"

"Josef has been asking to see you." Paul crushed his hat in his big hands. "I moved our supply day up to a Saturday so he wouldn't miss any school."

Annika smiled at Josef. "How is school going?"

"I can read the whole first primer, but I can't do sums as good as Jakob."

"I can't wait to hear you read it to me. What have you been up to besides school?"

"Farming."

At Annika's questioning look, Paul tousled Josef's hair. "This young man's been helping out at the Hubers' on weekends. He likes looking after the lambs and kids."

"And how is Fritzie?"

"He's into everything!" Josef rolled his eyes. "Sometimes Frau Huber has me watch him. It's harder than minding the animals."

Annika laughed. "Ja, I imagine it is." She checked the clock. "It's time for me to have lunch, so let's go get something to eat."

As they passed a cheesemaker's, Annika said, "Let's get some goat cheese."

"Mutter sent wheat bread." Paul held the door open for her.

"Excellent. It's too damp to eat outside today. We can eat at my place."

Josef was so excited on the walk to Annika's he could hardly contain himself. "Run on ahead," Paul told him. "Go through the Kornplatz and down the left street until you get to Engelsgasse."

Josef tore down the cobbled street, dodging carts and pedestrians.

Annika took Paul's arm to step around produce spilled from

a handcart. "He's full of energy. Such a difference from before."

"Ja. He's a lot better, but I don't know what's going to become of him." Paul's blue eyes looked sad. "The bakery doesn't have enough work for him. Business is slowing down. We don't bake as much as we used to."

Annika sighed. Everyone was feeling the pinch of hard times.

A child's scream split the air.

"That sounded like Josef!" Paul broke into a run.

When Annika reached the two, Josef was pinching a bloody nose.

Paul rescued their packet of cheese from the cobblestones. "He got hit in the face by a plank hanging out of a wagon. The driver didn't notice, but a man passing by gave him a handkerchief."

"Hold the hankie tight. My brother Matt used to get nosebleeds all the time. Let's get you home and cleaned up. I'll soak your shirt to remove the stain while we eat."

Paul took Josef's hand, and Annika led the way. By the time they reached the top of the apartment stairs, blood was dripping through the handkerchief onto the stairs.

Annika grabbed a towel and laid it on her bed. "Lie down with your head on the towel. It should stop soon." She rummaged in a drawer for a clean handkerchief and passed it to Paul who swapped it for the bloody one. "Put the dirty one in the washbowl and pour the rest of the water over it. There's not much in the pitcher. You stay with Josef, and I'll fetch more water. We're going to need it to get him cleaned up."

On her way down the stairs, Annika swiped at the drops of blood with a rag. *Frau Hoffmann won't like these steps to be stained. I'm going to need soap.*

After getting her lye soap, she swabbed each bloody spot

with a dab of soap. She was going to need water to scrub the stains out of the wood. Although she hurried, there was a line at the fountain, so the chore took nearly an hour.

When she returned to the attic, Paul was sitting in a chair. He held a finger to his lips. They both tiptoed into the bedroom to examine the sleeping Josef. Paul had managed to clean some of his face, but his shirt was a sorry mess.

As they were exiting the bedroom, Gustav appeared on the stairwell, leaning on a crutch. He stopped short and blinked. "Hussy! Frau Engel told me Paul had been by the dress shop. You weren't expecting me home, were you?"

Paul stepped between Annika and her irate husband. "It's not what you think."

Gustav's lip curled into a sneer, and he balled his fist as he reached the top step.

Too late, Annika remembered the soap.

"Ahhh," Gustav bellowed as he tumbled down the stairs. His voice cut off as he hit the floor.

Annika rushed to the stairs. "Be careful, Paul. There's soap on a few of the steps where there's blood."

Paul picked his way down the steps, towering over the form crumpled at the bottom of the narrow staircase.

Uhrich appeared in the hall. "Should I run for the doctor?"

Paul felt the side of Gustav's crooked neck. "No, son. He's got no use for a doctor."

Annika lurched down the steps and fell to her knees beside the body.

Frau Hoffmann appeared and helped her to Dorothea's bedroom. "What happened?" she asked Paul.

Paul ran his hands through his thick hair, making it stand on end. "We were going to have lunch, but we were doctoring

Josef through a nosebleed. The blood got on the stairs, so Annika was cleaning it with soap. Gustav slipped and fell."

"I wasn't expecting him. He thought…" Sobs choked off Annika's words.

"Everyone heard what he thought. There's no truth to any of it. Herr Becker, I'd be obliged if you'd find Erwin Weber to tell him what's happened. Dorothea will sit with Frau Weber while I attend to a few things."

Paul darted out of the house.

Frau Hoffmann disappeared to check on Josef who had been wakened by the noise. She sent Uhrich to fetch a shirt he'd outgrown and put him in charge of entertaining Josef. Then she went down to her kitchen to boil tea for Annika, who was shaking.

The good woman brought two cups of tea back up to the bedroom. "Dorothea, there's tea for you downstairs. Let Herr Weber in when he arrives."

Chapter 49

Before Paul returned with Erwin, the constable arrived with a list of questions. He examined the staircase and talked with Josef, Uhrich, and Paul before questioning Annika.

Finally, he said, "I'm ruling this an accidental death. There's soap all over the bottom of the crutch."

After everyone left, Frau Hoffmann urged Annika to eat and rest. "Your little one needs it." She gestured to the thickening of Annika's waist.

"What am I going to do?" Tears sprang to Annika's eyes. "This little one's not going to know his Vater." A sense of relief flooded her as she thought of his temper and last words. Shame followed.

"It wasn't going to get any better," Frau Hoffmann whispered. "It probably would have gotten worse."

Annika couldn't meet her gaze.

"It's difficult right now, but you're young, beautiful. It will be all right." Frau Hoffmann patted her shoulder.

Annika didn't dare show her face in church the next day. Everyone would be talking about Gustav's death and Paul's presence in their apartment.

Olga bustled in with a basket of food in the afternoon. "I let everyone I talked to know that Josef was with the two of you."

"Danke, Olga." Annika's mind turned to her other big worry. "Do you think Frau Engel will let me work after I have the baby?"

Olga looked away. "I don't know about bringing the baby with you, but maybe you can work here."

Annika's heart sank as she looked at the poor afternoon light streaming through her only front window. She brought herself back to the present. "The funeral will be tomorrow. I hope you can come."

"I've already spoken to Frau Engel. She's going to close the shop so we can all come."

"I appreciate it."

"What can I do?"

"Just be here." Annika clung to her friend. "Erwin's taking care of all the arrangements. Paul stayed until he knew when the funeral would be before he took Josef and went to tell my family what happened." Shame colored Annika's face. "I hope he doesn't repeat everything Gustav said."

"Herr Becker seems like the kind of man who will only divulge what they need to know."

"He does choose his words carefully. And he would never do what Gustav thought he was doing." Annika sighed. "I can't believe this all happened. I should have..."

Olga took her hand. "This is *not* your fault."

"But it is! *I* put the soap on the step. Gustav was angry with *me*. He's dead because of *me*."

"Annika, were you doing anything inappropriate with Herr Becker?"

"No. There wasn't any more water, but Josef needed cleaned up from a nosebleed, so I went to the fountain. When I got back, I went to check on Josef, so Paul and I were coming out of the bedroom together. It looked like..." Annika hid her face.

"Things aren't always what they seem." Olga took bread

and soup from her basket and set them on Annika's table. "Gustav had a temper, and it contributed to his death more than your innocent actions. Did he let you explain what was going on?"

"No. He yelled the most awful things, and he was trying to hit...someone."

"Let's be glad you and Herr Becker weren't hurt." Olga found bowls and spoons. "You need to eat."

Josef climbed out of the Becker's wagon with Lucie, Fritzie, and Frau Becker. "You came to my ma's funeral. I should be here with you."

She cried while Lucie and Frau Becker hugged her.

"Paul's gone to stable the horse. He insists he needs to be here to squelch the gossip." Frau Becker looked her in the eye. "You've done nothing wrong, child, so don't act like you have."

With Matt, Dora, and Josef surrounding her and the Beckers in the pew behind her, Annika made it through the service, reciting the oft-repeated words, "'Even though I walk through the darkest valley...'"

How could she be here again?

The entire congregation recited, "'I fear no evil; for you are with me.'"

Are you with me, God? You seem so far away. How am I going to take care of this baby by myself?

A thought rippled through her mind. *How would you have protected this baby from Gustav's temper?*

It didn't seem right to think about Gustav's faults now that he was dead.

The whisper came again. *But it's the truth.*

Maybe she would be better off without him. Frau Engel was

doing fine as a widow.

"'I shall dwell in the house of the Lord my whole life long.'"

A home with God. How could she find that?

Erwin and five other strong young men shouldered the coffin. Matt offered Dora one arm and Annika the other, and the mourners followed the coffin to the graveyard. Annika felt like a weight pushed her down, and she sobbed, losing her footing. Matt caught her around the waist and supported her until they reached the grave where the casket had been lowered.

Everyone bowed his head while the reverend prayed one last prayer. Annika lifted her eyes after the "Amen" to find Adele Zeigler glaring at her from across the open grave. Her stylish black dress outshone Annika's widow's garb. The two women's eyes remained locked until Annika recoiled at the thud of earth on Gustav's casket.

As she stood in the drizzle, the crowd melted away except for her family and friends from Braunfels and Erwin and his cousins.

When the grave had been filled, Erwin approached Annika. "I've arranged for a headstone with Gustav's name and the dates of his life. Would you like anything else added?"

"I don't think so. Danke for arranging everything. My head's in a muddle."

Erwin took her hand. "I'll come see you soon. If you need anything, send for me at the Kellers'."

Annika nodded before she turned and followed the Beckers from the cemetery.

Lucie held her as tears slipped down Annika's face. "Consider coming home, Anna. We love you."

Annika dried her tears on the handkerchief Lucie had given her for her birthday. "Thank you for coming. I know you need to get back to Braunfels."

Dora stepped in to put an arm around Annika. "Matt and I are spending the night with you. The children are with Lina, and Vater is home to take care of the chores."

After Annika waved good-bye to the Beckers, Dora steered her toward the Hoffmanns'. "It's been a difficult day. Let's get you home to rest."

Frau Engel had left a parcel of meat and cheese along with a message that Annika didn't need to work the next day. Dora prepared fried ham and potatoes. Paired with Olga's bread, it was a feast.

"It was kind of your employer to send so much food." Matt dug into his second helping.

"She feels bad that she told Gustav Paul was here. When Gustav arrived in Wetzlar, he went to the shop with her order of pink cloth. He was coming home for a few weeks to recuperate from a railroad injury, and the Webers wanted to save the cost of shipping. She feels almost as guilty as I do." Annika laughed bleakly.

"She's a good woman, but I don't know if she'll keep me on after the baby is born." Annika picked at the food on her pewter plate. She looked around the attic room crowded with three adults and sighed. "This place would be big enough for me and the baby, but I don't know if I'll be able to pay for it." She grimaced. "By the way, I'm expecting."

Dora patted her hand. "Paul told us."

"How did Paul know? The women I work with know because I fainted one day. And Frau Hoffmann figured it out."

"I don't know. He's quiet but perceptive. Maybe he heard one of the women talking." Dora buttered her bread. "He cares about you."

"He looks after you like you're family." Matt pushed back

from the table. "Anna, I hate to tell you this, but Vater said you can't come back to the farm."

"Matt and I tried to reason with him, told him you could sleep with Charlotte. He said there wasn't enough room. We thought we could talk him into it eventually, but with the baby..." Tears formed in Dora's eyes. "I'm so sorry, Anna. We'll still share food with you."

Shocked, Annika cradled her belly. What would become of her and her child?

Chapter 50

Annika returned to Engel's on Wednesday to pleat the bodice of the pink gown. The laughter and gossip that usually filled the workroom were absent. Even Greta was quiet.

When Greta left to wait on a customer, Olga sat down across from Annika.

"I can't go home to the farm! Vater said I couldn't. He doesn't even know about the baby."

"Why can't you stay where you are?"

"It was a stretch to pay the rent before..." Annika couldn't frame the words. "When there were two of us. I might be able to keep up if I work full-time, but you know how it was over the winter. And I have the funeral costs."

"God has a place for you, Annika."

"I wish He'd show me where it is."

On the last evening in April, Annika paid her rent.

"Gonna be hard to meet your rent after this?" Herr Hoffmann mumbled around the pipe in his mouth.

"June's will be paid. I don't know after that." Annika's lips trembled.

Hoffmann leered at her. "We could come to an agreement."

Annika's stomach roiled, but she had to ask. "What kind of agreement?"

"I could visit you some nights, not for the whole night, just a little while."

Bile rose in Annika's throat.

"Don't worry. We'd keep it real quiet. Not like Gustav and Fraülein Zeigler."

"What?"

"You hadn't heard? Word is the Fraülein is expecting, and Gustav was the Vater."

Annika sank to the floor. Could it be true?

She was rescued by the return of Frau Hoffmann and the children from May Day preparations.

"What did you do to this poor woman?" Frau Hoffmann demanded, peering into Annika's white face before helping her stand. "Frau Weber needs rest and peace. Ulrich, go fetch her some buckets of water. She's in no condition to go to the fountain.

"Here, dear, come into my kitchen. I'll boil water and you can have some tea. Is your stomach upset?"

Annika clutched her landlady's arm and nodded. Her stomach was agitated, but it wasn't from her pregnancy.

Frau Hoffmann made toast and tea while clucking over Annika like a mother hen. Tears slipped down Annika's cheeks.

On Sunday, Erwin appeared at the Hoffmanns' to escort her to church. She didn't want to go. She wanted to rest, but it would take too much effort to explain. On the way, he informed her that Frau Keller had invited her to lunch.

"It's too soon for me to socialize."

"I'm family, and the Kellers are like family."

Annika didn't have anything to do except nap. Eating with the Kellers would also stretch her food stores. "It's kind of her to offer. I'll come."

For the remainder of the short walk, Erwin told her about his week at the machine shop, and Annika didn't need to say much. When they reached the cathedral, they joined the Kellers in their pew.

The cathedral's calm seeped into Annika's soul. She couldn't sing a note due to the lump in her throat, so she gave up trying, closed her eyes, and listened. The music carried her to a better place. She was sorry when it ended, but the Reverend's bass voice reading the Scripture was also comforting.

The psalm started with David's lack of fear. Annika had felt nothing *but* fear since Gustav's fatal fall. David asked God for one thing—to live in His presence. Annika had asked God for many things. She hadn't received all of them, but He had answered the ones about a job for Gustav and her pregnancy.

She nearly missed the next verse.

"'For he will hide me in his shelter in the day of trouble...'"

Annika's breath hitched. That was exactly what she needed. She was in more trouble than she'd ever been in. She needed God's shelter. She shuddered when she thought about Hoffmann's proposal and came to a decision. No matter what happened, she wasn't going to accept it.

"'Hear, O Lord, when I cry aloud...'"

Annika's heart cried out to God. *Please, Lord, take care of me and this baby you've given me.*

"'Your face, Lord, do I seek.'"

Yes, God, I want to know you.

"'Do not hide your face from me.'"

Please, God.

"'Do not turn your servant away in anger.'"

God's anger! That's what Annika deserved. Her complete inability to measure up to God's perfection earned God's wrath.

How could she escape it so she could live in his presence?

"'Believe on the Lord Jesus,'" Pastor Brandt had said at the end of nearly every sermon. All she needed to do was believe what Jesus had done for her. It wasn't hard. *Lord Jesus, I believe you died for my sins on the cross to take away God's anger. I want you in my life.*

"'If my father and mother forsake me, the Lord will take me up.'"

It seemed like the most beautiful promise Annika had ever heard. She might not know where she was going to live after June, but now she truly belonged to God. He had made a place for her in His family.

"You seem a little happier." Erwin escorted her home from the Kellers after Sunday luncheon.

"I am. I'm glad I went to church with you." Annika hesitated. How could she explain what had happened? "I... experienced God in a new way."

As Erwin opened the door for Annika, he noticed the yoke in the entry hall. "Could I get you some water?"

"I'd appreciate that. I get tired easily these days." Annika paused again, uncertain how much to share. "I'm expecting a child."

Erwin's blue eyes looked troubled.

She didn't want his pity. "In September if all goes well."

Erwin cleared his throat. "I'm sorry my brother missed this. He would have been proud."

Annika doubted that, but maybe. Who could know now?

The first full week of May slipped away as Annika worked on a yellow silk gown for Frau Zeigler. Although ten dresses had been ordered for the month, Annika was able to leave at lunchtime on Saturday so she could search for housing. None of the rooms seemed safe, well-lit, and affordable. Remembering the Scripture "he will hide me in his shelter in the day of trouble" kept Annika going through the next week.

"I trust You to provide," she whispered every morning before breakfast and every night before falling asleep.

Although she didn't find a suitable room, God sent her an amazing gift.

She was cutting out a skirt with the last of the pink cloth when she felt her baby move. She froze.

"Are you all right?" Olga sounded worried.

"I'm better than all right. I can feel the baby."

Olga's plump face creased into smiles. "Wunderbar!"

"Ja." Annika laughed, tears streaming down her face.

Olga dropped her sewing and gave Annika a hug, which Annika returned with gusto.

"You seem to be doing remarkably well."

"I am. I finally understand what it means to belong to God. I'm still concerned, but I know He's my home, no matter where I live."

Olga hugged her again. "I'm so glad. I can tell a weight's been lifted."

"Why wouldn't you stay where you are?" Greta asked from her place by the window.

"Too expensive. Not enough light to sew by." Annika turned back to her task.

A little while later Greta finished the hem and left the room. When she came back with Frau Engel, she was beaming. "I know where you can stay."

"You do?"

"Ja, if you don't mind not having a window."

Annika deflated. "I need light to sew."

"Not if you're still working in front of these windows." Frau Engel gestured to the large windows.

"I can bring my baby to work?"

"What if you lived and worked right here?" Greta asked.

Annika's mouth dropped open. "How?" She pictured the tiny upstairs living quarters.

"We don't have enough cloth to fill the supply room anymore. We'll store some on shelves in this room and the rest under the counter in the showroom. It will be more convenient anyway." Greta tugged Annika toward the door. "Come see the space."

Annika followed, hardly daring to hope.

"It's not very big," Olga said as the four women peered into the room.

"Is it big enough?" Greta asked.

"We'll share our kitchen with you." Frau Engel lit a candle so Annika could get a better look.

Annika figured her bed, washstand, and chest would fit along with a cradle. It would work for a while. "How much would you charge?"

Frau Engel took a pile of fabric off one of the shelves. "For this small space, only a thaler."

"That sounds fair. Even in the winter when there's not much work, I can have that much set aside."

Greta's homely face was wreathed in smiles. "It's settled! I can't wait. Can the baby call me Tante?"

"Absolutely."

"It's awfully small," Olga muttered.

Annika nudged her in the ribs. "God's provision."

Olga didn't look convinced.

Chapter 51

F rau Hoffmann's face fell when Annika told her she'd found new lodgings. "I was looking forward to a little one in the house."

"You've been so good to me. Come see me at Engel's after the baby's born. It really will be better." *For both of us.*

"You're right." Frau Hoffmann sighed as she pushed her considerable bulk up off the front stoop.

Annika surprised them both when she hugged the kind woman. "I'll never forget what you've done for me."

Annika asked Paul to move her furniture on his supply trip in May. She'd decided to move out early to avoid any unpleasantness with her landlord. The Schumachers had already taken the couch since they had extra space. The Kellers agreed to store her table and chairs in their attic. The rest of her things were crowded into the Engel's Kleider Shop storage room.

June's pleasant weather and long days coaxed Annika outside when she wasn't sewing. Olga said it would make for an easier birth if Annika kept active, so Annika and Greta walked through Wetzlar or in the fields around the town almost every day. While they walked, Greta talked about her plans to marry and run the Kleider shop. Annika started to feel like her older sister.

Paul stopped by Engel's when he came into Wetzlar in June, but Annika didn't want to visit the farm. "Vater made it clear the farm's no longer my home. Could you take this note to Dora for me? I'll visit in July if Matt can bring me back on Sunday."

"If Matt can't bring you back, I will." Paul mashed his hat in his hands.

"Danke. Tell Lucie I'll be sure to visit."

"I'll take you by her house." Paul handed her a basket of bread and pastries. "Mutter sent these for you."

Annika peeked into the basket. "Strudel! My favorite."

"No one makes strudel like Mutter."

"Would you like to have some of this with us? Since Frau Engel is here, there wouldn't be any...talk."

"Is there still gossip?"

"The Schumachers and Frau Hoffmann have squelched most of it." Annika didn't mention she still heard some snide comments. "There are new things to talk about. Adele Zeigler's gone to Berlin, to visit relatives according to her family, but there's gossip that she's pregnant." Annika's voice dropped to a whisper. "By Gustav."

Paul tore a chunk out of his worn hat. "Oh, Anna! No wonder he was quick to believe we were...together." His hands clenched into fists. "If he weren't already gone..."

"I can't believe he left me with this mess."

"You deserved better."

"Thank you, Paul." Annika made the effort to push her troubles away. "Now, do you have time for some Kaffee and strudel?"

"Ja. I'll take the wagon to my supplier and come back while they load it."

"Perfect. I'll start the Kaffee."

The day of Annika's trip to Braunfels, her ankles had swollen and her back ached by the time they reached Lucie's.

Paul assisted her as she clambered out of the wagon. "We'll return to Wetzlar in the buckspring. It should be easier on you."

Annika shot him a grateful look but became distracted when Fritzie toddled out the door in the pantsuit she'd sewn him. "Aren't you the most handsome little fellow in Braunfels?"

Fritzie laughed as he latched onto his Onkel's leg. Paul picked him up and threw him in the air. Fritzie chortled, and Paul and Annika joined in.

"What am I missing?" Lucie asked as she came out of the cottage.

"Nothing. Your little boy's spreading joy. I'm sure you see it every day." Annika hugged her.

Lucie raised her eyes to the heavens. "When he's not causing mischief."

"How about I take him out to the barn to find Fritz while you two catch up?" Paul lifted his nephew into the wagon.

"Perfect." Lucie took Annika's arm and pulled her into the house. "Let's find you a cold drink. Do you need to put your feet up?"

Annika sank onto the couch and propped her feet on a stool while Lucie prepared a tray with cold milk and boiled eggs. "I'm sorry there's not more. I'm baking bread tomorrow. The garden's taking up my time this year."

"How is your garden doing?"

"Fair. I'm pulling bugs off the plants every day and having to water at least once a week. The cows got in and trampled some of the turnips. Fritz mended the fence this morning. At least those naughty cows give us plenty of milk and cheese this time of year. Would you like some cheese?"

"That sounds good."

Lucie fetched some cheese and sat down next to Annika. "How are you?"

Annika wiped crumbs from her fingers. "I'm feeling well. My room is small, but it's a safe place for me and the baby. I get along well with Frau Engel and Greta. We eat together since I share their kitchen."

"Are you missing Gustav?"

"He'd been gone for months before he died, so not much." Annika stared into the fireplace. "He wasn't always a good husband. He liked to drink and sometimes...he'd hit or grab me. Not often, but if he'd lived, it probably would have gotten worse."

Lucie stared at Annika wide-eyed. "I had no idea. He was always so charming. I'm sorry, Anna."

"I think I'm better off without him."

The women sipped their drinks.

"Would you consider remarrying anytime soon?"

"Greta's been chattering about marriage. She has several beaus. Listening to her talk makes me think I'd like to try again."

"I'm glad. Promise me you'll give careful thought to anyone who asks."

"Ja. I can't live in a storage room with a child for too long. I'll just have to be more careful about who I choose this time."

Lucie picked up their dirty plates. "Let's go through the clothes Fritzie has outgrown to see what you can use for your baby."

"You'll need them for your next baby."

"They're a loan. You can give them back when the time comes."

The women had just finished sorting through his outfits

when Fritzie burst through the back door.

Paul followed. "Ready to go, Annika?"

Annika hugged Lucie. "This will be my last visit to Braunfels for a while. Will you come see me after the baby's born?"

"Of course. Mutter will come too."

Annika's family welcomed her with open arms. Even Vater treated her with more kindness than usual. He let Matt take the women and children to pick blueberries one afternoon while he continued working in the fields.

After Annika recreated her Oma's famed blueberry Kuchen, he almost smiled. "If your little one's a girl, maybe she could be called Katarina after my Mutter."

"Katarina's a beautiful name. I'll think on it, Vater."

On Saturday, Annika and Dora weeded the garden for hours before picking scallions and green beans. While Dora fried them with bacon for dinner, Annika picked mint and rosehips so she'd be able to brew tea over the next few months.

"That was the last of our bacon. We still have a ham, but I'm already looking forward to hog butchering." Dora poured beer for the adults and milk for the children.

"Will you come again this year, Tante?" Charlotte carefully set a plate on the table.

"I might be able to. The baby should be old enough."

"When's it going to be born?" Charlotte put forks next to each plate.

"In two months."

"That's a long time."

"I agree." Annika put Helmuth in a highchair. "But it will come."

Dora brought the pot of bacon and beans to the table. "And then Tante will have her hands full. Go out to the barn and tell your Vater and Opa that dinner is ready."

Charlotte ran with her braids streaming behind her.

On Sunday, the entire family walked to the Schlosskirche.

Annika basked in the pastor's closing blessing: "The Lord lift up his countenance on you and give you peace."

She held back while the other parishioners shook Pastor Brandt's hand and headed home. When her own family started down the hill, she clasped his hand. "I finally understand what you've been telling me about Jesus all these years, Pastor."

The pastor's gray brows lifted.

"Jesus is my home. I have peace because I believe in Him."

Pastor Brandt smiled. "I'm so glad, child, so glad. Losing your mother and now your husband have been hard trials."

"It's been the problems that got me to this point."

"Tante Annika!" Charlotte ran back and tugged her hand.

"Go with God, Frau Weber."

Chapter 52

Annika held onto the peace from the chapel service for exactly three days.

"Frau Zeigler's coming in this afternoon." Greta pinned the pieces of a black linen skirt. "Mutter has some burgundy satin to show her. We hope she'll order several dresses so there will be enough work next month."

"It would be a pleasure to create a satin dress again." Annika smoothed out the linen bodice she was attaching sleeves to.

Olga straightened from her work at the cutting table. "There are usually a few satin gowns for fall."

When the shop's bell chimed mid-afternoon, all three seamstresses stopped talking and strained to listen.

Frau Zeigler's disdain carried clearly to the back room. "I've been informed that one of your seamstresses is *living* in your storage space. What's your establishment come to? I'd almost decided to take my business elsewhere, but I made this appointment and was determined to come find out the truth of things for myself."

Annika exchanged frightened looks with Greta and Olga. Engel's couldn't lose Frau Zeigler. She was their best customer and had recommended their services to several other ladies.

"It's a temporary arrangement while my widowed seamstress has her baby," Frau Engel said. "It seemed the Christian response to a difficult situation."

"There's going to be a bawling baby too?"

"Frau Schumacher and I would be pleased to make house

calls for you to select fabric and be fitted so that you won't be inconvenienced in any way."

Silence stretched. "I don't know. It's the principle of the thing. Good dress shops don't have workers living on premises with their babies."

The women heard the rustling of fabric. "Let me show you some material I think you'll like. It would make a magnificent fall dress."

"Ah. This is finer than anything I've seen for a long time. Let me think it over. If I decide to continue my patronage of your shop, I'll send a message for you to bring patterns to my home." Frau Zeigler swept out of the shop with the jangle of the bell.

Greta dropped her sewing and rushed into the showroom. "Mutter, what are we going to do?"

Frau Engel came into the workroom with Greta trailing behind. "I don't know. I want you to stay, Annika, but I won't have work for you if Frau Zeigler doesn't order any dresses."

Greta mashed her lips together. "Worse, she could cause such a problem other customers might leave too."

"I don't think her objections have to do with living arrangements." Frau Engel looked at Annika. "I hate to ask, but are the rumors about Gustav and Fraülein Zeigler true?"

Annika bowed her head. "I don't know."

"I think Frau Zeigler believes them."

Greta gasped. "Why would she take it out on Annika? Annika didn't do anything wrong."

"No, but Frau Zeigler's hurting for her niece, so she's lashing out at Gustav's widow."

"Doesn't make much sense," Greta protested.

"No. It's a good lesson not to be ruled by your feelings."

"I'll find somewhere else to live so Frau Zeigler will remain a customer." Annika's lips trembled.

"But where can you go?" Greta asked. Annika had confided in her about Herr Hoffmann's indecent proposal.

"In the short term, I can probably go to Kellers', but that might not work once I have the baby. I'll just have to deal with one thing at a time."

"Maybe you could remarry, someone with a house, or at least good prospects." Greta wiped her eyes on a handkerchief.

Annika laughed. "I feel like a cow. I can't imagine any man wanting to marry me right now. Maybe in six months."

Olga looked at her sternly. "You're beautiful, inside and out."

"A widower with children would consider marriage now. I can think of several," Frau Engel said.

"No matchmaking, please. I need to write a note to the Kellers. Greta, could you take it to them after dinner?"

"I'd be happy to."

Frau Engel sighed. "We're all too worked up to sew. We'd only make mistakes. Annika, why don't you go up to the kitchen table and write it now? The rest of us will tidy up and then Olga can go home early."

Chapter 53

By August 1, Annika was settled back into her old room at the Kellers'.

Late one night as she sat with a cup of tea, Erwin wandered down to the kitchen. "Couldn't sleep?"

"It's hard to get comfortable when you're this big."

"I hope I won't ever have to test that theory." Erwin patted his slim waistline.

Annika gave him a half smile. "Probably not. The water's still hot if you'd like a cup. The herbs are from Dora's garden."

Erwin made himself a mug of tea. "What are you going to do once the baby's born?"

"I don't know. The Kellers said I can give birth here, but I can't take the baby to work. Engel's most important customer would complain. Maybe I can find a wet nurse to care for him during the day, or maybe I can work here for a while."

"I've been thinking about your...situation." Erwin wrapped his hands around his mug. "I've been saving money and can rent a small house. I found one not far from the cathedral. Annika, why don't you marry me? I'll provide for you and the baby."

Annika pinched herself to see if she were dreaming. She'd never imagined this possibility. But did she want to marry another Weber? Erwin didn't seem as volatile as his brother, but she didn't know him well.

"We haven't courted, but we could for a few weeks. Take your time to think about it."

"It's a generous offer, Erwin. I don't know what to say, but I'm honored that you asked. I will think about it."

Annika was struggling to breathe. When Erwin took his tea upstairs, she started a letter to Werner.

Dear Werner,

I'm sorry I've neglected writing lately. As you know, I'd been living in a small room at Engel's, but our best patron complained. In order to save all our livelihoods, I offered to leave. So I moved back in with the Kellers.

I feel like my life has moved backwards. Here I am again, unmarried, but this time I have a child to think of. I can't continue at Engel's in the same capacity as now and care for a baby. Yet the baby and I must have a roof over our heads and food to eat.

Erwin, Gustav's brother, has just offered to provide for both of us. He has the means to rent a small home. I've been married to one Weber and am not sure I want to marry another, but what else can I do?

I wish you were here to discuss these matters in person. I pray you are well. Send your return letter to Engel's. They will make sure I receive it, no matter where I end up.

Now that I've written these thoughts, I think I can sleep. It's late.

Your cousin,

Annika

Annika was all thumbs the next day but brushed off everyone's concerns. She didn't want to marry Erwin, but what else could she do? She tried to pray. *Hide me in your shelter, Lord. I'm crying out to you. You gave me this baby. I know you'll make a way for me to take care of him or her.*

The week dragged on. Annika dreaded getting out of bed in the mornings. How could she refuse Erwin's proposal? Her vision often blurred with tears as she sewed.

She hoped Paul would visit when he picked up supplies, but he didn't appear on August fifteenth. He must have been too busy to see her. At least she didn't need the baked goods he always brought. She was eating well at the Kellers.

"It's normal to feel a mite down this close to delivering a baby," Olga comforted her. "But I sense there's something more."

Annika sealed her lips and bent over the sleeve she was adding lace to.

"I'm here if you need me." Olga returned to the cutting table.

A week later the outer door chimed, and Frau Zeigler's voice reverberated through Engel's. "I've come to order my fall and winter dresses. I've heard there's a room where I can examine fabric."

"If you'll wait for just a minute, I'll make sure it's tidy." Greta gestured for Annika to go upstairs when she passed through the workroom on her way to the former storage room, which she had fitted with a couple of comfortable chairs after Annika moved out.

Annika went up to the kitchen with a pair of sleeves to line.

"My niece will be home soon. Of course, she ordered some gowns in Berlin, but she might still need a dress or two." Frau Zeigler's voice drifted up the stairs.

Annika grimaced. It wasn't likely. Adele's measurements had been the same for years, up until her last gown, that is. If Adele had given birth, she wouldn't be the same size, and she wouldn't dare order from her former dressmaker.

The shop bell jingled again, and a deep voice asked for Annika.

Annika froze. She was hidden upstairs so as not to provoke Frau Zeigler, but she needed to see a friendly face from home, maybe talk her situation through. Talk in the supply room had ceased, and Annika knew everyone was listening to the conversation in the showroom.

"She's moved, Herr Becker. You'll need to deliver the items to the Kellers' home."

The door chimes rang again.

Annika swallowed her tears.

A few minutes later, Frau Engel came upstairs and whispered, "He'll be waiting at the Gasthaus on the corner once his supplies are loaded. I figure that will give us enough time for Frau Zeigler to make her selections."

Annika fidgeted as she waited for Frau Zeigler. When the woman finally left an hour later, Annika hurried to the Gasthaus, praying she wasn't too late. She waved when she caught sight of him in the corner. Several customers gave her nasty stares as she moved toward his table.

Before she could reach him, Paul threw a coin on the table and escorted her outside. "I'd have liked to buy you something, but those patrons were in an ugly mood. They barely tolerated me, and when you showed up, they turned into wolves." He turned to her. "Why didn't you tell me how bad it is?"

"There are whispers, but no one has seemed threatening. It was probably the sight of us together that made them angry."

"You're the innocent one! You shouldn't have to live this way."

Annika bit her lip and looked down the street. "I'm just glad I caught you. It's good to see someone from home."

"Why don't you go straight to the Kellers'? I'll get the things I brought and meet you there."

Annika sat down in the parlor and let the maid admit Paul.

"I brought you something I hope you'll like." He set a wooden cradle at her feet.

The walnut gleamed with polish. "That's not the Lange cradle. Did the Roths make it?"

"Nein." Paul looked at her with a sheen of tears in his eyes. "I carved it...years ago."

This cradle had been meant for his firstborn. Paul's wife Gretchen had died trying to birth him.

"I know neither of our lives have turned out the way we imagined, but I've come to love you, Anna. Would you do me the honor of becoming my wife?"

Annika was overwhelmed. Wouldn't marrying Paul give credence to the rumors about them?

"It doesn't matter what people think, Annika. We did nothing improper. Widows and widowers marry all the time. Besides, we'll live in Braunfels in my cottage." Paul jiggled his foot. "It may feel cramped."

"It will be more room than I'm used to."

Paul took her hands in his. "There's one more child I'd like to include in this family. I want to adopt Josef."

Annika hid her face in her skirts and cried.

"Anna, please don't cry. Forget whatever I said that's making you cry."

She drew a shuddery breath. "Nein. It's all perfect. I'm crying because I've wanted to adopt him since we first met him. I'd be honored to become your wife."

Paul put an arm around her.

"What about your dream to go to America?"

"We'll wait and go next year when the baby is older. I don't want to risk a newborn's life on a sea voyage."

"But will the land be gone?"

"We'll trust God to make a place for us."

Acknowledgments

Thanks to:

Tori Aul, Helen Hoover, and Lisa Simonds, my critique partners who followed Annika through all the ups and downs

Christine Sears for visiting German locations with Dad and me, translating, and providing other German contacts and information

My dad Al Spires for visiting central Germany with me and taking my author photograph

Severine and Arnaud, Airbnb hosts in Schöffengrund, Germany

Gerhard Adam, a Braunfels historian who sent me information, answered questions, and set up a tour of Schloss Braunfels

Alex Conrad and Linda Sweet for critiquing and correcting my German usage

Stacy Evans for editing

The German American Society of New Braunfels, TX

Alyssa Velez for proofreading

Discussion questions

1. What was Annika seeking to satisfy her after her mother's death?

2. Have you seen problems arise when couples plan their weddings? What could have alerted Annika that the issue with her dress was revealing a deeper problem with Gustav's character?

3. Annika thought she found a "home" in Gustav. Can another human being provide lasting satisfaction?

4. Frau Becker and Olga both mentored Annika. What role have mentors played in your life?

5. After Gustav's death, what options did Annika have for supporting herself and her baby? What path would you choose for her?

6. How were Annika's needs met in ways she didn't expect? How have your needs been met in unexpected ways?

7. What needs does God fill in your life? Do you need to ask Him to fill others?

About The Author

Rebecca Velez

Rebecca Velez loves a good novel. She also enjoys baking, walking, and crafting. She lives in New Hampshire with her husband, daughter, dogs, and parrot. Although a New Englander, she's not fond of winter and prefers to escape on vacation.

Books By This Author

Such A Time As This

Such Deliverance As This

Such Redemption As This

Esperanza Ranch

Made in the USA
Middletown, DE
09 February 2024

48864892R00186